Humber
BOY
B

Ruth Dugdall

Legend Press Ltd, The Old Fire Station,
140 Tabernacle Street, London, EC2A 4SD
info@legend-paperbooks.co.uk | www.legendpress.co.uk

Print ISBN 978-1-9103945-9-5
Ebook ISBN 978-1-9103946-0-1
Set in Times. Printed in the United Kingdom by Clays Ltd.
Cover design by Simon Levy www.simonlevyassociates.co.uk

Ruth Dugdall is an award-winning British crime writer, whose debut novel *The Woman Before Me* won the CWA Debut Dagger Award and the 2009 Luke Bitmead Bursary. Her second novel *The Sacrificial Man* was published in 2011.

Ruth worked as a Probation Officer for almost a decade in high security prisons in Suffolk, including work with children who have been convicted of murder. Ruth's writing is heavily influenced by her professional background, providing authenticity and credibility to the crime genre.

She currently lives in Luxembourg and volunteers at a local prison.

Visit Ruth at ruthdugdall.com
follow her @RuthDugdall

To Amber & Eden
With Love

Deep inside
In that silent place
Where a child's fears crouch

Lillian Smith

1
The Day Of

Down the grassy bank, under the shadow of the Humber Bridge, a teenager walks on her hands in the shallows, blonde hair hanging into the water so the tips are soaked dark. Flipping back up, she sees black specs of grit on her palms from the waterbed and tries to wipe them off along her upper thighs, newly fleshed out. Her swimsuit digs in at the top of her legs; it's too small now but she hasn't got any other and it's a warm day and she longs to be in the water. Too warm, there must be a storm coming.

Yards away, her father is cocooned in his canvas chair, one hand rested lightly on the shaft of his fishing rod, beside him in a shuddering black bucket a grey fish gasps in its death throes. Her father's face sags, his downturned mouth makes him look as though he's bored, but she sees him wipe first one eye, then the other. His posture is his prison but also a shield, the best way he knows to keep the feelings inside. She knows why he's upset, but she blames him too, so she offers no comfort.

The girl punches her arms up towards the mottled sky, where grey patches mar the perfect blue. She wades to a deeper place and twists backwards, her spine arched as her palms land and she freezes in a wobbly crab pose, her legs shaking with the effort. She has been going to gymnastics since she could walk, but just recently the positions have become harder for her to achieve. Her body is finding new ways to move, and no longer wants to be twisted into unnatural shapes, made to split or bend, but she's forcing it now, demanding it to stay still.

"Dad! Watch me."

The girl lifts one hand, touches her thigh, and quickly returns it to the sand for support. She used to be able to hold this pose for minutes, he used to time her, but the water is lapping at her shaking wrists and he barely glances her way. She releases herself down into the water.

Roger Palmer sees his daughter for just a moment and then turns his attention back to the brown murky waters of the Humber, the bucket by his side now still. He thinks again of the conversation that has been replaying in his head since it happened, keeping him in a fitful state of wakefulness through the night, so now he is so tired his very bones ache. When he thinks of yesterday's argument he can recall Jessica's sad but determined face as clearly as if she were with him now. He should have said he loved her, that they could work it out, forced her to change her mind. But he hadn't seen the end coming. He hadn't been prepared to fight for it.

"You never watch me," Cheryl complains. "I might as well be invisible."

She slaps the water in irritation and turns her back. Gravel and mud are stuck to her shoulders in the shape of angel wings. A surprising gust of fresh air makes her shiver and look up to where a dark cloud hangs, so close to the bridge it looks as though it is tethered there, as if the weather belongs to this part of Hull alone.

"I want to go home, this is boring. And it's going to rain."

The father rummages in his rucksack for their raincoats, tosses Cheryl hers and pulls on his own, a black kagool that goes over his head like a plastic jumper. He huddles into it, his shoulders closing into his chest as he gazes at the end of his rod.

"A summer shower won't kill us. Why not read your school books? Surely you have some homework to do."

Cheryl scowls, why should she do homework on a day off? No-one else would be, he's only suggesting it because he's a teacher. She tosses the raincoat aside – it's too small for her now anyway – throws herself on the bank and gazes up at the beautifully monstrous Humber Bridge as she feels the first spit of rain.

A scream, an animal in pain or a human in terror, sounds from high above.

The noise makes them both start, the father is immediately alert, knocks his rod from its stand as he gets up. It is the worst sound of all: a child in distress. To his horror, Roger Palmer sees, high above, near the gathering thunder clouds, a small body hanging from the bridge.

"Oh God, no… "

"Dad!" Cheryl points, her eyes are sharper than his. "It's the gang from earlier, the boys who took your fish."

She doesn't say that she gave one to them, or anything of what followed. She washes her hands in the water but there are no remaining signs of what took place, just the evidence of the boy, on the wrong side of the safety barrier.

Roger panics, looks about him desperately, his brain grabbing then discarding ideas. *Run around and up, get onto the bridge. Is there time? There are two other boys on the bridge, so much closer to the hanging child than him. There must be other people on the bridge too. Why hasn't a car stopped, why is no-one doing anything?*

One of the boys, too small to be strong enough, leans far over the bridge towards the child. Roger squints to see what's happening. A blur in the sky, a brick – no, a trainer, red – falls to the water, lands with a sorrowful splash. There seems to be a scuffle, quick movement from the boy reaching down, a hand grabbing at the dangling child. Then, with the awfulness of inevitability, the hanging child drops, gravity takes him.

His body is like a starfish as it falls, limbs curling in then stretching wide. Roger recognises him and the thought cramps him in two. It is Jessica's son, Noah. How is this possible? The boy whom they argued about just last night, is now falling from the sky.

Noah drops under the cold, grey water leaving a ripple like a halo.

Roger doesn't wait to remove his sturdy shoes or kagool, he jumps into the water, despite his daughter's screams. He dives, comes up for air, dives again, in and out of the circle in the centre of the tidal river though soon the only ripples are caused by his own movement.

Noah and his red trainer are long gone, the sun is hiding. Rain is absolute.

But still he continues to search for the boy, heavy with wet clothes meant for a day fishing at the water's edge, his feet awkwardly encased in walking shoes, water becoming heavier as he refuses, again and again, to be too late. It is Roger Palmer who is hauled from the water by Humber Rescue, he who sits on the banks swaddled in a red blanket.

"I wasn't fit enough, I couldn't dive again. I have to live with that."

Roger Palmer says this many times, first to the rescue team, then to paramedics and finally to the police. Also, in a quiet moment just before Noah's funeral, to Jessica. She touched his hand for a fleeting second then pulled it from him, nursing it to her chest like she was wounded. He watched her husband, whom he knew she didn't love, lead her back to her pew. He knew in that moment that their lives were changed forever, and so was his.

And always, always, that reproach: *I should never have stopped trying. I will never forgive myself.*

Two brothers watch from the railing of the bridge. They

know the diving man, he's a teacher at the primary school. His daughter is in high school, one of the popular girls in year ten. The older boy's lips are still sore from her rough kisses. He grabs his brother by a shivering arm and urges him to move.

Together they run from the bridge as if the Devil himself is at their heels.

2
Now

Please help me find my son's killer.

Noah's mum: It's been eight years but it could have happened yesterday, I'm so raw. It's hard to think that time moves on, even without my boy. For other people, that is. Time stopped for me.

The parole board sent a letter, that's all I got, just a single sheet of paper. He's out. Just eight years after he murdered my son and he's free to do it again. The parole board say he's served his sentence, but I'll be living this hell forever.

Humber Boy B should be locked up. It's a sin that's he's been set free.

So I'm starting this page because I need help. He's out there, somewhere. Will you help me find him?

3
Cate

Cate Austin finished reading Roger Palmer's witness statement, the first in the Crown Prosecution dossier, and closed her eyes. For a moment she was there, in the Humber, feeling the water lap above her head, the numbing exhaustion of diving again and again for the boy whose bloated body re-surfaced days later, six miles further down the river. The poor man didn't get out of the frigid water until the emergency services arrived, and by then he was suffering from shock and exhaustion, his teenage daughter Cheryl hysterical by the river bank.

When she was finally able to string a sentence together, Cheryl said that she knew the boys, she recognised them from school and she'd spoken with them earlier. The older one was in her year, he was wearing a Hull Rovers football strip and this helped narrow down the search, along with CCTV footage. Just two hours later Humber Boys A and B were in police custody.

At age ten, Humber Boy B was surely too young to understand the finality of death. After fifteen months on remand, a six-week trial under the media spotlight and eight years in prison, he did now. And it was Cate's job to make sure.

"I can't believe this weather," Cate said, "September never used to be hot. Must be global warming."

"I know, I thought I'd put these sandals away for the year." Penny Rickman rubbed her heel as she spoke, adding, "Which would be a relief to the world with my bunions."

Cate looked at Penny's feet, noticing not bunions but glittery painted toenails, then at her own, hidden in sensible flats. She half-shrugged off her jacket and then gazed over Penny's shoulder into the conference room where three men were taking their seats, pouring glasses of water and leafing through paperwork. She pulled her jacket back on.

"There's coffee if you want it?" Penny pointed to the machine in the hallway.

"I'm alright with water, thanks. Day like today."

"I'd still drink coffee in the desert," Penny said, going to the machine and swiping her card, pressing buttons so the machine gurgled into action. "Especially considering what we're about to discuss."

Cate checked her watch. "He'll be leaving the prison now. He's expected at the probation office at one."

"Then we'd best get a move on." Penny opened the door to the conference room and the three men, all seated around the head of the table, looked up.

"Gentlemen, I'm Penny Rickman, victim liaison and witness protection. And this is Cate Austin from probation, Humber Boy B's supervising officer."

"Hi, Cate." Stephen Flynn, now Detective Inspector, welcomed Cate with an expression she interpreted as, 'you always get the strange ones', and offered her his hand, which she took, glad of the warm welcome.

"Good to see you, Steve. How's life?"

"Weird and wonderful, just how we like it."

It was a standing joke between them since they'd first worked together on the case of Rose Wilks.

Cate's attention was seized by the man to his right, whom she could immediately tell wasn't a police officer; his face was too refined, his clothes well cut. He was neatly handsome in a way that you would associate with public relations or shaving foam adverts, not catching criminals. When she offered her hand in greeting, his was soft and moisturised.

"Cate Austin. Probation."

"Olivier Massard." His voice was accented, his watch sparkled at the wrist.

Steve paused for a moment, until Cate had retrieved her hand, then explained, "Detective Massard is on secondment to Suffolk constabulary for six months. European exchange, part of the EU's desire to have us all working like robots," Steve looked down at his paperwork to hide his expression but she could tell from his voice that he was pissed off by the idea. "Isn't that right, Ollie?"

Cate saw the detective wince at the nickname.

"Not at all," he replied, in perfect English. "Because of the sterling police work with your Suffolk Strangler, we have become aware of this county. It is being held as a model of excellence, and I am here to observe and learn. Nothing more."

"Seconded from France?" Cate asked.

"From Luxembourg, actually. Though I'm three-quarters French, so good guess." He didn't say what the other quarter was.

Mystified, Cate turned her attention to the third man, who to her relief she could more easily classify by his worn jacket and pale pudgy face as a civil servant.

"I'm Ged, we spoke on the phone. From Ipswich borough housing."

"Oh, great, good to put a face to the voice. So, do you have an address for Ben?"

"I do." Ged picked up his pen and started to toy with it. "Though I'd prefer it was out of my area."

Cate wouldn't care where it was, so long as it was an address. She'd been envisioning last minute calls to local B&Bs, which would be scandalous given the nature of Ben's crime. If the papers ever got wind of something like that... well, it didn't bear thinking about.

"He has to live somewhere, Ged."

Ged sniffed. "Since there's no death penalty in this country."

Cate supressed a sigh. "He was ten when he was convicted. He hasn't had a breath of free air in eight years."

She became aware of the French detective listening closely and felt her colour rising. When she met his eye she saw a look of amusement on his fine features, apparently he was enjoying this minor clash of values.

Ged delivered the coup de grâce: "Unlike his victim, who'll never breathe again."

Steve tapped the desk, "Alright, folks, so now we're all on friendly terms shall we get to work? Sit down, Cate, you're blocking the sun."

The police conference room was on the top floor of the squat building so its windows showed the tops of trees and a blue Suffolk skyline. It was the view that Cate tried to paint when she had time. In another life she would have liked to have been an artist, spending her days with images rather than words, with beauty rather than the ugliness of human behaviour. But she had never made it to art school and there were bills to pay. Canvas stacked against canvas in the laundry room, all the same blues with shots of white and grey, all not quite right somehow but the activity filled weekends when Amelia was with Tim and Sally. Looking out on the blue there wasn't a cloud in sight, the sky was bleached clean.

"Okay, so, this is us," Steve said, rotating his pen in a circle around the table. "Buck stops here. Penny and I will be managing the police end," he said, "making sure Ben's registered on the Schedule 1 list and checking that only those who need to know are in the loop, and everyone who doesn't stays in the dark. And thanks to Ged his housing is sorted."

Cate picked up a pen to make a note, "So since the gallows weren't an option, Ged, what's the address?"

"We've allocated him a flat in the new affordable housing

section of the block overlooking the docks. The new waterfront, Ipswich's pride and joy."

Steve whistled, "Whatever would the neighbours say?"

Ged looked panicked, but Penny swiftly answered for him, giving her police superior a warning glare.

"Nothing. Because they won't know." Penny made a bridge with her hands and rested her chin. "He's got a whole new identity, he hasn't used his given name in eight years. And even though there are photos out there, he was just a kid when he got sent down, so there's no way people will recognise him."

"What photos?" Cate asked.

"Pictures of them messing around under a sprinkler in the garden, playing football in the street. Regular family snaps, taken by Jessica Watts – that's Noah's mum. She's started up a Facebook page and since the victim and Ben were friends, she's got a lot of pictures of our guy from just before the murder. All in the public domain."

Ged sniffed. "A kid who murdered a kid. And we're giving him a prime flat in the marina." He pushed a piece of paper across the desk, "Here's the address."

Cate made a note and handed it to Penny who continued to update them. "Jessica is posting on Facebook, 'please help me find Humber Boy B' et cetera, but she's just fishing, she has no idea where he is. If we can just keep this from the press and vigilantes we'll be fine. Things will die down after a few weeks. He needs to live like a hermit, one on a vow of silence."

"I'd like to think we can do more than that, and give him a chance at a normal life." Cate said, quietly but with feeling. "He was only ten when it happened. Barely formed."

"Still ten in here," said Steve, tapping his temple. "Don't go thinking you can make a silk purse from a sow's ear, Cate. Keep his identity secret and he can rot in his flat for all I care. At least he's got a view."

Beyond the conference room window the blueness of the

sky now seemed oppressive in its constancy.

"Have you met him yet, Cate?" asked Penny.

"Our first meeting is today."

"He's strange. Of course, he's been locked up since he was a child. But he's not our usual sort."

"What's our usual sort?" Cate was genuinely interested, having lost the notion years ago that such a person existed. Working in the prison with Rose Wilks, then supervising the Suffolk Cannibal, Alice Mariani, Cate didn't make assumptions anymore.

"You know how it usually is, young man, just out of prison. How they blag, how pale they are and cocky, fluent in Hackney patois and bullshit. Ben's different. Looks like a choir boy. But evil."

An evil choir boy sounded like something from a tacky horror film.

"What he did was evil." Cate said, thinking of Roger Palmer's witness statement, the boy in the single red trainer hitting the water with the weight of death. "But he was just a child. There's got to be some reason, some sort of explanation."

"There is. He's evil. End of story," said Ged, now standing. "Are we done here?"

4
Ben

Something's wrong.

At first I think it's the sun, it's too bright and making me blink. There was a storm yesterday, grumbling thunder then cracks of lightning, but today the sky is as blue as… as…

I haven't seen blue in very many different ways since I was ten, so all I can think of is blue as a prison shirt that's just come out of its plastic. I only had that happen once, a prison shirt that hadn't been worn by fifteen other sweaty bodies. As blue as the water after that shirt's first washed, when the dye seeps into the milky bucket. I saw that a lot when I was working in the laundry, last prison but one. It was a good job, a privileged one for cons close to release, but my fingers wrinkled and cracked and then got itchy. Turns out I have eczema. So when I was moved to Suffolk, my final prison stay in open conditions, I asked for a different job. My personal officer said I should be working in the community anyway, get some experience of the outside world after being locked away for so long, so I got placed down the road with the Suffolk Punch horses. I'd never touched a horse before, not even a normal-sized one, and a Punch is a giant. When I was told I'd be grooming Axel, the stud, I was scared. I had to learn how to move around the horse, not behind its back, and slowly, so it could see what I was doing.

That horse was just like me. It just wanted to see what was going on and not be taken by surprise, no-one could be blamed for that. An animal only kicks out because it's scared, but the kick will be vicious and a bone is easily broken.

And then I realise it isn't the sun that's the problem, it's that I can't see all that's going on and there are people behind me, moving and talking. I want to kick out because I'm afraid.

For the first time in my life I'm on my own. I haven't been alone in eight years. Our home was a narrow terrace, upstairs was only Mum's bedroom and a smaller room that I shared with my brother, Adam. Half-brother, technically, and his dad Stuart lived with us too, when he wasn't on an Icelandic trawler out in the Arctic somewhere. Sometimes, Mum would get tired of waiting for him to show up with the brass so other men would come and go, and we'd eat for a few days. Stuart would always return eventually, with a pocket of cash and enough fish so we'd be sick of it after a fortnight, telling us about waves as high as buildings and fish as tall as a man. Cuffing me round the head every chance he got, giving Adam treats, then disappearing again for weeks on end, sending Mum into a spiral of sadness that meant she slept lots and there would be no food again, not even fish, and we knew it wouldn't be long before we'd hear strange noises coming from her bedroom. It was Adam who got me up for school, who made me wash, who stole milk from the neighbours early each morning. Whoever came or went, whatever was going on with Stuart and Mum, Adam stayed the same. And, always, it was Adam and me against the world. Until the bridge.

After that, we got separated.

First, I was with a police officer who looked at me like I was rotten, then a social worker who looked at me like I was ill. Later it was secure unit staff, psychiatrists, prison officers, teachers and other inmates. But I was never alone and now what's behind me is the closed prison gate and what's ahead is a place I don't know – how can you know anywhere if you're in a locked room all your adult life? – and a new home and maybe work and even a new name. The name I used to have, the one Mum gave me is gone now, thrown into the Humber with everything else that died.

I keep walking, down the gravel path that leads to the train station, checking again that the train warrant is in my pocket. It's all I have: a train warrant to take me to Ipswich, the address of the probation office and a duffel bag with my drawings and some letters, along with the handful of birthday and Christmas cards that Mum remembered to send. On some she'd signed Stuart's name though we all knew what he really thought about me, he'd told a whole courtroom.

Letters and cards, not worth much, and I shouldn't keep them. Not with my new life, new name and everything. But if I destroy them, then what have I got to show for the ten years I lived before that one moment on the Humber Bridge?

Melton train station is small, a village outpost that happens to be just a few miles from the prison. It must be obvious where I've come from; the prison stench hangs on me, even in my new T-shirt and jeans. My shoes came from a catalogue. I saw a picture of some I really liked, red canvas they were, but Kevin, my personal officer, just laughed at that and instead he picked out a cheap white pair. He said they wouldn't last but they were all my allowance would stretch to. My jeans came from a proper shop, I picked them myself while Kevin waited a few steps away, trying not to look obvious about the fact that he was watching me. My T-shirt I hesitated over. I kept thinking, *But would Ben like it?* I'm still new at being Ben and maybe he likes different things to the old me. So I chose a blue T-shirt with a cartoon of Superman on it because I thought it was tacky and babyish and so surely something my old self would hate. Also, because Superman takes off his glasses and he's a better person, a hero, and I'd like to transform like that.

Only I wouldn't go from ordinary to hero but from villain to ordinary.

The station is a platform and a track. That's it. I need to wait for a train to take me to Ipswich and I can see the timetable on the wall. I couldn't have read that eight years ago, but now I can see the times and work out that the train will be here soon.

I used to be into trains, Adam and me both were, back when we watched *Thomas the Tank Engine* while Mum slept off the booze or blues and Stuart was gone to sea again, with no notice of when he might return. Adam would take me to the toilet and fetch me water from the tap when I complained of hunger. The cartoon made me forget any of the bad things and we both liked that the programme was repeated, again and again, over weeks and months when he should have been at school and I should have been at nursery, but at least we could both say the lines of the Fat Controller, so we were learning something. We learned not to answer the door, too, after the social worker found us eating out-of-date Smash from the box, the only food we could find, and surrounded by empty milk bottles. She asked us how long it was that Mum had been in bed, and when Adam had last gone to school, and we told her the truth. When Stuart came back from sea he had to go to a meeting and he hated those. His muscly frame squeezed into a shirt, his bald head that looked tough on the dockside but thuggish in an office. When he came home he was in a foul temper and I got the worst of it. He said that if we ever, ever, told the truth to anyone again then we'd both be taken away and put into care. And even though I didn't think I'd miss Mum too badly, and I'd be glad to get away from Stuart, I couldn't let them separate me from Adam so I kept my mouth shut. I thought if I always kept my mouth shut then Adam and me would always be together. But it didn't work out that way.

Watching Thomas on TV wasn't preparation for this. I

haven't been on a train, not ever, and I feel the warrant in my pocket again.

The train arrives so fast I have to jump back from the edge. When the doors open I step inside, look around and take a seat next to a window. There's no-one else on the train, just a man bursting out of a blue shirt and navy jacket walking towards me, brandishing a machine, something to check that I'm legal. Fat Controller comes to mind but I know that's not right, that's from years ago when I wasn't Humber Boy B.

I show him my warrant and he slides it into the machine, which spits it back out. Fat Controller looks down at me, he knows I'm from the prison. This must happen a lot, maybe it's why they keep the train stopping at that station when all the locals must have cars and the village is tiny. He can't see it, where my badness is hidden, can't do anything but hand my warrant back and walk back down the train, a futile search for other people to check.

The train rumbles along the track, rocking me. I feel a bit sick, then I remember I've felt sick since I woke so it's not the train causing it, but still I worry about vomiting. What would Fat Controller say if I puked on the floor, would he throw me off onto the next platform? Then how would I get to Ipswich?

Stuart had no patience with illness. "You think you feel sick, you wanna try being on a boat in a storm," he'd say. "That'd stop your mithering."

The train pulls into Ipswich, the platform is busy with businessmen, women in dresses, kids in blazers and ties, all stood chatting and reading papers and drinking coffee. It's early, before nine, and they're going to work or school. I hitch my duffel bag over my shoulder and start to walk towards the town centre, to the probation office. My first task in my new life as Ben.

I try not to think about my old life because it hurts. Since I got found guilty the nearest I got to Hull was Swinfen Hall Prison in the Midlands, though that hardly counts as north.

Anyway, a prison is a prison and I never saw the outside world. I was near the Scottish border for two years but I never saw a loch or a mountain. The local news was my only way of knowing what the closest town looked like and I'd crane my neck to see beyond the newsreader for a glimpse of green or blue in the picture behind. But then they moved me to a Suffolk prison and the parole board thought it would be safest for me to be released here too. I'd like to be farther north, near my family, my mum and especially Adam, even if I can't see them, but that isn't possible. And Suffolk looks good to me so far.

How often do you look up into a tree? Sat down below, leaning on the tree trunk, do you ever look up to where the massive boughs hang above your head? You'd never expect it to fall and hurt you, though things happen like that. Things happen. The thing on the bridge happened when I was just ten. Just two weeks before I'd had a cake with candles and a football from Mum. It needed air, and we didn't have a pump so I never got to use it. It was the last thing she ever gave me. The present from Adam was the best though.

It was a bow and arrow, not from a shop, but one he'd made with a perfectly bent piece of wood and some twine he'd nicked from somewhere. He made the arrows from doweling, sharpened the tips with his penknife and scored the butts for the best bit: real feathers. He must have searched for ages to find such perfect feathers, large and grey. I didn't know what bird had gifted these, which tree gave the wood, I just loved it. He always knew what I wanted, even before I knew myself.

On my tenth birthday, playing with my bow and arrow, I had no idea that in just two weeks I wouldn't have a brother anymore or a mum or even myself. I had no idea what was coming.

Mum wasn't so good at birthdays but for my tenth, apart from forgetting a pump for the football, she got it about right. On Hull's waterfront there's an aquarium called The Deep, and we'd go past it if we were out Hessle way trying to kill a few hours. I'd always whine a bit, trying to pull her towards the long line of lucky kids. "Think I've got the brass for that?" she'd say. "Not meant for the likes of us. You want to see fish, you watch that Nemo DVD I got you. Or look in our freezer."

So who knows where she got the money or what changed her mind but on my birthday we went. "It's special, being ten," she said. "Double digits. Besides, they take Tesco vouchers."

The aquarium had promised so much over those forlorn walks past the outside, the posters of squid squirting black ink, the fluorescent jellyfish with tentacles like something from outer space. As I pushed through the turnstile I felt like I should just keep pushing, going round and round, forever trapped in that wheel of perfect anticipation so I didn't get let down like when dad sent a postcard to say he'd soon be docked in England and he'd be sure to visit, but he never showed up, or when I had a parcel to open at Christmas and it was a hand-me-down jumper from my mum's cousin who lived in Goole.

But I needn't have worried – the aquarium was magical, walking through tunnels of glass as sturgeons and horseshoe crabs and wide-mouthed sharks swam above and around. Even Mum was impressed.

There was a section called Under the Humber. I remember two bicycles, covered in clams, the wheels all wonky. There was a play area built like a boat that the lady from the aquarium told us was an exact replica of a herring boat wrecked at the bottom of the river. I climbed into the bottom of the play-ship, amazed by the boxes of rope and rigging, replicas of things that rest at the bottom in a watery grave.

Still rest.

I can't think about what else is under the water now, along with the broken boat and the abandoned bikes. A lost shoe, a boy's scuffed red trainer. The Rolo wrapper from his pocket.

No. I can't think about that, it is lost to the Humber.

My life isn't really divided into two, it's in three. Before I was ten. My time in prison. And now. A new start.

Ipswich. My new home. I hitch my bag up again and follow the bulk of the walkers towards town, following the flow of the buses and traffic, and hoping I'm not late for my first appointment at the probation office. My new life has begun.

5
The Day Of

Roger Palmer woke, not feeling like Mr Palmer, Sir, form tutor of 4P and deputy head of year, but feeling like himself. This was because school was closed.

Not a political man, Roger had hedged and ducked months of staff room conversations and debates, but he had still put his name on the sign-up sheet for the coach to London to march on parliament with the NUT.

"The bus leaves at eight, so make sure you frame," announced Jessica Watts, head of year, organiser of Christmas plays, summer fetes and now strike action. And his lover for the past fourteen months.

Jessica was the reason why he'd put his name down for the coach, hoping to sit beside her on the journey, to maybe go for coffee in Covent Garden after the main event and talk some more about when she was going to move in with him and Cheryl.

He woke knowing none of this would happen now, last night she had ruined everything.

He peered at the alarm clock – eight-forty. The coach would be long gone. He couldn't go and let her see him like this. He was angry that she'd ended things, just when they had started to plan for her to tell Dave about the affair. She'd been with her husband since they were seventeen, but that marriage had run its course. Once Noah started school, Jess had decided to turn her life around. She had completed an access course, then a degree and trained as a teacher, caught up on everything she'd given up when she fell pregnant. Now she was moving forward and leaving Dave behind. Her affair with Roger was part of that, her new life, she'd told him so, hadn't she?

But now she'd gone and changed her mind.

"I can't, Roger. I want to be with you, God knows I do, but I can't take Noah away from his dad."

She'd rubbed the salt in a bit, saying how she couldn't expose Noah to the pain of parental divorce, playing on Roger's own experience when Rachel left. All the times he'd told Jess how damaged Cheryl had been by the split, how she sometimes acted out to get attention. He'd been called to the high school on a few occasions because they said she was bullying younger girls, locking them in the loos and making them cry, but he'd soon sorted it out and made sure she didn't misbehave again. "I'm doing my best with her, but her mother walked out on us," he told the school counsellor, who was starting to interfere. The woman had changed her tone then, a look of pity on her face, saying it can't be easy, a man raising a teenage girl alone. Jess had said the same thing, and he wasn't above taking advantage of such sympathy. It was true, after all, that they had both been damaged by Rachel's selfish behaviour. But his own words were now being used against him as a reason for Jess to stay with a man she didn't love. Jess, the feminist, having to concede that Noah needed his dad, needed the convention of two parents under the same roof, even if those parents didn't love each other. It was utter bullshit.

"Noah will be happy, he'll adjust," he had tried to reassure Jess. "Children are so resilient. Look at Cheryl, she's much better now, hardly ever has tantrums and that silly bullying phase has totally stopped. And she never even mentions her mum. And we'll make sure Noah understands, won't we? We'll be a new family for him."

Roger wondered why he wasn't enough for these women, not just for Jess but for Rachel too. Since his divorce he'd been the sole carer for his daughter, one of the few men who worked at Bramsholme Primary and not even faculty leader because each evening, each holiday, he rushed home to look after his daughter. He'd told Rachel, in no uncertain terms, that if she left, she was never to come back. She'd be walking out on both of them.

He had thought that with Jess there would be a fresh start, a chance to try again. Seemed he was wrong. She was just like the rest. If there was one thing he promised himself it was that Cheryl wouldn't turn out that way. Not if he had anything to do with it.

On the first day of his heartbreak the sun was shining and his daughter was unusually quiet, though he could hear the cheery tones of presenters on CBBC – he could only guess they took drugs to stay so perky, to allow themselves to be dressed so garishly, as if wearing red jeans and yellow T-shirts would make children feel comfortable around them. Neutered adults, with clown smiles.

"Switch that rubbish off, Cheryl." She wasn't even watching the screen, but concentrating on the iPad on her lap. "No more Facebook or Instagram or whatever it is you're doing. We're going to get some fresh air."

"I thought you were going to London?"

Dull voice, the tone that meant she'd been hooked up to her electronic babysitter for hours whilst he'd overslept.

"Change of plan."

Father and daughter looked at each other, Roger wondering if he would get away with saying as little as this.

"You said it was important to stand up for your rights," said Cheryl, sulkily. "So why aren't you there?" She jabbed a finger at the iPad, which was showing a scene in London, teachers with placards.

"Because I'm here with you. And we are not going to

waste today. We are going to do something interesting and healthy. And educational."

"What's that, then?" Cheryl asked without enthusiasm.

"Get dressed. We're going fishing."

6
Now

FACEBOOK: FIND HUMBER BOY B

Nicky: Did HBB have a birthmark on his chest? We went swimming yesterday (Manchester city pool) and there was a skinhead thug giving another boy a hard time. The thug had a large birthmark that looked like Brazil over his right nipple. Could it be him?

Noah's mum: I'm publishing this photo of him playing in our garden with Noah. They were having a water fight so both boys are topless and as you see, no birthmark. But please keep looking.

Nicky: Sorry I couldn't help.

Noah's mum: You're trying. Every day is a struggle, knowing he is free, but this site gives me hope that one day I'll get the answer I need. You can see in the photo how both the boys are happy. This was just a week before the murder. So why did it go wrong, why did my boy have to die? The only person who can answer me is out there, somewhere. Please help me find him.

Silent Friend: I'll do my best. I promise.

7
Cate

The trial notes sat on Cate's desk in a fat tower. She had never seen a dossier like it.

"Fuck. It's going to take me a month to wade through that lot. I've only read one statement so far and that took me an hour it was so long."

"So don't," Paul said, grabbing a handful of crisps from the open packet on her desk.

"Hey! Buy your own lunch," she said.

"I'll buy you lunch too, Cate, if only to stop you wasting time with that pile of paperwork. That was all written eight years ago and you have the real live boy coming in any minute. Just talk to him, that's the magic formula. You won't find the answer in that stack of legalese."

Cate's stomach growled. Breakfast had been hours ago.

"Okay. But it better be quick. He's expected at one."

She reached for her jacket and followed Paul out, tempted by the thought of a proper lunch but still unconvinced that he was right about the paperwork. Every case she had worked, every single one, she had read the Crown Prosecution papers in full. To not do so now, simply because of the size of this task, felt not just lazy but negligent. She knew that she would work her way through those papers, because she owed it to the boy who died, and to his family, to work this case right.

She also owed it to Ben.

When he was first interviewed, Ben didn't have any

explanation, no insight into why he had thrown Noah from the bridge, but maybe someone who'd submitted a witness statement did. The top one had been from Roger Palmer, a teacher at their school, the man who'd witnessed the attack from the riverbank below and tried to rescue Noah. Other statements, other views on what had taken place, would be deeper in that pile.

"Come on, Cate! Let's talk catwalk fashion and latest hairstyles and forget about crime, even if only for half an hour."

"That could be a very short conversation," Cate said, considering her reliable but boring navy suit, "but I'll give it my best shot."

She was back at her desk forty minutes later when she got the call from Dot on reception to say Ben was in the waiting room.

"Better come get him," Dot said, always quick to assess the individuals in her waiting area. "He's looking at the door like he could bolt at any second."

When Cate first saw Ben he was sat on the edge of the chair nearest the exit and she could see what Dot meant. He looked terrified.

"Ben? Come this way, please."

She led him to her office and let him settle, arranging himself awkwardly in the chair, his bag precariously propped against the wall. As he bit his thumb and looked around, Cate considered the boy in front of her. Penny had described him as looking like a choir boy, and Cate knew exactly what she meant by that. He was small with fine blond hair cropped close to his head and, unlike most teenagers who swaggered into the probation office, he had clear skin. He had neat ears, a small nose, as if being locked away had stunted his growth, and the way he curled his hands and slouched didn't help. His Superman T-shirt and jeans made him look even younger. Why hadn't the prison staff given him some advice

33

on clothes? Eighteen-year-olds don't wear cartoon T-shirts and they don't wear jeans that dark and neat.

Ben rolled his shoulders and Cate could see all the trapped tension in his body, bunched up inside. She saw that being in an interview situation was torture for him. The paperwork could wait.

"Okay, let's get out of here," she said.

He frowned. "Where are we going?"

"To see your new flat," Cate said, picking up the key from her desk.

The docklands area had climbed many social rungs from what it had once been, and Cate noticed all the changes as she passed the new dance academy, the Italian delicatessen, even the sweet shop looked expensive with jars of aniseed balls and pineapple chunks lined along the window, sweet enough for the middle class' insatiable appetite for retro. Other shops were empty, with To Let signs in their windows instead of the anticipated goodies. Most of the flats hadn't been snapped up by young professionals, so they had been converted to affordable housing, the only way to stop it becoming a ghost town, so how much longer the deli and the sweet shop would last was anyone's guess.

"Don't be tempted to buy food in these places," she told Ben. "It'll cost you an arm and a leg."

"Okay."

"Did you do any shopping as part of your pre-release? Learn about prices or anything like that?"

Ben shook his head, looking down.

"Well stick to supermarkets for the moment. We can do a budgeting plan, help you work out how to spend your first giro, which you collect tomorrow. I've arranged for you to sign on at ten."

"Sign what?"

Cate was so shocked she stopped. "Really? They didn't even teach you about benefits?"

Ben shrugged. "Maybe. It all felt a bit unreal when I was inside. I didn't really believe they'd ever let me out."

Cate nodded, looked at the nearest flat to check its name. "Come on, let's keep walking. The planners obviously decided against numbers when they built these apartments, too helpful. Your block is called Wolsey."

They walked along the waterfront. Beside them, tethered boats knocked hollow sides and seagulls were screaming at each other over scraps. Ben seemed lost, his eyes darting from this place to that, he flinched occasionally and looked over his shoulder. Cate thought how this client would be a change from the others on her caseload. She would need to work in a way probation officers used to, before everything became about offending behaviour. Ben would need to learn life skills: budgeting, cooking. Surviving. She'd have to be teacher and social worker and maybe counsellor all rolled into one. The poor kid didn't seem to have a clue.

"Here it is. Your block."

They went to the pristine main entrance, and with the key made their way into the lobby. Here, everything changed. Junk mail was piled up on the filthy carpet and the paintwork was scored with black marks at the exact height of buggy tyres. From the lower ground flat, rap music was blaring, and the door had a dent from where someone had kicked it. However much the local area was attempting to deftly climb social rungs, here the ambition had stumbled, landing in a heap at the bottom of the ladder.

She pressed the button for the lift and it opened its doors crankily, but when Cate stepped in, Ben remained rooted to the spot. The door began to close and she had to keep it open with her foot.

"Come on then."

He didn't move and his eyes darted towards the stairwell.

"You're on the top floor, Ben."

"I'll meet you there," he said, and in a split second he was gone.

Cate let the door close and the lift take her up, a glass panel giving a clear view of the marina below. She caught sight of herself and saw she had a toothpaste mark on her jacket, mornings being a rush of hair and teeth and cornflakes. Paul had spent their lunch hour telling her to go shop, to get back out there, and she'd made the mistake of mentioning the French detective, knowing Paul would enjoy the details of his well-cut linen suit, his glossy hair. She hadn't mentioned how Olivier had seemed to be looking at her every time she glanced his way.

The lift came to a jerky halt and she focused back on her real life; tonight she would sit down with Amelia, listen to how her first day of the new term had been, the start of her final year at primary school. In just four weeks Amelia would be eleven, and they should start thinking about her birthday party. Her little girl was growing up.

The sun sparkled on the water below but Cate knew that summer was almost over, despite the heat.

The lobby on level five was small but clean, a charcoal carpet that was so new it still bore the fluff from where it had been cut to fit. Ged had told her that Ben would be the first person to live in this flat. When he finally arrived on the landing, huffing from the exertion of the stairs, she handed over the key.

"Welcome to your new home."

Inside was a surprise for both of them. They stepped into the lounge and stood in silence taking in the large glass windows that looked directly onto the blue sky, the boats down below looking like toys on a pond and the Orwell Bridge like an iconic landmark in the distance. The grey blinds had been pulled back so the view was dominant.

When Cate finally turned back to the room she saw that the small lounge had a simple sofa and matching chair in slate grey and a low glass coffee table. It was quite lovely, and she wondered who had picked it all. Not Ged, he didn't look like he'd have such taste, and anyway she suspected he'd deliberately pick something nasty to spite Ben. Maybe this had been the show-flat, back when the architects hoped to sell it to an ambitious commuter.

"No TV. Still, that view would take some beating."

Off the lounge was the small galley kitchen, with a sink, built-in oven and fridge. "You'll have to eat in the lounge until you get a table in here," she said, opening the fridge. It was brand new, the ice containers were still wrapped in plastic. "Right. Just one room left."

The bedroom was a reasonable size, with a double bed and wardrobe, as well as a pine bedside table. The room had an en-suite bathroom, also small but with a powerful-looking shower.

"I think," she announced, "that you've landed on your feet here Ben."

But he had turned back to the lounge and was once again stood by the window, staring out. Not at the sky, but down to the waters of the dock below.

8
Ben

My first night of freedom is bad.

Night is always the hardest part of the day. Even in secure I was always most worried as I lay in bed, fretting over what the newest arrival might do to me the next morning in the showers, more scared than I ever was when it was actually happening. Held fast under the tepid water, waiting for the dull thump on the jaw as he proved himself by ragging on the fragile. Because they always found out, in the end, that I wasn't a burglar or car thief. Once, at a secure unit in Birmingham, a kid came in from Lincoln and recognised me from some Panorama Special that had been on the previous month called 'Kids Who Kill'. I'd been the main focus of the programme, so I was told. I never watched it myself but Mum ranted about it in another of her letters, the ones she'd write when she was drunk and angry and feeling sorry for her lot in life. Anyway, this new lad remembered the artist's sketch, the one drawn in the courtroom that has hounded me ever since. I still had my Hull accent back then. He put two and two together and yelled "Hey, Humber Boy B!", right across the dining hall so everyone saw when I looked up. They moved me overnight. 'Ghosting' they call it, whisking you away like you never existed, spiriting you in a van through the night, full of fear, to somewhere new. New but the same.

It's fear I feel now, waking to my first day in my new home. I wish I could hear the lock turn, have the safety of knowing I can't leave. I could make this flat another prison, but what kind of life would that be? No. I have to go out. Besides, Cate told me that I have to collect my giro at ten and even though it's not yet eight I need to find the benefit office. Start to get my bearings.

At half past ten I'm staring at the money on the post office counter, £20 notes which I've never seen before and £2 pound coins, which I have – though I haven't handled too many. I can hardly believe this money is all meant for me.

"Thank you so much," I say to the grouchy woman behind the glass, guiltily scooping up the notes and coins. Fifty-seven pounds and forty-five pence seems like a fortune to spend in one week. I don't even have a wallet so it all goes into my back pocket and I instinctively look around for anyone who might nick it, but there's only an old woman with a shopping trolley and a mother looking at birthday cards with her toddler. She glances up at me and I tense, but then she looks back at the cards and I breathe out. She doesn't know who I am, what I did. No-one here does. I reach for a random card, which happens to have a picture of bright balloons on the front and a bottle of champagne with the word 'Congratulations' underneath. I push it under the grille to the grouch.

"And this please, with a first class stamp."

Outside there is a brisk breeze and I gulp it in, tasting the warm then cool that must be what September is like, this air that can't seem to settle on being summer or autumn. I'll soon need a jacket, and that will eat into my fifty-seven pounds and forty-five pence. Despite this, I long for rain, for snow, for blistering sun and all the other types of weather I've missed, I want to know the seasons, to recognise winter and spring. I want rain on my skin and sunburn too because that's what it means to be free and even though seasons changed throughout the years I was locked away, it all happened beyond the bars. My clothes never changed, I never needed a coat or sunscreen. My world was a constant cool, always the smell of bleach and cooking fat.

I'm finding the noise of birds to be deafening, the sounds of traffic and people and the world is too loud. It's as if my senses are just waking up.

With my body weighed down by the fortune of cash in my back pocket I walk from the post office towards the town centre, forcing myself to look up. It was in prison that I began looking at the floor, a way of trying to avoid a fight. "What you gawping at?" one boy had said, just after I arrived in secure, and promptly punched me, bloodying my nose, which was swollen for the rest of the trial. The social worker dabbed at me with a tissue, "Well this won't look good for the jury," she said, as if a bruised nose could make anything worse.

I taught myself to avoid eye contact and now I'm in danger of tripping up.

Cate told me to go to the supermarket for food, and there's a Spar on the corner of the docks near the cinema, a red and white sign, people coming in and out.

I follow a man who looks like he knows what he's doing, copying him by taking a silver trolley, though mine has wonky wheels and skids me into the stack of pot plants. Fruit is first. Fruit is good, but there's so much of it and not just apples and oranges. I pick up a spiky yellow fruit, then put it down. I might hate the taste. What food do I like? Chips and porridge and sausages. I've never had a pointed fruit so instead I choose a bag of apples that say Value on them and go to the next section, which is dairy. The fridge in the flat isn't big, so I just buy milk and margarine but even then there are so many different types and I don't know if I want sunflower or olive oil or butter, or skimmed or full fat milk. I push the trolley, still mostly empty, round to the checkout because I'm worn out and it's already taken too long to buy just the few things I have. Also, I'm worried about the money side of it even though I know my milk and apples can't possibly come to fifty-seven pounds and forty-five pence. I'm lined up behind other trolleys when I realise that I want to try something new, that I'm Ben now and my life is different. When it's my turn to put my food on the conveyer I see that the woman on the till is watching me, a pleasant face with deep wrinkles worn by smiles.

"Hello, love." Her name badge says SHIRL.

I think of Mum suddenly, this woman is about her age, and I wonder why she never smiled like that, why she was always in bed with a headache when a job would have helped her feed Adam and me. I can feel my face going red as I think about these things so I concentrate on placing my items on the black belt that moves them towards the woman: bread, milk, beans, coke.

"Do you need any help packing?" she says, and I don't know what she means, then she laughs and I realise it's a joke because I only bought a few things.

"Can I go and get something?" I say. "Something I forgot."

Shirl looks behind me, where other customers with heaving trolleys wait in line. "Be quick," she says, and I dash back to the fruit aisle and pick up the strange pointed fruit. I run back with it, and the man behind me, the one I followed coming in, glares at me as I hand it to Shirl.

"What's it called?" I ask, hoping it's okay that I don't know.

"Star fruit," she tells me. "But don't ask me what it tastes like."

She tells me how much I owe, and I take one of the notes from my pocket,

"Thanks, love." No-one would smile at Humber Boy B or call him love, but she's smiling at Ben, so I smile back. "Here's your change."

"Thank you," I say, as she places it in my palm. I awkwardly pick up my food, lodging the milk into my elbow, but then she says, "Here," and hands me a plastic bag. What an idiot I am, not knowing to ask for a bag. She opens it and takes the milk, then packs the bag for me and passes me the handles.

"See you later," she says.

See you later. It's nothing, just a saying I've heard on films or TV, but it's friendly. My first trip out and I've done well. Back in my flat, I put the milk in the fridge and wonder whether apples go there too. I should have bought cereal. I'll have to go back to the shop, maybe tomorrow. I line up my other purchases on the kitchen counter, labels facing forward, just like I used to organise my shower gels in prison. Lots of us collected them, because there wasn't anything else and it was a pop of colour in an otherwise grey cell. Lemon or orange shower gel was the best because it was almost like having a bit of sun in that god-awful place. But now I have coke and beans and bread and a yellow fruit shaped like a star.

I'm Ben. I still don't feel like Ben. Ben lives here, in this flat at the top of Wolsey block. Ben buys star fruit. I look at it like it's a prize I won, but don't know if I should peel it or not. The skin is thick and waxy and I bite it then spit it out. I can't see how to peel it so I use my teeth to suck out the juice inside, which isn't sweet like I expected but has a flat, dry taste. Ben decides that it's delicious and when he next goes to the supermarket he will tell Shirl so, and see if she smiles at him again.

I walk around the flat, looking at my new home. You travel light in prison, so I don't have many belongings and around me is everything I own in the world:

One grey jumper (well worn), burgundy jogging bottoms, cheap trainers, four pairs of ragged boxer shorts (more than my just my bottom has been in them).

It all goes in the bedroom, on top of the chest of drawers because it looks too bare if I put them inside.

There's English literature coursework. That goes in the lounge, neatly on the table.

My CV and GCSE certificates. (Eight. An A star in

English.) Also on the table, but maybe I'll buy some Blu-tack and put them on the wall. Would that be showing off, or is that what normal people do?

There's one photo of Mum and my brother at the aquarium on my tenth birthday. I'm ripped out of the picture, so there's a gap where I stood in the middle, my mum smiling tightly, my brother draping his arms around the space where I was. This goes beside my bed, on the bedside table until I decide that my own face being removed is too much of a giveaway, so I place it inside the drawer.

Letters. Some from my mum. A few from Dad, but years apart. My dad, as absent to me as my face in that photograph, cut from my life. Three years he went without writing and when the letters started up again it was like he didn't realise I hadn't lived in Humberside for three years, so all he could ask is how Hull Rovers were doing in the Rugby league, as if I still cared, as if I could ever watch a match without thinking of Noah. Anyway, what do you say to a boy whose life consists of a building smaller than a school and a patch of stubble grass? No cinema, no McDonald's. No trips to the zoo, no swimming. No parties. That's it. All I knew was a concrete wall and bars. But I liked the part when he told me about his job, and where he was in the Atlantic, about the Black Sea and how cold it was and how numb his fingers felt even though he wore gloves to his elbows, how the waves got as high as a tower block. Then the letters stopped, and that was the end of my relationship with him. The only time I think of my dad is when I look in the mirror and see my white-blond hair, my pale skin. So unlike anyone else in my family.

Finally, Adam's letters. The ones he wrote to me after he got released. The biggest pile, my most precious possession.

I put all the letters back into my duffel bag, and slide it under my bed because I know I shouldn't really have them at all. They are dangerous, because they reveal that I am not Ben at all, I'm a fake.

9
The Day Of

"No school today! Jammy!"

Adam jumped onto Ben's bed, one leg either side of his brother's slumbering form, and bounced so hard his body rose from the mattress and the headboard banged hard against the wall. There was a replying bang from their mother's room.

"Stop yer roaring! I'm trying ter sleep!"

Ben pulled the duvet higher so it covered his ears and rolled onto his side so he didn't have to see Adam's jubilant face or hear his yelps of joy.

Adam kicked his brother's ribs, "Nah then, runt. I'll get yer a stick of peppermint rock, No need to bawl."

"Give over," Ben muffled into the bedding as Adam landed on the floor with a thud and began to tug at clothes from their shared pile, trying to find something clean, something suitable for a day at the seaside.

"Mam!" he shouted at the wall, "I can't go in me kegs. Where's us shorts?" Mam didn't answer, so he started muttering to himself.

Ben tried to return to sleep but Adam was noisy, cursing that his Hull Rovers T-shirt had sauce stains down the front, crowing that his dad said he could go to Peaseholm park, promising he'd swim naked in the sea if he couldn't find his fucking shorts. Though the Hull Rovers top was in need of a wash, Adam pulled it on.

Finally, he left the room. Ben heard their mother's door

being opened and then the shocked wail.

"Dad? Where's me dad?"

Ben removed the pillow from his head to listen, but their mother could not be heard. Adam was loud and accusing.

"Hasta been rowing again, even after all you said? And what's this?" There was more banging, something being thrown to the floor, a bottle maybe. "You promised the social worker, Mam. You said you wouldn't drink!"

There was a reply, a pleading female voice, then Adam spoke again, no longer angry. It was a quieter voice that Ben strained to hear through the partition wall. "This time he's really gone, hasn't he? He promised us, that if he did he'd take me too. But he lied."

Ben placed the pillow over his head, not wishing to hear any more.

Adam's dad had left many times previously, he had broken many promises. There was no reason why this day, this promise, should cut any deeper, but for some reason it did. Adam returned to the bedroom and pulled off his Rovers T-shirt and the shorts he had searched so hard to find. He lay in his pants on the bed, face down, and only his shaking body revealed that he was crying.

Ben watched, neither smug nor surprised. "Peaseholm park is lame anyway."

There was a long silence, so Ben thought his brother hadn't heard him until he mumbled into the mattress, "Nobbut the battleships are cool."

Ben had to acknowledge that the battleships were a highlight, as he'd discovered when they all went to Scarborough last summer, a rare moment of family calm, just after Stuart's last return and the departure of yet another social worker.

Stuart had taken them all for a mini-break to his static caravan, his home when he was not with their mother. It was crammed full with unusual glass smoking devises and replica guns that both boys had to solemnly promise not to touch. They eagerly agreed, glad to be by the beach, happy to be a family. They spent the day in the park, watching the battleships with their steamy funnels and bubbling motors, but the day had turned sour as the sun dimmed and the adults' voices began to slur from too much beer. A caravan is a small space for four, and Mum and Stuart each had large personalities and loud voices, so it wasn't long before the neighbours had rapped on the flimsy caravan door followed by the sound of a police siren. They had to cut the trip short and returned to Hull the next day in a car filled with adult rage and childish confusion, but Ben remembered the battleships with fondness.

Mum appeared in the doorway, wearing only an 'I hate mornings' long T-shirt and scratching her head. "I want you boys out of my hair today." Ben noticed her mousy hair, which looked matted and crispy, and wanted to agree.

"I've got a headache so I'm going back to bed. Just be quiet. Okay?"

Both boys knew better than to argue but Adam's anger was still driving him. "You need to give us some brass so we can get us some grub."

Their mother looked shocked, then angry. "You mardy fucker! I just said I'm ill. Now get that miserable look off your face and leg it. When I was your age I was out all the time, not laying on my bed sulking. Get some bloody clothes on!"

And then she returned to her own room.

They heard her door slam closed and knew that would be the last they saw of her for a while.

"Fuck them, who needs Scarborough? We're goin' on us '-olidays, right here," Adam said, sitting up and reaching again for his Rovers top. "Me and you."

Ben felt an ache. He loved to be with Adam and knew his brother was hurting badly, but he couldn't help him. He looked at his bedside clock, which was only approximately right. "Noah'll be here any second. His mum's gone up ta London for the strike, so we're looking after him."

Adam gave a snort. "Do I look like a babysitter?"

"Not you, our kid. Me and our mam said we'd have him. It'll be a laugh. Noah and me will go scooting up the ten foot or we'll knock a ball around the park."

"Lame," was Adam's verdict.

"Then Mam will cook us summat, from the brass Noah's mam gave her."

"Like she'll remember that. You saw the state of her," said Adam. "We'll look after him, you and me. Best we don't bother our mam anymore. You know how she gets."

Ben looked at Adam, wild eyes catching his brother's anger. Their room was so stuffed with frustration and hurt that neither boy knew what to do with it. "What'll we do? We don't have any brass."

"Maybe we can find us summat better to do than football. Like I said, this is us '-olidays. And I have an idea."

10
Now

FACEBOOK: FIND HUMBER BOY B

Noah's mum: I just had a call from a reporter with *The Sun.* Now HBB is out, the calls have started, dragging up the past, but this journalist seemed very sweet. She wanted to give me the chance to say what I think about him being free, and I said that it was a betrayal of my son's memory and I would do anything in my power to change it.

I told her to get me in a room with him, that's what I really want. For that, I'd go on TV, be interviewed for any magazine. I just want to look him in the eye and ask why he murdered my Noah.

The one question no-one in the courtroom ever asked. I've asked God, but he never answers either.

Silent Friend: That's the only question that matters. I hope you get to ask him yourself one day.

11
Cate

"Neither brother told anyone that Noah was in the Humber River, they just ran home," Cate says, shaking her head slowly. "If they'd only told someone, called 999, then it may have been okay."

Paul winced. "I doubt it. River water can be icy and that boy dropped from a height."

"But why didn't they? I mean, an anonymous call. There's a phone box on most bridges, there's surely one on the Humber."

Paul's face had a look of disgust. "Evil bastards."

"Come on, Paul, you know it's not as simple as that. You've been a probation officer how many years?"

"More than I care to count."

"And how many people have you met who you'd really call evil?"

Paul hesitated. "Not many. But this case isn't exactly run of the mill."

Cate looked at the pile of paperwork as if it was a haystack and she was tasked with finding the needle. "He was ten years old for God's sake!"

"You can be evil at any age. You just better make bloody certain he's cured now, or exorcised or whatever the opposite of being evil is, because I don't want him doing anything like that in Suffolk."

"Don't fancy your mug shot in the *Daily Mail?*"

Paul smoothed down his red velveteen waistcoat and made for the door. "That I don't, unless it's a photo of me sipping Bollinger because I just won the EuroMillions," he said, as he stepped into the corridor.

She looked up at her old friend.

"And not so close to retirement."

He closed the door behind him, leaving Cate alone at her desk, contemplating the next witness statement in the case file, which was that given by Ben's mother, Yvette. Paul was right, the best they could do for Ben was to keep him safely hidden. This was the highest profile case she'd worked, and her main priority was making sure no-one discovered who he really was. But her other priority was simpler, more primal than that: what had made a child kill another child? She needed to know, and so far the case file hadn't revealed any trigger points.

There had been cases she'd heard of, everyone knew about Jamie Bulger, the grainy CCTV image of him being led from the shopping precinct, hand in hand with the boys who would kill him later that day. Ben's case had also made the news. She remembered Humber Boys A and B, the image of them walking onto the bridge with Noah, their friend, who would soon be lost to the water below. In the file were photocopies of newspaper articles, some of which she'd read when they first came out eight years ago.

Cate, like most of the nation, had followed the case with morbid interest, both shocked and saddened as the details of the Humber brothers had been splashed across the papers. It wasn't a surprise to her that the boys had come from a deprived background, the absence of a reliable father figure blah blah blah. But then it was, because that was so many people's lives, so many people who turned out fine, and even those who didn't rarely stooped to murder. What was it about Humber Boy B that made his life path veer so badly? What was it that made him lift his friend over the side of the Humber Bridge – not a split-second act, it was several feet

50

high and even now he's not tall – and tip him into the water below?

And then, another big question, how would she discover the answer to that question when the likelihood was that Ben didn't even know it himself? If he ever had, it would be so deeply repressed by now that she may never find it.

The phone rang. Dot's voice was even but quick and highly assessing.

"Cate? Your lad's arrived. Still looks like he could run for the exit at any second."

"Hi Ben. How are you enjoying life on the out? Feeling settled?"

"I'm getting there."

Cate wondered if Ben knew about the Facebook page, *Find Humber Boy B*. The latest picture posted by Noah's mum had been a scan of the artist's sketch of Ben as he was during the trial. In it he had a swollen face, a bruised eye. He looked so damaged, so out of control, that the young man seated before her seemed like an imposter.

"I'll be honest with you, Ben, I've worked with people who've been in prison for years, but none who went there when they were ten. I can't even imagine how strange everything must feel."

She could see him silently weighing her up, wondering if she could really help him. He must have met so many professionals over the years, the whole gamut.

"I bought a star fruit," he said, something that would be odd ordinarily, but she could see that for this young man such a purchase was a miracle of sorts.

"Good," she smiled at him. "But go easy on the exotics until you get a job. Okay?"

"A job," he said in wonder, then his eyes narrowed with suspicion that he was being mocked. "Who'll employ me?"

"Plenty of people, actually." Cate raised both eyebrows, acknowledging the irony that usually she had trouble placing offenders in work, but as Ben's past had been erased he would be a cinch. The only question was his skill set. "You passed a lot of exams inside, very impressive. Of course you can't work with children… " He gave her a hurt look, as if this was a surprise. "But other than that you have lots of options. Where would you like to work?"

She could see him marvelling at the question, the many varieties of job jumping around his brain, too fast to control.

"I like animals," he said, cautiously. "I worked with the horses at my last prison."

"Okay. What else?"

"I also worked the laundry, but that gave me eczema." He bit his lower lip and looked up shyly. "I'd really like to learn to cook."

"Right, well, give me a bit of time, and I'll see what's available. I might start with the Community Punishment department, get you some unpaid work experience. If we can build your CV, just get you a few hours' work each week until you get settled. How does that sound?"

"I'd like that." He smiled for the first time, and she saw that his adult teeth hadn't grown straight and weren't gleaming, prison not being known as a haven for excellent dentistry, but his smile was broad and genuine.

"It would be really good to get a job. Thanks, Cate."

"Thank me when I've found something. In the meantime you just get used to Ipswich, okay? And no contact with anyone from Hull, no family or friends. I can't stress that enough. There are people out there who would hurt you given half a chance. You can't risk anyone finding you, especially now when your case is bound to hit the press."

"Why?"

"Because you're free, Ben. And that is headline news."

12
Ben

"Yeah, man. That's the first thing I'll do when I'm free."

I heard it again and again. Wherever the secure unit, whichever the prison, the other lads all spoke about getting out and what they'd do. You'd think they'd be planning on going to college, or being married and having kids, something big and life-changing, but mostly they talked about getting a burger, a proper one, from McDonald's.

I never told any of the others that I've never tasted a Big Mac or a McFlurry, it was too shameful to admit. McDonald's existed when I was a kid, so maybe I did go, but if so, I can't remember it. I can't remember us ever going for a meal anywhere, what with Mum always being strapped for cash and two hungry boys to feed. Sometimes one of her boyfriends might chuck us a couple of quid to get us out of the house and we'd buy chips with extra scraps that we'd eat in the shop, but that doesn't really count as a restaurant. Stuart could have taken us out, I suppose, but he always came home from the Arctic carrying his own weight in fish so when he was back it was fish pie, fish stew and towards the end of the supply it was curried fish. Stuart said fish was good for us, and he liked to be fit. He said his strength was what kept him alive when he was reeling in those massive nets while being battered by twelve foot waves, so when he was home he lifted weights too. He kept them in the bathroom and when he was gone they'd just get in the way. I'd fall over them when I went to the loo in the night but I never dared move them because I knew he'd be back, and if he thought I'd touched his things there would be trouble. At least when Stuart was around we ate, even if I got so sick of fish just smelling it made me gag. It was better than when the cupboards were empty. Adam would search down the sofa for some money and then it was economy bread and beans, washed down with milk nicked from someone else's doorstep.

But no Maccy D, not ever.

What this meant was that when the other prisoners described the thin yellow fries and the thick juicy burgers with sloppy cheese and gherkins (whatever they are) my mouth learned to water and I would agree and say, "Me too. I'm going to go large." It was their desire, but I made it my own.

I feel like I owe it to them, to do what I said I would, and find a McDonald's.

Three days since I left prison and so far I haven't been far from the flat, only to the post office for money and the supermarket for food, and I'm guessing I'll have to go right into Ipswich town centre. I'm nervous about it, because I don't know this town, I've been to the probation office but that's not in the centre. I can't shake the feeling that I look like I am, that even the person who serves me fries will be able to see right into my tar-black heart. I push the thought aside and start walking, in the same direction as the line of cars that must be heading for the busy part of the town. It's twelve o'clock and lunchtime, or at least it would be in the prison, so my stomach is growling and I walk quickly.

The cars seem to be driving too fast, and even though I'm on the pavement I flinch when I hear the revving sound that means yet another car is just yards away from my back. My legs feel wobbly and I'm breathing hard, the sun seems to be right above me and I'm wearing my thick hoodie, my first pair of new jeans. In prison the uniform was thin and worn-in by other bodies, so these jeans feel stiff. But I love the hoodie, the thickness and feel of its fleece layers, even though it's wrong for this weather. Sweat gathers in my hairline and I wish I was fitter. The PE teacher at school always said I was useless, a wimp, and no-one ever wanted me on their team in games. PE was a big thing in secure unit too, and the popular boys wore the coloured bibs over their T-shirts and got to pick the team. I was always last to be chosen, and if I could get out of PE, volunteer to help in the library or give one of the teachers a hand, then I would.

I know I'm not strong, not in that way anyway. But I survived, I got through eight years and there were others who didn't make it. Suicide was an occupational hazard in prison, the posters were tacked up everywhere, and I've known boys end it with a shoelace or a sheet. It was something I never considered doing, though you'd think I would have, especially after Stuart told *The Mail on Sunday* that he wished I'd never been born, that I ruined our family unit and led Adam astray. But for me it was always about surviving, I knew there were people out to get me, that some would kill me if they had the chance, and maybe the fact that my existence was so uncertain removed the question of whether I'd end it myself.

I reached the finish line six weeks ago, it was the final meeting. I'd already been told I'd won my parole, but this was the official announcement, and everyone involved in the case was invited down to Suffolk to discuss the release. That's when I found out that Noah's mum had set up a Facebook page to try and find me.

My personal officer, Kevin, had written my parole recommendation and he got the job of breaking the bad news. We went to one of the education rooms before the meeting, just the two of us, and he unlocked his iPhone. When he showed me the page I was shocked. There I was, a headshot of me in my Bramsholme Primary uniform, missing two teeth at the front, pale skin and scruffy white-blond hair, blue eyes staring out at the camera like it was a gun. I hated having my picture taken, and I was shocked at how malnourished I looked.

"She's asking people to look for you, Ben. You're going to have to be very careful when you get out."

Kevin scrolled down the page, and there were other photos, ones she'd cut and pasted from other websites, some she'd taken during those few weeks when Noah and me where inseparable.

I had to go back into the meeting, my joy at getting parole suddenly damned by fear because I knew that the outside world was still interested in me, that no-one had forgotten, they were waiting for me to walk out. In that meeting the talk was all about the danger I was in.

Mum said that wasn't news to her, she'd been living it for eight years. She said people had spat on her in the street, someone had put dog shit through her letterbox. Then she glared at me, because it was all my fault. "You wait," she said, as if she was looking forward to me finding out just how unpleasant the world was. I think she thought I'd had it easy, while she'd had to face the flack.

Right from the start Mum didn't visit me much, but she came to that final meeting because two Hull police officers came too, the one who first interviewed me after Noah died and another who brought me cans of coke during the long hours I spent at the police station. I sometimes wonder if it was his own money he used, he seemed so kind. Until my solicitor arrived and told me to say 'no comment' to every question, and then he changed. There were no more cokes then.

They wanted to be sure I wouldn't be returning to Humberside, and they drove her down. Maybe Mum wanted to see me, or maybe she just fancied a day out, but at least she came even if she barely looked at me. The kind officer said they'd been in contact with Noah's mum, and they'd told her that if she posted anything to incite violence then they would prosecute her. Mum pulled a face.

"I bet that went down well. Jessica Watts is our local saint, people would go ballistic if you arrested her."

The police officer said there was nothing else they could do about her page, I had to wait until someone posted a death threat or something. It didn't sound promising.

Even without a death threat the page was a problem. Noah's mum had shared all those pictures hoping that someone would recognise me. Mum got upset, then angry, and said the page shouldn't be allowed but the police officer just sighed. "Even if we asked her to take it down," he said, "another will come along, then another. This is the world we live in and we have to manage it as best we can."

It wasn't the world I lived in. I'd never had a mobile or a laptop and had only used a computer in the education block for lessons. It was all a bit of a mystery to me, all I knew was that Noah's mum hated me and I was in danger. The other police officer spoke then, he said that they believed Mum was also in danger, that if they couldn't find me she'd become a target. She'd stayed in Hull, despite the dog shit and spitting, and brazened it out but once I was released they thought pressure would build, so they had a proposal for her. I realised then that this was why they had brought her here, to the Suffolk prison. To place an offer on the table.

"Once Ben is discharged he'll be starting a new life in another part of the country. We're offering you the chance to go with him."

"Where?" Mum looked suspicious.

"We can't say. It's best if you know as little as possible, but it will be to a town with no connection to you or to his crime. A totally fresh start. If you choose, we could make it a fresh start for you too." They looked at Mum hopefully, and I could see they thought that she'd say yes, especially with me in the room. They assumed that she loved me.

"Any road, what would I do?" she asked, folding her arms over her bony chest. "In this new town?"

As she spoke I felt my heart get heavier as the prospect

of having my mum – really having her, in a way I never had before – became less and less likely. I could see from her face, her posture, she'd already decided. Mum would never leave Hull. Not for me, not for her safety, not for anything.

"You do realise," the police officer said, "that Ben won't be able to visit you? There can be no contact. He won't be allowed into Humberside at all."

Mum looked at me and her sad but cold eyes told me that she'd lived nearly eight years without me in her life, what would the rest of it matter? She was always a pragmatist.

"Can't Adam come with me?" I asked the officer, even though I knew it was impossible. My brother was also my co-defendant and I had more chance of fitting into my new world if I was on my own. But I was holding on to this last scrap of hope that Adam would give up his life in Hull for me. Mum may not love me, but he did.

"You need to wash your ears out, our kid," Mum snapped, irritated so much that her face reddened and beads of sweat appeared around her nose. "You can't move in with Adam. You can't even see him, or any of us. This is goodbye, and there's nowt more to be said."

I don't want goodbye, so I push the Congratulations card into a red post box. I didn't write much, just that I'm safe and that I've been shopping. But I write my address too, because what if Mum changes her mind and then she can't find me?

By now I've reached what must be Ipswich's high street with its shops and delicious-smelling roasted nut stands, too many people, mothers forcing sunhats onto babies' fat heads, men in suits walking alone, shouting and mad-looking until I see an earpiece and realise they're on a phone. No children, of course, they will all be in school. There are a group of men, all wearing red tabards, holding clipboards. One sees me looking and I realise my error when he makes a bee-line for me, holding his clipboard like a shield. "Can I tell you about the work we're doing for child soldiers in Africa?" I put my head down and walk quicker, but not so quick that I can't hear him say "Wanker" to my back. In my haste I knock the shoulder of an old man who has paused to take off a jumper, "Watch it!" he tells me.

I turn, hot and sweaty, confused about which way to go, wishing I was back at the flat, but the crowd moves me along and I walk past shops I haven't seen in years, Poundland, WHSmith, shops they had in the centre of Hull. We had a corner shop on our estate, with a sweet counter. I went there with Adam if either of us had any coins, and if we didn't we'd slip a chew in our pockets or dare each other to grab a Mars bar. We were never caught, or maybe Mrs Patel who owned the shop felt too sorry for us to say anything.

And then I see it. McDonald's. Red and white and yellow, glass frosted with condensation.

I've seen the adverts and can whistle the theme tune, but I've never been in one and the door is unexpectedly heavy. Inside are lines of customers, so long I can't see the till, and I'm unsure which line I should join. One moves forward and I stand behind an old woman who leans heavily on a walking stick which is pressed into a sachet of tomato sauce that someone dropped on the way to the bin. The woman's head is shaking as she peers into a battered leather purse.

"Oh, my eyes," she mutters, then offers the open purse to me. "Which is the two pound coin, dear? They all look the same without my glasses."

I hesitate, doesn't she know I'm not to be trusted? And then I worry that I'm also unfamiliar with coins. Luckily, there are only a few in the purse so I reach for the largest and place it in her palm. "Bless you," she says, and I feel something weaken, right under my hoodie, under my skin, inside my ribs. Because she trusted me and now she's blessed me and I'm about to have a burger.

The menu is mind-boggling, choices and options, meals and sizes. In the end I order the simplest thing I can see, a hamburger, and still a torrent of questions are fired at me about fries and sauce and meal deals and drinks, and I just nod, say yes to everything, watching as the bored-looking server presses buttons and shouts my order with a speed that leaves me breathless. This is one place I know I couldn't work.

With the paper bag in my hand, I leave McDonald's, hoping to find somewhere cool to eat my meal. There are benches along the high street, but I daren't risk sitting on one, it's too exposed with all the people passing by, prams and dogs and wheelchairs. So many of them are peering at their phones and I wonder if any of them is on Facebook, right this moment looking at my photo. I want to get back to my flat.

I walk back quickly, urged on by the thought of food. The burger wrapped in its white paper, the carton of yellow chips, a few of which I can hear rattling at the bottom of the bag. In my other hand is the sweating cup of coke, and I sip it as I walk, tasting how the melted ice has watered the drink but glad of it all the same. The traffic is less now, though the sun is as strong, and I keep to the shadows where it's cooler. Finally, I'm back at Wolsey block, wearily climbing the stairs as though I've run a marathon. My arms tingle with the effort, and I wish I was brave enough to use the lift. I wonder if I'll ever conquer my fear.

Inside the flat is cool and, when I split open the bag, so are the chips and burger but I'm determined to enjoy them. I sit on the sofa, the torn bag in my lap, first sucking the salt from the chips. I bite their crispy layer and tell myself they're delicious while a part of me is wondering what the fuss is about. The burger isn't thick, either, but a floppy slice of meat under an orange gummy slice of processed cheese. It tastes of nothing, sweet and salty, greasy, but no real food flavours as it hits my tongue in all the right spots. In twenty seconds the whole meal is gone and I still feel hungry but I have nothing in the kitchen. I crunch the bag into a ball, ready to toss, then reach into my jean pocket and look at how much money I have left. Thirty-two pounds and eighty pence. It sounds a lot, but in prison the wages were low and all there was to buy was shower gel and chocolate. I look around my new home and think of all the things I'd like to buy. Top of the list is a TV. Every day, after tea, we watched the telly in the association room and I miss this dip into life, the news, EastEnders, Coronation Street. I don't know how much a TV would cost, but it must be more than what I've got. And anyway, my priority should be bowls and cutlery and proper food. If I'm going to make a life for myself, I need to stop eating like an animal. I put the rubbish in the kitchen bin and tell myself that, from now on, I only eat on a plate.

13
The Day Of

It was only when Roger Palmer led his daughter from the house to the car that he saw she was wearing a thin party dress, white and delicate, with sequins along the hem. He saw too how her flesh was pressing into the fabric, new breasts spilling out of the sides of the straps.

"Go get changed, Cheryl. Now!" He was annoyed with her, embarrassing him like this. She had surely done it deliberately.

"I like this dress." She tugged it down so it sat better at the waist, but it was still hopelessly small for her and revealed too much thigh. He saw, as he'd seen a few times the last few months, that she was changing. No longer his little girl, but a teenager. Puberty had filled her out and she had started to adopt that stubborn expression, so very like her mother, that he had to fight the urge to shake her.

"We're going fishing, it'll be muddy. Please go get changed."

"Alright! Why are you so narky?"

Cheryl didn't wait for his reply, turning quickly as if afraid of his response. He watched her walk back towards the house as if the weight of the world was on her shoulders, and felt a sting of guilt. This was her day off too, and his breakup with Jess wasn't her fault. She wanted a step-mum as much as he wanted a wife, maybe more. To have another female around, someone to chat with about what was happening to her body, about boys. Someone she could talk to.

"And bring a towel," he called, as a peace offering.

She turned, her face broken by a half-smile, not quite believing her luck.

"We're going swimming?"

"We're going to the river, so you can paddle. Now quick quick!"

If Roger switched on the TV he'd no doubt see coverage of the rally, which would have reached Trafalgar Square by now. His teaching colleagues campaigning for a pay rise that he certainly wanted, and believed that all teachers deserved, but he wouldn't be missed in the crowd. Was Jess missing him? She'd said she loved him, even last night, when she was breaking his heart.

It hadn't meant to be so serious. He was a middle-aged divorcee who knew his best years were behind him and Jess was a newly promoted bright young thing, still in her twenties despite having a ten-year-old son. A woman who'd made a mistake at seventeen and was making her life count for something, and she looked up to Roger. He had supervised her final placement when she was a trainee, interviewed her for the role of teacher after she qualified. He already admired her, but hadn't acted on it until then. It wouldn't have been appropriate.

But she was wrong to think she could just walk away. Jess needed an older man like him, she was frustrated with Dave, and she had so much still to learn. He enjoyed taking her to films at the art house cinema, recommending books she should read. And now she was being silly, saying she was going to stay with Dave. As if a man like that could give her what she needed. Just like Rachel, these women never knew what was good for them. And Cheryl looked in danger of going the same way, if he didn't start to take action.

Cheryl ran back out, dressed more suitably in denim shorts, though they were too skimpy for his liking, and there was a smattering of sequins on her vest top. She was also clutching her swimsuit and a towel. "Let's go, Dad," she said, as though it was she who had been waiting.

Roger drove carefully, pausing at junctions, getting petrol even though the tank was half-full, and finally stopping at Mrs Patel's shop for drinks and sandwiches.

"Wait here," he told his daughter. "I won't be a minute."

Alone in the car, Cheryl reached to the driver's side and tugged the indicator switch, then fiddled with the headlight lever, but nothing happened as the ignition was dead. She pulled down the mirror and studied her face, touched the sticky lip gloss, peeled a flake of blue mascara from her eyelash and regretted picking the spot on her chin which was now a red sore. She put her feet on the dashboard and tried to touch her toes but it made her stomach ache. Now she thought about it, her stomach had ached since she woke up. She looked out of the window and saw three boys from the rough part of the estate. Adam was in her school year, and she'd known him for years, and she also recognised his kid brother. But it was the younger boy who took her attention, Jessica's son, Noah. *Little wanker,* she thought, though it was hardly his fault that his mum was a bitch.

Her dad was stupid if he thought Cheryl hadn't noticed what was going on, she'd known he hadn't been to the snooker club when he came back smelling of perfume, she'd seen the way he suddenly wore trendier clothes to work. She wasn't an idiot, and she liked Jess. Liked that her dad wasn't on her case so much, that he had someone else to think about. This was the main reason Cheryl more than liked her, she needed her. But Jess had gone, just like her mum. Jess was a bitch.

Noah was pushing a silver scooter, but the other boys were walking. Adam had his hands in his pockets, kicking the grass as he tagged along behind.

She opened the car door and stood behind it, one foot stretched out like a ballerina, using the car door as a barre.

"And where are you going?" she demanded, with the tone of a child who had been raised by a teacher.

Adam looked up, startled, then seemed to realise she was speaking to him. He was a bit of a nothing, a gap in her knowledge, since he never went for school plays, didn't play in the orchestra and only did the egg and spoon race on Sport's Day. He was barely at school come to think of it. She'd heard her dad talking about his family to other teachers and knew social workers had been involved, but there her knowledge stopped. Today was the first time she'd ever spoken to him directly.

"Answer me, then. What you lot up to?"

"We're having us a little holiday." Though he was fighting it, Adam looked bored, or sad, she didn't know him well enough to know which. "You?"

"Nowt." Cheryl gave up on the ballet and kicked the tyre of her dad's car. "Fishing. Boooring."

Noah, who had been standing with Adam's kid brother, both of them listening, suddenly perked up. "I love to fish. Where you going to do it?"

The last thing Cheryl wanted was her dad's ex-girlfriend's son joining them so she ignored his question and said to Adam, "I'd rather go to town but he won't let us."

"We can do what us likes," said Adam. "No-one cares."

She was interested in this, and stepped closer to him. He was wearing a rugby top, Hull Rovers, like all the boys did. It looked like it needed a wash.

"No-one cares what you do?"

"That's right."

Cheryl had just grabbed Noah's scooter from him, and was scooting in perfect circles around Adam, when her dad came out of the shop carrying two bags of food. He stopped still, staring at his daughter.

"I told you to wait in the car, girl."

"But you were ages."

Roger hadn't noticed Noah until he said, "Hello, Mr Palmer."

"Oh, hello, er… " It was awkward, seeing him like this, though of course the boy had no idea about his relationship with Jess. Until yesterday evening, Roger had hoped he would be his step-son, and now he was just another pupil. "Hello Noah."

Then, in a more sarcastic and definitely less reverential tone, Adam said, "Hello, Sir."

"Adam. How are things at high school?"

"Pretty shite."

Roger looked at his daughter, "Come on, Cheryl, give the lads their scooter back. It's fishing time," he said sharply.

"Where'll you fish, sir?" asked Noah.

"The Humber," said Roger, warming to the idea once again, settling his purchases onto the back seat of the car where his rod and bucket waited. "Under the bridge."

14
Now

FACEBOOK PAGE: FIND HUMBER BOY B

Noah's mum: September is always a hard month for me. The local children have just gone back to school and it makes me think about what Noah should be doing now. He'd be nearly eighteen, probably about to start university or college. Leaving home for the first time, instead of leaving me forever when he was just ten years old. Sometimes I allow myself to think about it, how he'd look, what he'd wear. Other times it's too painful to even remember that I had a son. People say it gets easier but it never seems to. People at church are always praying for me, and that never helps either. What would help is for HBB to be back behind bars, where he belongs. Then I could rest.

Jenny: So sorry to read this. Sending you hugs, and a reminder that you are STRONG.

Silent Friend: Help doesn't come from the heavens, but from your friends. I would do anything to take your pain away. I hope one day soon I get that chance.

15
Cate

"It's so stuffy in here. Bet it's nice outside, though."

Cate cracked open the window of her office and bunched her hair into her hands, lifted it from her neck and waited for a breeze. The weather showed no sign of breaking, yet Ben was wearing his jumper, the hood pulled up so it covered his head and fell on his forehead. With his pale face and wisps of blond hair he looked like a ghost. Or an angel.

"So, you survived your first week of freedom?" As soon as she said this Cate regretted it, not meaning to remind Ben of the danger he may be in. "How's it been?"

"Alright."

Ben looked tired, there were dark shadows under his eyes and he'd lost weight – it showed in his cheeks.

"Are you eating enough, looking after yourself?" Even as she said it, she knew she sounded like a mother. Not a probation officer.

"Yes, I'm really fine."

Cate smiled at his bravado, a trait that must have helped Ben cope while locked up. No vulnerability can be shown in prison, as she well knew, and he had survived his sentence in text book style. No adjudications. No back-staging. Always returning to the prison on time after any trip out. And everyone, from the chaplain to the PE staff, had said he deserved parole.

"You don't need to pretend any more, Ben. It's okay. This

room may be stuffy but it's also a place you can be honest."

He blinked at her and she caught the glimmer of tears.

"But you write everything down." He looked at her notebook, at the tower of court papers. "Just like they all did. Assessing me, analysing."

Cate knew it was true, and also that some of the staff had used his story. The first social worker to meet him after Noah's death had even published a book: *The Face of Evil.* She turned away from her desk and put her hands in her lap to show she had no pen. She wasn't making notes.

"I feel scared when I'm out of the flat. But I still went to McDonald's. I helped a woman find the correct money."

Cate nodded, smiled, "That's a great start. If you can manage the queues at McDonald's I'd say nothing could beat you. Personally, that place brings me out in hives." She paused. "But you haven't spoken with anyone, no-one knows?"

"Course not." He looked angry, and she reminded herself that he had kept his secret for years. "I'm not stupid." He pulled a ragged piece of skin from his thumb with his teeth. "I know I can't tell anyone who I really am. I said goodbye to family."

"I'm afraid that was necessary," Cate said, though she could hardly imagine how tough it must be. She hadn't seen her father and sister in many years and knew how painful this sometimes felt, but at least she had Amelia. To have to say goodbye to everyone, to everything you'd ever known, and at such a young age, she couldn't begin to comprehend.

"If anyone finds out you'd have to move me," Ben stated in a flat passionless voice. "It'd be a lot of work."

"It's not about that, Ben. You could be hurt," Cate said, carefully. "Most people talk about Humber Boy B as evil. You're a demon to them. There's a Facebook page set up purely with the intention of tracking you. No-one can know who you really are. You're Ben now. This is it, your chance to begin again."

They looked at each other for a long moment and Cate felt his desperation. She was Ben's hope for a normal life, his guide in this new start.

"Okay, Ben. We've got you a place to live. Now we need to move on to step two, a job."

Over lunch in the staff room, Cate made her announcement, gnawing on a piece of celery as she told Paul, "I've got Ben a work placement. Something to use his skills."

Paul gaped at her, reached up with one hand and closed his mouth in a mocking gesture of disbelief. "You're utilising his skills in throwing people off bridges? Where is this job, Go Ape?"

"Funny." She finished her salad and closed her plastic lunch box, one of Amelia's old ones with Hello Kitty smiling on the lid. Cate cocked her head to one side to look at her friend. "But I'm really determined to help him."

"Cate, this isn't the eighties, you can't just 'help him'. Whatever would the parole board say? You need to address that boy's offending."

"I know that, and we'll get to it, but I need to work differently with Ben. He's just a kid."

"You've worked with teenagers before."

"Not teenagers who've never been to the cinema, who don't know how to open a tin of beans."

Paul squirted a fish-shaped carton of soya sauce onto his M&S sushi, took his mini chopsticks and tucked in. "So," he said, chewing on raw tuna, "where's the placement?"

"I've spoken with the Community Punishment team, been through all their contacts. Ben fancied something with animals, so I found the next best thing and got him a placement at the aquarium."

Paul poked a chopstick into the fish. "Oh, nice. I've always fancied working with animals myself. Oh, wait… I do! And so do you, Cate. Remember?"

"Thing is Paul, he's not. I know as far as Facebook or *The*

Mail are concerned he's evil, but he's just a messed-up kid. At least if the vigilantes are looking for a monster with two horns they won't find our boy."

"He's not 'our boy'. He's a convicted killer. Now go and see if anyone left some birthday cake in the fridge, Cate, and start focusing on that."

16
Ben

At the aquarium a man is seated behind the desk, he's an old bloke with glasses and not much hair on his head but a bunch of it coming out of his ears. He reminds me of my old primary school teacher, Mr Palmer, so I think he's going to be strict, but when he notices me he smiles, and his face changes. I see that to the side of the reception is a small room and the door is open so I can hear the sound of voices, chatter and laughter. I start to step away, but then I hear the jingle and realise it's not a group of people, it's only the TV.

"Hello, lad. You must be Ben?"

I jolt, eyes open and nod. To the side of reception is a tank, and inside are orange and black clown fish, prettily darting between lime green plant tentacles.

"So, Ben, the lady from, y'know, probation, she told me you like fish?" he asks, conversationally.

"Yes. I especially like the… " I want to say atmosphere or peace but something tells me this is the wrong answer. "Carp." I haven't thought about carp in eight years, yet the word just popped out.

"Hmm. Sullen buggers they are. Never ones to break a smile or a sweat, just bob around in their own sweet time. We've got a tankful of big 'uns just like them, through there." He points with his rolled up newspaper to the lower part of the aquarium. "Moody buggers, they are."

This makes me smile and he grins back. I imagine he

doesn't have many people here to appreciate his humour, the place seems empty. He unrolls his paper and I look back at the clown fish, feeling more awkward now that the silence has been broken.

"Okay, so my name's Leon. I'll show you round, but first do you want a cuppa?"

"Please." The truth is, I'm gasping for a drink. I still haven't bought a kettle, so all I've had for breakfast is tap water and a chocolate bar.

"The staff room is in there," he jerks a thumb to the small room. "Make me one too. Milk, two sugars."

I realise that this means something, that he's giving me my first job. It may mean he accepts my presence, or that he can't be arsed to make his own tea, but either way I'm glad to once again have someone telling me what to do.

The staff room is a cupboard with no windows. There are posters taped up, a football league table and a picture of a cat hanging from a branch by its claws. The officers in prison used to put posters in their office, the prisoners had pictures of women on their walls, but I never did. I couldn't think about girls, not properly. Not when the last time I spoke to one was eight years ago, just moments before my life was about to change forever. That girl was with her dad, and she was doing gymnastics in the Humber. She was wearing a vest top and cut-off shorts and was every bit as pretty as the girls in the wall posters. But her face became mixed up with what came after, so I can't stand to think of it. I fill the kettle with water, and while it boils I watch the TV.

It's an American show, loud voices, tanned skin, big hair. An older woman with a plunging neckline is giving three other woman, also with plunging necklines, advice on finding a man. "Don't give it away!" the busty woman orders. "Make him wait for it."

I can hear the water in the kettle bubbling so I pour it into mugs, not sure whether to use one teabag or two. I opt for one, dipping it between the cups, then agonise over how much milk to add. This simple thing, another lesson I have yet to master.

I return to reception, where Leon is reading the creased paper, and hand him his mug. He sips, then smacks his lips. "Perfect," he says, and I feel unreasonably delighted with myself. Because I don't want the moment to end, and I have nothing better to say, it tumbles out of me.

"That show on the telly is weird."

"Yeah?" He raises his eyebrows. It's just background noise to him, and he probably doesn't even know what's on right now.

"It's dating advice. But like a quiz game too. These three women, they all want to date this man who's a millionaire."

The man whistles. "I wouldn't mind advice on that, meself. Then I wouldn't have to work in this crap-hole."

My mouth sags. The aquarium seems so peaceful and calm, how can it be a crap-hole? I think he sees how upset I feel and then he says, more softly, "If you like fish it's different. Me, the only fish I like come battered with chips." Then he shrugs. "But it pays the bills, so I shouldn't complain."

Not for me, though. This job is voluntary, to get work experience that Cate said is important for my CV. Leon seems to realise his gaff.

"One thing, Ben. I know you're here as part of your Community Service or whatever they call it now, so you've done something wrong. I just want to say this: your probation officer never told me what you done and I never asked. As far as I'm concerned, you're here on work experience and as long as you keep making tea this good you and me will get on just dandy. Okay?"

17
The Day Of

The damned sun was still making its way into the room, even though Yvette had pegged the curtains together and piled two pillows over her head, which was throbbing like a swollen toe. She hadn't even drunk that much, though the vodka bottle was empty. It was mostly Stuart, and spirits always made him angry. He shouldn't have bought the bottle anyway, that money was meant to buy food. She had a splitting headache, but not 'cos of booze. It was stress, she probably had a brain tumour. Damn that man. Fuck him. Leaving again, just like he always did. Letting Adam down, pissing off just when she'd started to think that this time he'd stay for keeps.

She hadn't seen it coming. Stuart had talked about quitting the trawlers so he could be here more often. He was trying to get in at Smith and Nephew's, knew a bloke who knew a bloke. But instead he was gone again, with his duffel bag and his all-weather kit. He couldn't give up the sea, but he could give her up.

It was over. So he said.

He'd said it was her drinking, he said it was the way she couldn't get her act together, then he'd said it was Ben. And that was the part that really stuck with her, the reason she thought most likely. He couldn't live with 'that kid' and when she asked what he meant he'd said something about a 'constant reminder'.

Yvette occasionally looked into Ben's face and remembered

that time when Stuart had been gone too long and she was lonely, grateful for a little bit of kindness from a man who was indebted to her, but mostly she just saw Ben. Her kid, her son, no-one else's. For ten years, Stuart had never let it go, not that it was the only time she'd had another man but here was the evidence, walking around their home. It was why Stuart hated Ben, not that the kid could help where he came from.

A moment of defiance, maybe it was high time that Stuart pissed off. *Good riddance! Why should Ben have to put up with a step-dad like that? They were better off on their own, the three of them.* Then the anger was gone and she simply felt defeated.

How would she cope without him? When he came home, there was brass and there was food.

If only she could get some damned sleep, get rid of the headache, the world would feel a whole lot better when she woke, but Adam was in the bedroom next door, roaring about T-shirts and getting ready for a day-trip that wasn't going to happen. He'd find out soon enough. She groaned and slid deeper under the covers, putting off the moment, but then the bedroom door was flung open and she knew the moment had found her anyway.

Adam looked around the room.

"Where's me dad?"

She could hear in his voice that it had taken just a second for him to know Stuart was gone again. Doing what he always did when the going got tough.

"Gone. On the Icelandic boat."

Adam's face was drained of colour, his lower lip trembled, and she knew as well as if she felt it herself that the disappointment was crushing. And she couldn't find the words to comfort him, she couldn't say anything, her son looked so broken hearted. Instead she just opened her arms, her fingers beckoning him, desperate to hold him and make it better. Tell him that his dad may be a shit but she loved him and that was what mattered.

But Adam glared at her accusingly, like it was she who had ruined the plan. He saw the vodka bottle on the floor and he turned back to his own room. To Ben, the only person he seemed to trust with his pain, and Yvette returned to her own.

18
Now

Noah's mum: Today is our sixteenth wedding anniversary. I met Dave when I was seventeen and he gave me our precious son, Noah, may he rest in peace. Did you know that half of all parents who lose a child, divorce within a year? Not us, though. Happy anniversary, Dave. Thank you for everything, and I'm only sorry that I can't always be there for you. But everything I do is for our boy, you know that, don't you?

Dave: Happy anniversary, Jess. I love you and admire you, my powerhouse of a wife.

Silent Friend: Congratulations. It can't have been easy for you to make it through.

19
Cate

"Mum! Stop staring at me."

"Sorry, love."

Amelia was right though, Cate had been staring as Amelia painted her nails, inexpertly, dripping blue polish on the white Ikea table, but that wasn't what Cate was thinking about. She was marvelling at how grown up her daughter looked. Ten years old and so fully formed, with whispery blonde hair and large green eyes, Cate was glimpsing the woman her child would one day become.

"I'll take my nail polish set when I stay at Dad's tomorrow night. Maybe Sally will let me paint Chloe's nails."

"You better pack pink then. I don't think you'll be allowed to paint your half-sister's nails blue. And take the remover, once you've finished wiping the mess from the table."

Amelia enjoyed having a half-sister, so much so that she got annoyed when Cate used that phrase. "She's my sister, Mum. There's no half about it."

No half about any of it, not with Amelia.

Amelia lazily put some remover on a cotton pad and began to half-heartedly wipe up the mess, noticing that Cate had a stack of papers in front of her. "What's all that?"

"Just work."

Cate had been reading Yvette's statement, and it had made her feel sick for the woman's lost opportunity to save her son. The woman came across as depressed, she'd given up on life so much she hadn't even noticed that her two boys needed her. If the woman had only got up that day, taken them somewhere, things would have been so different. Cate knew this was harsh judgement, borne from hindsight. How was Yvette to know the tragedy that was coming her way?

Harsh too because Cate knew first-hand you can't just 'snap out of it'. Yet she couldn't bring herself to feel wholly sorry for Ben's mother, not when there were other people who deserved her pity so much more. Like Jessica and Dave Watts. Noah's parents were the true victims, no matter how much Yvette's life had been fucked up by the murder. At least her son was alive.

"Criminals?" Amelia asked, leaning her chin on Cate's shoulder to see what she was reading.

"Yup." She pushed the notes aside, out of Amelia's eyeline, and turned to her daughter. "Just for a change."

She covered Amelia's hand with her own, pulling away to see a dab of blue on her own skin and as she moved, a photocopy of the trial proceedings slid from the file. It was the artist's sketch of Ben as he sat in the dock. Amelia noticed it too.

"Did he do something bad?"

"He did." Just recently Amelia had begun asking questions, as if she was beginning to understand the world beyond her own life. Cate wanted to tell her anything she needed to know, didn't believe in innocence as a means of protection, but questions about Ben were sure to be difficult to answer.

"But he's just a boy."

"He was ten. Your age."

Amelia's eyes didn't widen, she didn't even looked surprised. Was it only adults who failed to grasp that children had the same range of emotions, the same capacity for good and evil?

"But now he's a young man. And it's my job to make sure he doesn't do anything bad again."

Amelia blew on her nails, then went to collect her bag,

calling over her shoulder. "You're always working, Mum. Why don't you have some fun?"

There was an email on her laptop. She hadn't replied to it yet, because she wasn't sure how to.

It was from Olivier:

Cate,
As part of my secondment it would be most beneficial if I could discover more about the probation service.
As part of my weekend, it would be most enjoyable if I could discover more about Cate Austin.
So maybe we could meet to this end.
Yours,
Olivier (mob 0776245673)

Her daughter had suggested she had fun, and who was Cate to argue? Ten-year-olds were always right, as Amelia often reminded her.

She clicked Reply and typed: **I'm free tomorrow evening if that offer still stands.**

But before she pressed Send she looked again at Ben's dossier on her dining table. Two possibilities presented themselves, and though seeing Olivier may be fun it also terrified her. She hadn't been out with a man in four years. Reading a casefile was a much safer option, and besides she didn't have anything nice to wear for a date.

She deleted the message to Olivier, and so resolved to spend another Friday night working instead. A much safer option.

20
Ben

I have an hour, just sixty minutes until my next meeting with Cate and I don't know where to go. I'm slowly walking through town as I count each second down, wondering how time can drag more than it did when I was in prison. I thought when I was free I would never feel its weight again, but I don't know what to do with myself. I haven't enough money left to go to McDonald's and anyway it's busy. I'd like to go to the aquarium but just one hour wouldn't be long enough, and Leon might think it's odd if I turn up when I'm not supposed to be there.

Then I see someone, he looks about my age or a bit older, but he's walking with such ease that I know he's never been where I have and I start to follow him. It's only then that I realise why. He reminds me of my brother. He has Adam's dark hair, I can't see his face, but he has Adam's walk too; shoulders back and head up just like Stuart told him. Like me, he's wearing jeans and a T-shirt, but he looks like he didn't give it any thought, they fit so easily. I tag behind him, through town, trying to copy how he moves, swinging one arm, using the other to support the orange rucksack casually carried on his shoulder. If I can only learn to walk like that, to look around me that casually, then no-one would realise I'm a freak. He turns and I think he's noticed me following so I duck into a doorway. My heart thumps and I tell it to calm down. I'm not doing anything wrong. When I step back onto the path I'm just in time to see the orange backpack disappear up a side street. I follow, jogging to catch up, then stop when I see the building he's entered, not sure I can go any further because it may be restricted, a special place where I'm not allowed.

Then I see it's a library.

Ipswich library is a glass building with shelves stacked so close to the windows they look vulnerable, layers and layers of books. We had a library in prison, but that was just a room with a handful of books and an old teacher, Roy, who'd try and persuade us not to pick the slasher books, but to go for classics. The other lads took the piss, but I liked Roy and I grew to like the classics too. Especially American stuff, *Catcher in the Rye*, *The Grapes of Wrath*, *To Kill a Mockingbird* and *On The Road*. Boys like me in different worlds, making other choices. It excited me more than any of the talk about rehabilitation, this idea of another life. I wanted my new identity to be American and brave, fighting injustice, having sex. I wanted to be Dean Moriarty on a road trip, not just me trying to enter a library on a Friday afternoon without looking odd.

I steel my nerves, though I'm so tense my shoulders are almost touching my ears, and tell myself this library is for everyone. And if I can find the boy with the orange rucksack, I can watch him some more. I can learn how to be normal.

Inside the library is a warren of bookshelves, much, much bigger than any library I've seen in any prison, which was usually just a converted classroom. But at least books always feel friendly, I learned that much, and I study the racks with longing. I catch my reflection in the window and wonder if I could look like a student. My hair's short, prison-issue – better not to give them anything to grab onto – but my clothes might pass, they aren't so different, except for my hoodie which is wrong in this heat but I'm too scared to lift it off, as if exposing my pale skinny arms is what will give me away and not my face. As if the hoodie isn't fleece but steel, a protective armour rather than a cheap sweatshirt that right now I'm sweating in.

I look for the boy, for his orange bag.

The library is fiercely air-conditioned inside, cold pricks at my skin until my arms are bumpy, and then I start to shiver. It's like being trapped in a glass box, I feel that everyone walking by is watching me, and I don't know how to act. Inside are older people mainly, all looking like they belong whether it's checking out books or reading leaflets or – like the student – finding an empty desk and opening up a laptop. I need to choose a direction, and quickly, or someone might speak to me.

Next to the entrance is a cluster of comfy-looking armchairs where people sit reading magazines. Other magazines are waiting to be read, on glossy display in gleaming glass racks with headers of different hobbies, different worlds: *TOP GEAR, FILM REVIEW, CROCHET CLUB.* I'd like to sit and read one, any of them, just to lose myself in the possibilities life offers a free person, but the single vacant chair is next to an old woman reading *KNITTING FOR BEGINNERS,* and she looks distracted, flipping the pages like she can't find what she's searching for. If I take that empty seat she might start talking to me and then I'd be trapped so I keep walking around in a circle, searching for stairs, but all I see is a lift. I can't do lifts.

I study the floor guide:

Floor 1: Fiction

Floor 2: Children's Books

The lift is open, just one step and I'd be whisked to another level.

Come on Ben, keep moving, you can do this. I can't stop walking or turn around, that would attract too much attention. I must look like I know what I'm doing. I force myself to step inside.

The lift is also glass so when the doors close I'm in a prison where I can see all the people and books, but can't be touched. My heart thuds and my hands feel clammy. As the lift moves I'm scared it will go on forever but of course it doesn't. It knows where it's going even if I don't, and opens up to show me even more racks of books in a darker, larger room. Corridors of books, I've never seen so many, it's like a labyrinth where exits are blocked by people reading back covers or walking long rows with their fingers trailing along spines.

I have to walk past people, still searching for the boy who reminds me of Adam, and I'm aware of their closeness and the silence. I sense some glance up as I pass but I keep my eyes ahead and walk as if I'm not lost. I'd like to stop and look at the books, find one I've read before, something familiar, but I'm scared. Then I come to some stairs and realise that there was an alternative to the lift and I was stupid to think there wouldn't be. Wide wooden stairs with open spaces between, curving up next to the window. The wall outside is a silver mosaic pattern, squares and circles, and I know from all I learned during hours of education that this is modern art. Or design. Something to be valued, anyway, though I can see the rust and think how it's being wrecked, by the rain or wind or whatever the elements are. If it was inside, locked away, it would have been protected from that. The rust makes me think of my silver scooter that got left in the rain. The rust meant the wheels didn't spin freely, and because of that I met Noah.

I'd seen him around, we lived on the same estate, but we'd never spoken before I got the scooter. He was different; his family had a bit of money, he had a dad who left for work every day in a car and came back each night. We had nothing in common until that scooter. He watched me as I tried to kick the wheels back into action, shyly at first and then with the conviction of someone who knew.

"WD40."

He took the handle, positioning the scooter so he could see the rusted wheels.

"My dad'll do it for you. He's a mechanic, so he knows."

I snatched it back. "Liar! You just want to steal it."

His eyes widened in surprise. "Why would I? I've got a scooter that works."

I watched him wheel it away, telling myself it was broken anyway, that it didn't matter if he nicked it.

But the next morning when I left for school the scooter was propped on my porch, not only greased and working but also rust-free. Either Noah or his dad had cleaned it up, and it looked better than when Stuart brought it home from a car boot sale, on a good day when he was making up for beating me, back when he still bothered.

I can't find him, the boy with the orange rucksack has disappeared. I look on Level 2, Children's Books, but it's deserted.

Of course, it's two in the afternoon, but there are no pre-schoolers even. This doesn't calm me, because I know I shouldn't be here – I'm not a child – and I stand out more being the only one. Eighteen. Too young to be a father and too old to be reading teen books. Aren't I? I walk swiftly, trying to contain my panic as I pass through sci-fi, skirting through romance, and arrive into another room, one that is smaller and brighter. On the floor is a large fluffy rug with a teddy bear's head, and there are different coloured beanbags all around it. There's a long lime-green crocodile, its back is big enough to sit on. I love this room, I don't want to leave and can't stop looking at the colourful books, yellow and orange and blue, so big I'd have to use two hands to read one. I daren't actually hold one. This room feels perfect and it makes me want to weep.

I sink deep into a giant red beanbag. I can hear activity in the other room, where the teen romances are, the wheels of a book trolley. Roy, the prison librarian at my last place, had one of those, I'd help him push it down the landings when he got out of breath. I hear it rattling closer, then I see the trolley and a portly woman pushing it. The librarian, short and busty and severe in half-moon glasses. I hold my breath, waiting to be told to leave or recognised or accused but she doesn't even look at me, as if her book business is far more important than noticing people.

When she leaves I relax but only slightly because I know this room isn't meant for me. There's a doll dressed like a witch holding a magic book and a fluffy Dalmatian and crayoned pictures of pirates taped to the window. I long for it, all of these stories and playthings, to have been brought somewhere like this, to have been read to. This never happened to me. Mum didn't like books but Stuart would sometimes bring one back from his trips, thick paperbacks about spies and criminals and drug barons because there wasn't much to do on a boat in a storm, and the crew would swap books between themselves as the skipper tried to get the boat to even water. When he left, I'd find them and try to read, a finger under the line and mouthing the words, but they were too difficult.

I don't remember anyone reading to me but I know without a doubt, though I never asked him, that this happened to Noah. His mum would have read him something every night, a book to help him sleep. And for a sharp moment I forget he's dead and I hate him all over again.

21
The Day Of

Noah knew the day wasn't going right, that his mum would be mad. She'd arranged for him to be looked after by Ben's mum, who she knew from school and also lived nearby. She'd left the house early, so when he woke there was an empty bowl set out with his chocolate cereal and a note that told him to do exactly what Yvette asked and to be a good boy and that she loved him. But Noah hadn't even seen Yvette when he knocked at the door, he'd not even got beyond the doorstep before the brothers had pushed him back out and told him to frame.

"Your mam is supposed to look after me today. It's been arranged. Mum gave her some brass for summat to eat for lunch."

Adam made a noise in his throat that was halfway between a chuckle and a roar. "Forget that, lad. Our mam's already drank your lunch money," he said, now making small circles on Noah's scooter.

Noah felt his insides going watery, he didn't like the way Adam was looking at him and he didn't know what to do. Should he knock and wait for Yvette to answer? Or call his dad at the garage, ask him? Yes, that seemed like a better plan, though his dad would probably say that he should just wait in the house until he finished work.

"Ben, can you tell your brother to give us the scooter back? I'm going home."

Noah watched anxiously as Ben approached his brother, there was a tussle with the handlebars and then Adam turned, rode directly at Noah who froze, thinking Adam was going to scoot straight into him and send him flying. Instead, Adam pulled up short, yanked the scooter onto its tail and said, "Ay up, lad. Cool scooter."

Noah took the handle, feeling relieved to have his scooter but also wondering why his mum had done this to him, why she hadn't found a proper babysitter. He started to scoot away but Adam grabbed his wrist.

"Hey, where are you going?"

"Home." Noah looked at Ben for help. "Mam will be back soon."

It was a lie, her train didn't get back at Paragon station until this evening. And Dad would be back then too, but that still meant he had the whole day alone. He felt himself shaking, close to tears.

"You can go home," Adam said with a shrug, "if you want. But we're going down road to the shops. I'll get you summat, if you like?"

"What?" Noah asked, suspiciously.

"Whatever goodies you like. Chocolate. What do you like best, Mars, Crunchie?"

"I like Rolos."

"Fine." Adam showed Noah a pound coin he'd got. "Come on, then."

It was almost eleven o'clock and Noah's stomach was rumbling. If Adam was telling the truth there'd be no lunch from Yvette and his mum was miles away in London.

The three boys walked to the small stretch of shops nearest their estate that included their own personal Mecca, the Patel's corner shop that sold 5p sweets along the counter. Mrs Patel never said anything, even though she must notice that they never bought much but always seemed to be sucking blackjacks or jelly dummies when they left. She wore an exotic wrap of a dress and had a red spot in the middle of her forehead. She never looked directly at them, always just a little to the side, and Noah's mum said she was a workhorse. "In that shop all hours, poor thing, when her husband is God knows where." If Mr Patel was anywhere in the vicinity, the boys never chanced it, but today as usual it was just Mrs Patel, standing over her till as the bell above the door announced their arrival.

Adam strode up to the counter and started picking up different chocolate bars, then putting them back, as if he couldn't decide. Noah stood next to Ben, both of them itching to put a few of the chewy cola bottles into their pockets, when Noah felt something, a pressure, being slid into his pocket. It felt heavy, like a large rock, weighing him down. "Now leave!" Adam hissed into his ear, as he handed Mrs Patel a packet of Rolos and pound coin. "Just this, please."

The bell rang loudly as Noah left, feeling the bulge in his pocket and feeling certain Mrs Patel knew, even if she didn't say.

Adam ran from the shop, grabbed Noah by the elbow and together they scarpered, Ben running behind and yelling, "What's up? Why're we running?"

Once they had left the estate and arrived at a grassy bank on the edge of Hessle Road, Noah slowed, feeling the item in his pocket banging into his leg. He reached to see what it was, but Adam took it from him and held it into the air like a trophy. It was a globe-shaped bottle of something peach-coloured.

Adam gave Noah the tube of Rolos.

"Okay, lads. Let's get us party started!"

The drink tasted like bubble bath, the fruity stuff his mum liked, that he bought her at Christmas and Mother's Day. But after a few mouthfuls Noah felt warm in his tummy, and his head felt swimmy like when he'd stayed up too late watching

TV and was so tired he should be in bed but instead he fought it. Adam was lying on his back, telling them funny stories about other kids at his school, and Noah now knew that his mum was definitely wrong. Anyone who supported Hull Rovers had to be alright, and Adam was cool and funny and peach schnapps was fan-bloody-tastic.

"Hey, Noah," said Adam, finishing off the fruit-shaped bottle and tossing it into the undergrowth where a woman was watching her dog take a shit. She gave them a dirty look and yanked the dog onwards, not bothering to clean up after it. If she wondered why they weren't in school, she said nothing.

"Let's go see a film," said Adam, excited to have had an idea and fuelled by the cheap alcohol to a spike of happiness.

"How?" said Noah, huffily. "We've got no brass."

"Ah!" Adam jumped up, wobbling on one foot before righting himself, looking in his red sports strip like a rugby player ready to run for the ball. "But I know a secret way in."

22
Now

FACEBOOK: FIND HUMBER BOY B

Noah's mum: I went to the doctors today and she gave me some more tablets to help the stress and the not sleeping and that. It's horrible to think Noah's killer is out there, and I don't even know what he looks like now. When he was a boy I welcomed him into my home, made him sandwiches, gave him juice, let him come into the house to play with Noah. Both boys liked Lego and I used to keep a box in the sitting room. It's still there, I can't bring myself to part with it.

Humber Boy B played in my house, with my son, and now I could pass him in the street and not know. I'm feeling my search for him is useless, that I'll never be able to change the fact that he's free. And that's as painful as losing Noah all over again.

Dave: We can't give up, love. Someone somewhere knows where he is.

Noah's mum: The reporter from *The Sun* keeps calling, and I'm thinking this may be our best hope. The paper is read by millions, and it only takes one person to recognise him. I just want to be clear, this isn't a witch-hunt. I just want some answers. My son died, don't I at least deserve that?

Silent Friend: You deserve much more than that. And he can't hide forever.

23
Cate

"Mum, I want to go see *Frozen 2* with Chloe this afternoon. It's just opened, and they've got a 4D premiere, with real snow. Well, not real snow but you know what I mean. Dad said he'd pick me up after lunch."

Cate hesitated. Amelia had stayed with her dad on Friday night, as usual, and returned home last night. Sunday was supposed to be her day.

"Oh, well... Would I like the film?"

"It's only just out, so no-one's seen it yet, but you know how amazing the first *Frozen* was."

"Vaguely."

"You do, Mum! You know the song," Amelia broke off speaking to sing the chorus of Let It Go until Cate was singing along with her. "It's about two sisters, Elsa and Anna, but they have to be apart because one has got this secret, this bad thing that if she tells anyone they'll just... well, I don't know what, because when she does tell it's actually okay. But it's sad, because the sisters can't play together, but then one sister decides to sort it out. Anyway, I don't know what happens in *Frozen 2* but it's got to be brilliant. Please say I can go?"

Cate smiled at her daughter, whose face was twisted in earnest concentration as she tried to remember the details of the film. "Okay, I like the sound of that. I'll come too. We can sing that song again in the car."

Now Amelia looked panicked, a frown formed between

her eyebrows, marking her perfect face with worry. "Sally's going to be there, Mum."

"Oh." Being civil with Tim's second wife was one thing, sharing popcorn with her was quite another. Much as Cate liked the sound of two sisters sorting out their differences, she'd have to take a rain check. "Sounds like I'll have to skip on it then, even though I'd enjoy the snow."

Amelia's face showed her emotions swing from relief to concern. "But what about me? Please, Mum. Can I go?"

Cate gave in, keeping Amelia at home would be selfish. "Okay, sweetheart. Call your dad and say yes."

As Amelia rushed to the phone, excited and happy, Cate thought of what she would do with her Sunday now. Something had changed for her, spending the last few days immersed in Ben's casefile, she had an urge to shake free of its weight, to do something daring. And that's exactly what she was expecting Ben to do, she was asking him to live again, to work, to find some pleasure in life. Yet she was trapped, as trapped by her divorce as she had been when Tim first left. And Amelia, who had once been all hers, was breaking away, making choices about how to spend her time. Cate needed to take a risk. And she had an idea in mind.

She felt in her bag for her phone, and scrolled down her emails. Dare she reply to Olivier? His email had remained unanswered for three days. She sent one line into the ether: **I'm free to meet up today, if your offer still stands?**

Amelia was singing as she slipped on her coat, Tim was outside in the car, where he tended to wait these days now that he had so little to say to Cate that couldn't be communicated via text message. Cate waved her daughter off and forced herself to get a glass of water, all stalling tactics, before she finally returned to her phone to see if Olivier had replied.

Olivier: **That took you a while to think about! So is this a work meeting? Or pleasure?**

Cate hesitated before responding, she had to push from

her mind Tim's steely face as he had driven their daughter away, the pain this doomed marriage had caused her. Fun, that was what she needed and Amelia's talk of the snow in the 4D screening had given her an idea, but she wasn't sure that Olivier would be up for it.

Cate: **That depends. Can you ski?**

Olivier: **In September? Are we catching a plane?**

It wasn't Cate's first visit to the Ipswich ski slope, Amelia had her last birthday party here and had a great afternoon ringoing down the slope. She hadn't joined in herself, too busy setting out cake and sandwiches in the picnic area. But now she wanted to try.

"What is this?" Olivier asked, looking at the inflated plastic tube as if had landed from outer space. "Plastic hoops belong in swimming pools, not on a ski slope!" He placed the ring on the fake snow and then sat on it, it sagged beneath him, making him looking ridiculous. Cate laughed so hard she had to catch her breath. His beige jeans were too smart, his long sleeved shirt too fitted for the trip, but she enjoyed this spectacle, and his awkwardness as they queued with a line of youngsters waiting to whizz down the slope in a wet, slippery heap. Maybe the French didn't do 'casual'.

Olivier was first to ringo down the hill, much to the disgust of the serious skiers who were presumably practising ahead of their winter holiday. These skiers ploughed their way across the path of the children and people just having fun. At the bottom he stood, brushed the faux-snow from his thighs and shouted up to her, "Go on, Cate! I will catch you!"

She sat on the bouncy tyre, feeling how little control she had over its movements, how quickly it would slide once she pushed off from the flat section at the top. But this had been her idea, and Olivier was waiting.

She closed her eyes as the tyre slipped over the edge, then screamed as she gave in to fun, bumping down the snowy slope at a speed that took her breath and left her laughing hysterically in a heap at the foot of the hill, looking up at Olivier.

"Okay, Cate, so I have done as you ask and made a fool of myself along with a million school kids. Now can we get a drink?"

The ski lodge was three months ahead of itself with black and silver Christmas tinsel twisted around the dark wood railings that segregated the coffee drinkers from those eating lunch, but all the tables were the same fake mahogany, the wood all painted black around the windows which were covered with black slatted blinds.

"We can pretend we're in the French Alps," Cate said, knowing that beyond the windows was the car park and the other side was the docks. But with the dim lighting they could be anywhere, if not for Michael Bublé being piped from the speakers and the crowd being obviously British from their Hollister hoodies, ruddy faces and copious drinking of cappuccinos.

"I just have to drive two hours to ski from Luxembourg. The Vosges Mountains are beautiful and the restaurants, I promise, absolutely nothing like this."

"Snob," Cate teased, then drank her sparkling water quickly, thirsty from the physical exercise. "I know this isn't exactly Switzerland but what I like about it is that it doesn't feel like Ipswich. I could be miles away."

Olivier watched her keenly. "Indeed, travel of any kind can be good for the soul." He reached and touched her hand. "Thank you, Cate. This trip has been good for mine."

This time when she arrived home to an empty house, Cate didn't feel sad, she was too elated. She ran a deep bath, adding oils that would soothe her aching muscles. Before she stepped into the steamy water she poured herself a glass of wine and found the paperback novel she had bought in the summer but never got around to reading. It was a light romance, and she simply hadn't been in the mood before.

She settled in the water, sipped her drink and opened the book. And not once did she think about work.

24
Ben

Who will find me first?

This is my waking thought.

Which I suppose is progress, because on other mornings I've woken up thinking I'm late, that any minute a prison officer will fling open my cell door and haul me from bed, shout at me that breakfast is being dished up and do I think this is a bloody hotel? Or, on bad mornings, I've woken in a cold sweat thinking it's shower day.

That was when they used to get me. The new kid who wanted to mark himself out as tough, the gang leader who sniffed out my weakness, prisoners who knew enough to see that I don't fit in any box that says 'burglar' or 'junkie' or even 'nonce'. They knew I was none of those things, but they didn't know what I was, so they got me, in the shower, when the staff were turning a blind eye, when the sound of the water hitting the tiles covered up my cries. "Tell us what you did, freak. Tell us before we drown you like the rat you are."

At least I don't have to worry about that any more.

But when I was crumpled on the shower floor, blood leaking from my ear or nose, I knew someone would come to help. Eventually. Even if it was a prison officer who was well aware of who I was and let me know that, they still had to escort me to the medical wing, they still had to keep me alive.

Who will protect me now I'm free?

I'm an easy target. I'm small, skinny and pale. 'My fine-boned prince' Mum would say when she was happy or just 'runt' when she wasn't. My smallness was something she enjoyed more when I was little, but when I failed to grow and Stuart pointed out how weak I was, how Adam was so much stronger, she changed her mind. I've always been small, the other lads in prison thought I was a wimp, the lads who pushed weights in the prison gym and did sit-ups each night when we were locked in our cells, calling to each other breathlessly as they counted to a hundred before changing to squats. But they were wrong. I'm not a wimp. I may be skinny, but I'm more lethal than any other boy I met in prison.

Dangerous. That's why the judge had me locked away for so long, even though at ten I was only just legally responsible. That's why I have to be Ben, because the real me is so feared, so wanted, that even to keep my first name was a risk. Someone in the Home Office changed my name when I was still ten and, entering my first secure unit, I was re-named by some civil servant who'd never met me, but my shiny new name didn't keep me safe. For six years I was ghosted from secure unit to secure unit, up and down the country, then for two years I did a tour of the YOIs. If I couldn't hide in the prison system, when I was surrounded by scum, how can I hide in the open, among decent people? They may call this freedom but it feels like a bigger prison with more to fear.

After I've eaten a handful of cornflakes, with no milk because I ran out yesterday and forgot to buy some, and from the packet because I still don't have any bowls or spoons, I decide to walk.

My feet take me towards the bridge. It's not my bridge, this is the Orwell not the Humber, but it still makes my heart flip like a fish in a bucket, it's so huge and beautiful. Perfect in its concrete-footed steadiness, the even arches and straight, straight lines. From down here at the water's edge I can only see the tops of lorries magically moving down the bridge, like a remote control truck I had when I was a kid. Who got me that toy? Not Mum, certainly not Stuart. Could have been my dad, on one of his fleeting visits when he was docked in Hull and Stuart wasn't around. Before. Those lorries could be remote control, red lorry, yellow lorry, green. Spaced perfectly.

Can't see cars, not from down by the river, just Maersk and P&O and Quality. Only words over concrete. The blue sky around it, fluffy clouds like grazing sheep under a perfect disc of white, the sun seemingly bumping the only grey cloud in the sky.

The footpath is closed, which is a shame because it looks like it leads down to the water's edge: Danger Men Working. But there are no men here, unless you count me, there's only a single barrier, a foot maybe two high, and that sign. Adam would never be stopped by a sign, he was fearless. If I'd been more like him, things would have turned out differently. I walk around it and go down to the water anyway, finding it isn't so hard to ignore the warning.

The river is full, rippling in the middle with a band of stillness before each bank, so I know a boat must have recently passed, the water is still settling. I can see all this, but I can also see another bridge and hear shouting, Noah and Adam's voices as clear as if they were next to me, so I squeeze my eyes and come back to Ipswich and this moment and being Ben.

I need to put my feet in the water.

On the other bank, to the left, a line of red brick houses, crumbling, they must be way older than the bridge, they must have seen the river being the main route through, the docks in the distance with cranes reaching into liners carrying cargo. Now their view must be red lorry, yellow lorry, Bartrums and China Shipping. Dock lorries, from Felixstowe port to the rest of the UK, onwards to the rest of the world. This bridge allows all this travel but those houses just have to watch. Do they like it, the activity, the signs of life, or do they curse the sound of lorries and sight of the concrete bridge ripping across the sky?

A head appears, a man's face. I turn to go, thinking it's a builder and I'll be told off for ignoring his sign. Then I see he's wearing waders and carrying a fishing rod and walking towards the water. He too is ignoring the sign because he wants to fish. My mind flips back, I can't help it, to Roger Palmer. When I saw him in the courtroom he was a different man from the one I'd known in the classroom, like he'd been shrunk and all the colour had bled from him. The court trial was so long, six whole weeks, so tedious and stuffy. Boring, even though my freedom was at stake.

By the end of those six weeks, through the tedious repetition of facts, the struggle to keep awake, came the sharp realisation that what happened on the bridge didn't just change three lives, Noah's and Adam's and mine, it changed other people's lives too. And Roger Palmer's was one of them.

That man can't be Roger Palmer. My mind is playing tricks again, like it did when I thought the boy with the orange rucksack looked like Adam. It's like my brain hasn't caught on to the fact that my life has begun again. This is a different bridge, but I won't ever go to any bridge now without thinking about that red trainer going over the side, then the boy following.

When I arrive back at the flat I see I have a letter.

In the lobby are mail boxes, one for each flat and I wouldn't have even bothered checking but I could see the corner of an envelope caught in the flap. I use my key to open the box and there it is, a small white envelope handwritten to my new name, at my new address. It's Adam's handwriting, so I know that my card to Mum arrived, because that's the only way he could know my address.

I feel the thin paper between my fingers and the serrated edge, this page was ripped from a jotter, the biro-ink smudged on the page and I can detect the faint whiff of Lynx body spray. Even when he was fourteen Adam was vain, always thinking about what to wear. He can't have changed.

We shouldn't have any contact, Cate made that clear, it's a condition of my parole. A breach, and I could be hauled back to prison. Many people would cheer if I was back behind bars. I can't give them any excuse. The past puts me at risk, but he's my brother, my family.

I gently peel open the envelope.

Hey Bro.

How's life, then? Must be weird, being able to walk about and that. They've sent you miles – I didn't even know where Ipswich was until I looked it up yesterday on us computer. New start for you, our kid.

Mam got your card. She can't write just now, give her a chance to get used to it, okay? But she's fine, no worries.

Summat to make you smile. I've got a girl. SHE KNOWS. She started writing to me, a few years back. Really sweet letters. And then she wanted to visit us and that's rare, right, so I thought why not? I was so nervous I couldn't sit still, but she was lovely. Pretty. And she kissed us when she left.

We're thinking of moving in together. Seems like my luck is changing. Hope yours is too.

Anyway, I know where you are now so I might just come and see you one day. I've missed you, bro.

I check the postmark on the letter and see it was sent second class, two days ago, from Hull. Just that word mixes me up inside, and part of it is that he's there and I can't be. He's seen Mum, but she won't even write to me. Adam's given me no details, how could he when a letter could get lost, fall into the wrong hands. But even this isn't my main thought, the one that goes round and round is whether Mum knows that Adam has written to me. Does she care?

I read the letter again, this time zoning in on the fact that Adam has a girlfriend, and SHE KNOWS. The capitals are so he doesn't have to spell it out, but can she really know everything? Is it possible, that a girl can know about Noah's death and still want to be involved? Not be put off at all? Could I get a girlfriend too, someone who knows about my past and still wants to be with me? But then I remember that she's with Adam, not me. Adam wasn't convicted of murder. A girl may want him, but they'd never want me – how could they when my own mother doesn't?

I put the letter back in its envelope and go to my bedroom, yanking the bag from under the bed. This letter has to be put away along with the others, the ones I received during my eight years in prison. Inside the bag is one letter that I can't even stand to look at, but I know it by heart. My mum sent it, just days after the trial, and I was stupid enough to open it. The letter is worn thin by my fingers, the ink has rubbed in places under the pad of my thumbs and the folds are floppy and torn from all those times I read and re-read it, looking for one word of comfort or pity or even forgiveness.

I'll say it for you and save you the trouble – I'm a crap mum. There. Said and done so let's be straight with each other. Nowt you do from now on can hurt me anyway – I'm your mam so the blame was always gonna be put on us. Is that what you wanted?

Okay, so I admit it. I never loved you. I was rubbish at love because no-one loved me much either. Make you feel better, does it? I doubt it.

I try to not torture myself with the rest of the letter, though I can never bring myself to bin it, and even folded away the letter is still being read in my head. I was ten years old, had just been locked away for murder, and the letter exploded something inside me like a bomb, shocking me with its brutal honesty. Mum hated me. Even though she'd sat through the trial and heard all the evidence she still thought that what happened on the bridge was all my fault.

It wasn't my fault, Noah climbed over the railing himself.

Thinking about concrete and steel, the forever strength of the Humber Bridge, is so much more preferable to remembering Noah's face, the broken skin of his lower lip, which was puffed and bloody over his chin, dripping red down his front, splattering his T-shirt. Who would have known a lip could bleed like that?

And now, this letter from Adam.

Adam, who stuttered in court. Whose father pointed at me, and said I led his son astray.

"I'm Ben," I tell myself. "This is my new life. I have no brother."

25
The Day Of

Mrs Patel felt herself stiffen when she saw the three boys outside her shop. She knew about the teacher's strike, it was why her daughter Nazma was upstairs doing her maths homework, rather than sitting in class where she should be. These teachers did not seem to understand that teaching was a privileged occupation, and she found their demands for extra money vulgar. Why wasn't six weeks holiday each summer enough? She hadn't had a holiday in twenty-three years.

Through the window she recognised all three, two of them brothers and the third boy – the smallest – who would often come in with his mum. Polite boy, well-raised. The brothers she felt sorry for, though the oldest one made her nervous too. He was edging towards adulthood.

The bell rang as the door nudged open and in they came, bringing their vinegary sweat and old socks smell with them. They positioned themselves along the sweet counter, the eldest boy nearest to her at the till smelling heavily of deodorant and dressed in the sports top of the local team, then his brother with the white hair, finally the young one who hadn't looked at her once although when he came with his mother she always made him say hello. They thought she was a fool, pretending to be browsing the wares, when really they were looking for the chance to steal. Other shops had signs, not allowing children in groups, but Mrs Patel didn't like to do such things. She preferred to hope for better.

"Hello, Mrs Patel."

To be fair, the eldest boy always greeted her this way, and he had a nice smile even though he looked in need of a wash. She nodded, and waited by the till for him to hand her whatever chocolate bar he wanted, but the two younger boys were shuffling nearer to the smaller sweets, the ones that cost just a few pence each and were easier to slide into pockets. It was taking the eldest boy a long time to decide which chocolate bar he wanted, though her selection never changed and he had visited the shop hundreds of times. Finally, he chose a tube of Rolos and gave her the money. He then led the other boys from the shop.

She walked from behind the till to the window and watched them go. Once outside, they began to run. She turned to face the empty place on the alcohol shelf, where the half-bottle of peach schnapps had been. It was cheap and strong, it would probably make them sick. She wouldn't admit this to anyone, but she enjoyed this thought as she went to the stock room to replace the stolen bottle, the mental image of the three of them on all fours like dogs, vomiting into the grass. Then she placed another bottle in the empty space and returned to her position behind the till, thinking no more about it.

26
Now

FACEBOOK: FIND HUMBER BOY B

Sue: I saw a man today who looks like the boy in the photo you posted, but older. He was a right thug, roaring at his poor kid on the beach today at Scarborough. He had a tattoo on his neck.

Noah's mum: Thanks, Sue, but it can't be him. Parole Board say he's not allowed in Humberside. But please spread the word and we'll find him somewhere. At least when he was behind bars, I knew where he was. I'd sacrifice a great deal to have him back there again.

Silent Friend: This country isn't so big that he can hide forever. And I'm getting closer.

27
Cate

Resisting the urge to indulge herself on a Sunday evening by watching a soapy crime drama, Cate sat at her dining room table in front of her laptop, trying to concentrate. Her thoughts kept taking her back to her ski-slope trip with Olivier, and she was unsure if she enjoyed the tight knot of excitement she felt when she thought of him, something she had not felt since dating Tim, back when she was in her teens. She told herself to concentrate. Tomorrow at nine sharp was a Risk Management meeting, called by the police. Olivier wouldn't talk about it on their date, he'd simply said it was to do with a potential risk of attack, but the team would want to hear how Ben was, so she had written a report on his progress. It would be the first that they had heard of his work placement at the aquarium, and she didn't want any of them to say Ben had to stop. It was early days, but Leon who managed the aquarium seemed to like Ben and said he was doing well. She'd have to convince the panel that giving Ben a purpose, a structure to his day, would fend off the depression that usually struck long term prisoners following release. To her knowledge there had been no sign that Ben's identity or location was compromised.

The doorbell trilled, making her start. She wasn't expecting anyone and wanted to finish her report. Maybe it was someone collecting for the Blue Cross or something.

But through the glass panel of the front door she saw a

silhouette she recognised, and her heart dropped like a stone. It was her mother.

"Hello, Catherine." She said it primly, and Cate immediately felt like a naughty child. "I thought if I phoned first, you'd make an excuse not to see me."

Cate thought even more longingly of whatever crime serial was on TV, a bit of escapism from the drama in her own life that always seemed to start when her mother re-appeared.

"Isn't it a bit late for a casual visit, Mum?"

"It's only just nine."

"Yeah, but that's not exactly what I meant."

Cate's mother was smartly dressed as usual, but as she walked past her into the hallway, Cate detected a whiff of alcohol. "Where's Amelia?"

"Where she should be on a Sunday night at this time. In bed."

"Can I see her?"

"I'd rather you didn't. She's sound asleep." But it was too late, a call from upstairs revealed the lie. "Is that Nanny?" And then, as Amelia appeared in her nightdress at the top of the stairs, "I'm thirsty!" She clambered down and was immediately hoisted up in her grandmother's embrace.

"Well, Amelia, what a colourful nightie. Is that a princess on the front?"

"Yeah, it's Anna from *Frozen*. Dad bought it for me from the Disney shop in Norwich."

"Ah, well that's nice. She's got beautiful hair."

"That's what he said when he bought me the nightie. He said it was red like Mum's."

Cate raised an eyebrow in surprise that Tim would say anything complimentary about her. Sally must have loved that. Luckily, with the innocence of youth, Amelia carried on without noticing her grandmother and mum exchanging a look.

"Dad says that's why Mum has such a temper too."

Oh. Sally really would have liked that one.

"He says he might take me to Euro Disney next year, it's really for Chloe's fifth birthday, but they have a park that's all about films, so I bet there's a *Frozen* section. I'd like that best."

"Where is Euro Disney?" Her mother asked, vaguely, "Paris? Well that would be lovely, wouldn't it?"

Cate saw with detached interest that her mother was indeed capable of affection. Realising she was fighting a losing battle, Cate pointed her daughter and mother to the lounge. "Okay, Amelia, I give up. Tell Nanny about Paris while I get you some water. Want a drink, Mum?"

"Yes, please. A gin and ice would be good."

"I'll put the kettle on then."

From the kitchen, Cate listened to her mother ask Amelia about school, about dance class, about Chloe. She didn't want to leave them alone for too long, but when she re-appeared with the tray, her mum pulled a face at the weak tea.

"Look, Mum, I've got work to do for tomorrow and I don't want Amelia to be tired in the morning so if this can wait… "

Her mother stopped rummaging in her bag and wiped her mouth quickly. "If what can wait?"

"Whatever it is you came for."

Her mother tried to pull Amelia back onto her lap, but she was sipping her water and rubbing her eyes sleepily.

"Can't I call round to see my only grandchild?"

Cate shrugged, knowing there would be more to it than that. Her mother only turned up when something bad had happened, like some bloke had dumped her or someone had slighted her at the rotary club. And her eyes did look oddly focused, like she was really thinking about something or someone else. She took a deep breath, staring at the tea, which she no doubt wished was gin.

"Elizabeth called me."

So there it was. The real reason for the visit.

"Why?" Cate was incredulous.

"Is that your sister?" Amelia said, suddenly alert and no longer sleepy.

Cate was stunned. Her mother carried on regardless of Amelia hanging on every word. "Of course it is, Amelia, your Aunt Elizabeth who lives far away. She called to say she wants to see us."

"Amelia, time for bed now." Cate's voice shook. "Say goodnight to Nanny." Amelia reluctantly placed a kiss on an over-rouged cheek, pulling away as her grandmother held her too tight but still not making a move to go until Cate gave her a gentle shove. "Bed, Amelia. Now."

When she had gone, Cate turned on her mother.

"I can't believe it. Where is she?"

"She wouldn't say." Her mother sighed with a show of patience, as with a petulant child. "I know I made a mess of things, Catherine, but it wasn't my fault entirely. If your father had been a better husband, then things might have been different at home. You must take after me, when it comes to relationships. If only we didn't fall for such bastards."

"Don't bring Dad into this, or me, please. You're responsible for your own drinking."

"Is there any wonder I drink when my own daughter takes that tone with me? And what about Elizabeth? How would you feel if Amelia didn't want to see you?"

"Please don't compare me to you. I love my daughter." Cate said quietly, with barely supressed bitterness.

"And I love you, both of you. I must say, I think Tim may have had a point about that temper of yours. Do you think if you dyed your hair brown you might feel calmer?"

"Mum, don't be so impossible. You know you're just avoiding the truth."

Her mother primly smoothed down her skirt. "And what truth is that?"

"I'm talking about why you drank. If you hadn't been drunk all the time things would have been different. For me. For Liz. Maybe she wouldn't have walked out that day and never come back."

Cate's mother fell back into the chair, as if exhausted. "You're so selfish, just like your sister. Don't you think it's been hard for me? Don't you think I suffered, having to pretend everything was fine?"

There was a pause, a stillness, as they both mentally re-adjusted their positions, deciding how far this argument could go. Concluding that she was too tired, Cate said coldly, "So why does she want to see us now. What's changed, after all these years?"

"She says she'll tell us when we meet. She's going to call you."

"Well I'll have to see if I'm available. After all, I've been trying to find her for two decades."

Her mother was on her feet now, scrabbling for the keys at the bottom of her bag. On her way out she came face to face with Cate in the doorway.

"The thing with you, my darling, is you've always been so self-righteous. But has it ever occurred to you that you might have some responsibility for what happened?"

Cate listened to her mother drive away, her back to the front door, her chin pointed toward the light. Could it be true, that she had been part of the reason why Liz left? If so, it sounded like she might finally be about to find. And Cate, to her own surprise, discovered that the idea terrified her. Liz's leaving had been like a rock in a pond, but the ripples had now settled. Even if her life wasn't everything she wanted, it wasn't bad, and she didn't want Liz to change that.

28
Ben

The mop is frozen in my hand. I'm so mesmerised by the biggest tank, by the secret world of water and rocks, that I've forgotten I'm supposed to be cleaning the whole area. I'm hypnotised by the fish, all different types, swimming amongst floating jetsam, all sizes and shapes, getting along, bumping noses and not minding. How can they be so peaceful, despite the closeness, despite being so different?

My thoughts run on, unchecked, as the fish gape and float by.

River fish, the same fish that would live in the Humber, the type that gets hooked on lines or caught in nets. Was it fish like these that Noah saw as he drowned, bubbles of precious air leaving his nose and mouth, if it wasn't the impact that got him first.

A line of silver sharp-finned fish, each the size of my palm, peer out. Of all the fish in all the tanks these alone watched the watcher with bulging, accusing eyes.

"Penny for them?"

I jump, steady myself, and return briskly to the task of mopping the floor where a hyperactive toddler dropped a sippy cup of juice earlier this afternoon. Leon has already turned the aquarium sign to 'closed' and washed up our tea mugs.

"Sorry, Leon. I was just watching the fish."

"You're alright, lad. Nice to know you're so interested.

Now, I've a question for you. I'm wondering if you'd like to come to mine for Sunday lunch? Meet the missus."

Startled, I feel the colour rise from my neck to my cheeks as I scrub harder at the floor though signs of the spillage are all gone.

"Oh. When?"

"Sunday. Lunchtime." Leon laughs at his humour, then starts coughing. When he speaks again his tone is one of extreme politeness, "If you're free tomorrow, that is."

"I'm free."

For the first time the words mean something. I put the mop and bucket into the cupboard and wait, watching carefully as Leon draws a simple map of how to find his house, a buzzing inside announcing I am coping, I'm being 'rehabilitated' as the parole board put it. Sunday lunch, it sounds formal and proper though Leon is neither of these things so maybe it will just be a sandwich, like Leon brings to the aquarium each day wrapped in silver foil.

"And make sure you arrive hungry," he then says.

The prospect of a proper sit-down meal is both terrifying and thrilling.

Leon's pencilled map, with arrows and the bridge and pub sketched in, spent Saturday evening and night propped next to the bed on the bedside table. Now the map is in the kitchen, on the window ledge. I've studied it so carefully I could probably walk to Leon's house blindfolded, yet I still fold it carefully and put it in my back pocket.

It's just gone eleven, but I don't want to be late and I need to call at the Spar first. I've noticed before that they have flowers outside, in a black bucket, and I'm planning to buy some.

It's Shirl on the till again.

"Hello, love. Date is it?"

"Sunday lunch."

She looks me over, taking in the new shirt, the pale blue

one from my shopping trip with Kevin to buy my release wardrobe. This shirt is meant for job interviews. The collar is uncomfortable, unused as I am to fitted clothes, but Shirl looks like she approves. She turns her attention to the flowers.

"Nice. I love chrysanths." Shirl peels off the price label and wraps the flowers in pink paper, carefully taping them into a funnel, and hands them back to me like they are precious. "I hope she likes them."

I follow the map, taking the path that runs just under the Orwell Bridge, past The Star pub that Leon has indicated in the obvious way, and along until I see the line of red brick box homes and realise that he lives in one of the houses I saw the other day from the riverbank. Where I lived in Hull, there were lots of streets like this, the dog shit and litter, the taped-up windows. But when I get to Leon's home I see that it's not like my old home at all. The front yard is neat and cared for and the gate is dark with wood varnish. The gate has a wooden plaque with a squirrel painted beside it, holding number 3 like it was a nut. Opening the gate, I see that in the window of the front room sits another squirrel, this time pottery and red with pointy little ears. I reach for the door knocker, hesitate, then rap the bronze squirrel's tail onto the wooden door, too lightly to be heard, but the door opens anyway.

Leon beams at me, looking so different that I realise for the first time that what he wears at the aquarium, a navy short-sleeved shirt, is a uniform. Now he looks much more relaxed, in blue jeans and a burgundy T-shirt with a Native American pictured on the front.

"How!" he jokes, though I only get it when he holds up one hand in greeting. "Come in and meet the old gal."

"I wish I still was a girl." A woman is stood in the doorway to the kitchen. Behind her wafts the delicious scent of roasting meat. She has her hands in oven gloves, her body wrapped in a pink frilly apron, and her face lit with a heart-breaking warm smile.

One thing about prison, there weren't many women. Just a few officers, the odd teacher, but most of the adults I've known have been men. I suddenly worry that I won't know how to talk to her.

"Er, hi."

"Hello, love. I've heard so much about you. I'm Issi."

I thrust the flowers awkwardly into her oven-gloved hands and she holds them with such surprise and delight that I wish I'd bought chocolates too.

"Well, come on in. Mi casa is sur casa, isn't that what they say, Leon?"

"Something like that, love." He gives me a wink. "Come on, Ben. I'll get you a tinnie."

The front room is like no other I've ever been in. There are so many things, it's like a shop. Pottery and lace and cushions and squirrels, china ones and others sewn onto fabric and trapped in frames. And this makes it seem magical, like a fairy tale house and so unlike my home back in Hull, where the only ornament was an ashtray, no pictures hung on the nicotine-stained walls, and the sofa had long ago lost its cushions to the various usually vicious dogs that Stuart would sometimes bring home after a night on the razz, only to forget about them when he went back to sea leaving my mum to find them new homes or just let them loose to find homes of their own. Leon pushes a cool can of beer into my sweaty hand as Isabel calls from the kitchen.

"Show Ben the garden, love, while I finish the dinner."

The garden, though maybe only twelve feet square, is like a patch of Eden. Each blade of grass is so green and lush that they look edible, and the fragrant border of so many flowers makes me ashamed of my bunch. Issi could pick fifty flowers in her own back yard. There's a birdbath, a bench, everything so neat and perfect.

"Wow," I say, and mean it.

"See, it's not fish that I like, it's this," Leon points to the fences where a white flower is growing, covering the wood with delicate green leaves. "Gardening is my thing. Helps me relax." He sips a beer and raises the can. "Along with this."

It's good to see him like this and I'm enjoying my beer too. It's cool and not too strong, so though it makes me feel easy in my skin, I'm not going to get drunk.

"You're doing well at the aquarium, Ben," he says. "I'm really glad I took you on. I wasn't sure, you know. For the boss, taking on someone from Community Service is just free labour, and he only comes down from Great Yarmouth once a month, so if there was a problem he wouldn't be the one to deal with it. But it's worked out well."

He blushes, and I can see that though he planned to give this little speech it makes him feel awkward, so I sip more beer, say thanks, and then ask him some more about his garden. In the end, he gives me a tour of it, showing me all the plants and flowers, telling me about the soil, so in just twenty minutes I feel I know more about gardening than I ever learned when I was on the outdoor team at Glen Parva, and that was for sixteen months.

Finally, Leon sits on the bench, hands clasped on his knees and breathes deeply, looking at something in the corner of the plot, the sunniest spot. It's a ceramic statue, knee-high, of a footballer. A pottery boy kicking a ball, and at his feet is a plastic-framed photograph of a boy who looks about ten or eleven, wearing a blue and white football strip, grinning widely despite the goofy teeth.

I don't know Issi has joined us in the garden until she says, "That's our boy."

Leon clears his throat and looks at his shoes, but Issi comes beside me and grips my arm, gesturing to the photo with such a clear gaze of love and pain that I feel ill.

"Our Michael."

Then she releases me, so quickly that I wonder if I imagined it, and claps her hands together, changing the heavy atmosphere with the command, "Lunch time!"

Chatter over lunch is surprisingly easy. We talk about the aquarium, how hard Leon works, how much it's helped having me there. They tell me of their home, how they've lived here so long, how the neighbours came and went and had no decency. Finally there is a comfortable silence as we tuck into the beef and vegetables. I catch Issi watching me approvingly as I wolf down my third Yorkshire pudding.

"It's nice to see someone enjoying their food. Michael had a good appetite too."

"Issi… " Leon seems to be urging her to be quiet, and I'd like to say to her that it's alright, that I don't mind her talking about her dead son, but I can't do it. Instead I continue to eat, slower now.

"Leon doesn't eat much. I give most of his food to the birds. Nice to see someone enjoying what I make."

There's an edge of reproach and I nervously remember family rows over food, though we never sat down like this over roast beef. More likely over a Chinese curry on a Friday night, if Stuart was feeling flush, or a pot noodle if he wasn't, but get us all in the same room and something was bound to kick off.

Wanting to break the new mood, Leon grabs his girth and declares, "I don't think anyone would accuse me of being anorexic, love. I just can't eat for two."

It was there anyway. I could feel it. The gap in their lives, the space that Michael had left, with Issi unable to cook less food and accept he has gone forever. If only it could be fixed by simply by eating three Yorkshire puddings. I'm sitting in Michael's chair, but I can never be him. If these kind people knew what I did they'd ask me to leave, maybe worse. They've known loss, and I'm the bringer of it, so what else could I expect?

That night, back in the flat, my heart aches. In that lonely space between asleep and awake I wonder if Leon and Issi could ever love me. I've never kissed a girl, never had a crush even on a teacher, never felt anything like yearning before. And now I do, but it's not for a girl, or sex, but for two old people. Old people with squirrels and a memorial garden to a boy who'd liked football with goofy teeth. They never said how he died, or how old he'd been, but the gap was still there in their lives.

There's a gap in my life too. A mother who hasn't replied to my card, who didn't visit when I was locked away. A step-dad who sold a story to the papers about how evil I am. No, I can't go there. If I do, I just might start to wonder where Noah fits into the picture, how I became Humber Boy B, and that's something I can't bear to do. I decide to just think about the Sunday lunch, how this was a good day. How things might be alright, after all.

29
The Day Of

Nazma liked the window ledge, it was her favourite spot in the whole house. The ledge was wide enough for her narrow body, and with the curtain pulled across it felt cosy, but best of all she could look out over the estate, the houses and the park, and see what was going on without anyone even noticing. Somehow Nazma never really got noticed by anyone.

Now, she was sat with a book, losing herself in the story of a group of children who lived on an island with no parents. She liked to read, but sometimes felt she'd rather be outside if only someone would call and ask her to play. Sometimes she saw other kids from school, roller-skating or skateboarding up ramps on the kerbs, but she didn't join them. It was hard to make friends when you were different, and anyway her mum worried if she was out. Also, she told Nazma that working hard at school would mean that she would have a good future, a career. Her mother worked so hard in the shop, but the rewards were slight, and she repeatedly said that she wanted more for her daughter. Not more money, though this would hopefully come, but more respect.

"A doctor, an accountant. These are jobs that matter in the world," her mother often told her.

Nazma sighed, wished she had a sibling with whom to share this burden of responsibility to achieve and so please her mother, and turned back to her book, *Swallows and Amazons,* losing herself in the childish thrill of island life, the problem of how to start a fire with no matches. She did not want to be a doctor, she was no good at science or maths. She wanted to start a fire with sticks and build a tree house.

A movement outside made her look up from her book. Approaching the shop were a trio of boys. Two had their heads down, so she couldn't see their faces, but one of them looked up and she saw it was Noah. She'd known him for five years, ever since they both started primary school. He stopped, crouched down to tie his shoelace, and when he righted himself she raised a hand to the window and pressed the glass, it felt cool under her palm. He waved and she grinned at him as he disappeared into her mother's shop. She could hear the bell tinkling over the door and imagined him standing at the counter.

Nazma fantasised that in a minute her mother would call up to her, say that Noah had asked if she would like to go out and play. She closed her eyes and imagined laughing, running, the sun on her arms. She could tell him what she had learned from the book, how to build a raft with logs and twine. How to boil water and let it cool before drinking it. She would surprise him with how much she knew.

She waited. Eventually the boys re-appeared outside, quickly breaking into a run. Noah disappeared down the street without even looking back. She saw that his shoelace had come undone.

Nazma returned to her reading.

30
Now

Silent Friend: I've found him. I saw him coming out of his flat, a nice one too. What do you want me to do now?

Michael Farrow: They've given him a nice flat? That takes the biscuit. Do-gooders make me sick. Bring back capital punishment, that's what I say.

Silent Friend: I was thinking along the same lines myself.

Noah's mum: I don't believe in the death penalty. But I do believe in punishment, and eight years is nothing for what he did. Why does no-one listen to the victims until it's too late? Until we are backed into a corner with only one way forward?

31
Cate

Walking into the conference room on Monday morning, Cate's first observation was that Olivier's open-necked shirt revealed a surprising amount of chest hair. Her second was that he hadn't even looked up from his iPad to say hello. She had dressed so carefully too, choosing a green silk blouse that she'd bought in the summer sales but never had occasion to wear and a pencil skirt that she usually only wore in court. Even her make-up had taken longer than usual, and she'd dipped into Amelia's growing stash for a suitably girlish lip gloss. All of this had made her fifteen minutes late and he hadn't so much as glanced in her direction. The bastard was surfing Facebook.

"Morning, Cate." Penny, at least, looked pleased to see her. "You're looking good. Going somewhere?"

Damn. But at least Olivier was looking up now, his appraising glance sweeping over her and then locking with her own. He really did seem to have a lot of chest hair. Very dark.

"Er. Just celebrating the reprise in the weather, Penny. It's like summer."

"Not for me," said Olivier, fixating back on the screen of the iPad so she couldn't see his expression. "I went to a ski slope on Saturday."

That, at least, made Cate smile to herself. She forced herself to notice Ged, still in sweaty tweed, who gave her a

123

nod. "Hi, Ged. How are you?"

"Fine." But he didn't look it, arms crossed across his chest in a pose that clearly said he didn't want to be there.

Stephen Flynn entered, thankfully running even more late than Cate, with a fat file that he chucked into the centre of the table. "Bloody Facebook. I could sue that Zimmerman bloke, trouble he's caused."

Cate looked to Penny for an explanation but it was Olivier who pushed the iPad towards her, open at the page entitled FIND HUMBER BOY B. He touched the latest message with his pen.

Silent Friend: I've found him... What do you want me to do now?

"It could be a lie," Cate offered. "You know, all those people who make calls to Crimewatch just because they want to be involved with something."

"Possibly. Or maybe he thinks he has found Ben, but he's wrong." Olivier said, scrolling on the iPad and pointing out the picture of Ben playing with Noah in a paddling pool. "The pictures on this site are very old, no-one could be sure what this boy would look like in eight years."

"What makes you think it's a he?" Cate said. "Silent Friend could be a woman."

Olivier actually snorted with laughter. "It's not a woman! Women do not become vigilantes."

He said it with such pomp that Cate bristled.

"Never heard of Medea? Lady Macbeth? Women are no less... "

He interrupted her with a dismissive wave of the hand, "Tish tosh, these are fictional women. Real women are nurturing, they are homemakers and wives. It is a rare thing for a woman to be violent."

She couldn't tell if he was winding her up or being serious.

"I've got real life examples if you'd like me to give names."

Steve rapped the desk with his knuckles. "Okay you two, enough. If we're fighting amongst ourselves how will we

124

work together to protect Ben?"

Ged finally spoke. "I thought we were supposed to be protecting the public, not him."

For a wild second Cate wondered if Ged was Silent Friend. He knew where Ben was, and he'd made no secret of his revulsion at Ben's crime. But he wouldn't be so foolish as to post a threat when he knew the police were monitoring Facebook. And he'd be risking his career. He wasn't that stupid, surely?

"Can you trace the post?" Cate asked Steve. "Find out who sent it?"

"We've tried, but only got as far as the server. Whoever it is, is internet savvy, enough to cover traces. All we can say for sure is that the server used is in York, Humberside."

Relief flooded through her, more than she'd expected to feel. "Just a hoax then. Not someone in our neighbourhood, who may have actually seen Ben."

"It makes a hoax more likely," Steve agreed. "But we can't rule out that the danger is real. Not that it can change anything, not unless something actually happens."

"I can't move him," said Ged. "It was hard enough finding that placement, nowhere near a school, nowhere that other criminals might live. The marina is the safest option, if they find him there then we've done our best, but it was inevitable."

"Let's not jump the gun," said Penny. "I think it's best if we tell Ben nothing about the threats, no point in raising his anxiety. We just have to wait and see."

"Wait and see if he's attacked?" Cate asked, though she knew the answer.

32
Ben

Leon can't believe that I've never seen *Skyfall*. He looks so shocked that I feel I've made a blunder and try to remember anything I do know about it, blagging that I grew up watching James Bond, but he still watches me with disbelief. Finally I give in, shrug, and simply say, "We didn't see many films in my home." Which was true. Sometimes, in the secure unit, a member of staff would announce it was film night and we'd all get excited, even though the film would always be the favourite of whatever staff member was on duty that evening so if it was Kevin it would be *American Pie*, if it was Sue from the education team we always ended up watching *Harry Potter*. But film night was difficult, it was rare to get through the whole film without someone starting a fight or farting loudly or kicking a chair so hard that Kevin or Sue would get fed up and send us to bed, so they could finish watching their film in peace.

Leon is similar in a way, he wants me to watch his film so he can hear me say how brilliant it is but I'm happy, happy to be in the small windowless room in the aquarium where we make tea, watching the laptop screen and trying to make sense of why James Bond is jumping on trains and who it is he's following. I'm thrilled, though I can't show it because I sense that would be the wrong thing. He already thinks I'm odd.

"I brought these from home," he says, pushing a scone my

way. Made sure Issi packed enough for two."

"Tell her thanks."

"Tell her yourself. Come round and see us again. She'd like that."

I get a glass of water without asking, because I know that Leon won't mind, he wants me to feel relaxed here. I'm always respectful about Leon's tea and milk, though. I know how much these things cost and prison taught me not to take anyone else's things. But Issi has made scones, enough for two, already thick with butter and jam. I bite into it, delighted, my eyes following James Bond as he jumps and weaves over high buildings.

Leon is watching me, I can see it in the glass of the screen, and I wonder what it is he thinks I am, where he thinks I've been. He knows I've been in trouble, because I'm here through the Community Punishment programme, but he's never asked me what I did. Roy – the prison librarian – got me into Dickens, and I wonder if Leon thinks I'm like Oliver or the Artful Dodger, a bit of a scallywag but no more.

When the villain reveals himself on the derelict island I can't take my eyes from the screen. He's polite, dressed well, not like most of the criminals I've met. He seems friendly to James Bond, and then he asks him to play a mad game and see who can shoot a glass of whisky that has been balanced on the head of a beautiful woman. James deliberately misses, his bullet goes wide so the glass remains, but the villain shoots the woman right in the chest. She slumps to the ground, a bloody mess, as the glass shatters on the ground. 'I win. What do you have to say to that?' he asks.

What I have to say is that I think murder could be like that, like a game, and it's only afterwards when the body is on the floor and doesn't get up that it feels real. And you keep thinking, he'll get up, any minute now I'll see his head bob on the surface. But he doesn't, and then you're up on the Humber Bridge with your brother and it still feels like a game, because there's no blood, and you think that if you go home and don't say anything that everything will be alright.

"Ben? You okay, mate?"

I arrange my face to 'normal', bite into my scone and nod.

33
The Day Of

Hull Palladium wasn't the newest cinema in town, and round the back were the bins and a stinking mess of empty cans and wrappers and things that squelched underfoot.

"My mum would clout us if she knew I was here," Noah said quietly, then with more force, "she thinks I'm at your house, and your mam is looking after us."

"Shush! If they hear us we'll have no chance."

Adam moved closer to the younger boys and gestured to the grey door, which was open slightly, propped at the base with a brick. "Thank God for smokers, hey?"

Ben didn't see what smokers had to do with it, but he said nothing as Adam was pulling open the door.

"Help me," he hissed. "This is bloody heavy."

The door led into a corridor, dark and narrow, and the boys instinctively huddled together. They inched along to another door.

"Now when we get past this we have to act like we're meant to be here, okay? Like we paid."

The door opened and the boys were suddenly deafened by the booming noises of what sounded like a storm overhead and then shouting. They were behind the screen, just a few steps and they'd be in the audience. Adam grinned at the other boys, triumphant. "Best bastard place on earth, this. Let's go see a film!"

The boys slipped into an empty row towards the front,

trying not to be too obvious, but luckily the cinema looked almost empty so there was no-one to complain. Inside, the film was already playing though at first they couldn't tell because the screen was so dark. The only giveaway was the sinister music, and Noah started to back away.

"No you don't!" said Adam, giving Noah a hard shove. "All for one and one for all, remember?"

The screen became alive with a sharp blade and dark blood, then the sinister soundtrack turned to screaming. Ben and Noah sunk in their seats and even Adam looked shocked.

The film was a good way in, so it was hard to follow, but they soon became hypnotised by the darkness, the shared heat, and the wrap-around noise of the horror unfolding on screen.

By the time the credits rolled all three boys were wobbly on their feet, eyes dilated and senses spun out with blood and gore, their hearts hurting from the strain of palpitations. Behind them the few people began to move, the doors opened at the top to the exit. Adam placed a hand across the laps of Noah and Ben to stop them. "Be careful," he said, "and follow me."

But Noah didn't budge, he still stared at the screen. His hands were clammy in his lap and his body was bunched up small, into the padding of the seat. He was too scared to move.

Adam pulled Noah from his seat by the neck of his T-shirt and pushed him back in the direction they came from. To leave by the main exit was too risky, so instead of heading up the ramp to the foyer, Adam pushed them back to the screen.

"That was something else," Noah said, his voice quiet and unsteady but edged with awe. "It makes me want to do something crazy. I want to see if it's real."

"It's all real," said Adam, making his voice sound like a narrator from a horror film, "The Devil is in us all."

Noah's eyes glint. His breathing is shallow.

"Let's go do it then," he says.

The two brothers glance at each other, and follow where Noah leads.

34
Now

FACEBOOK: FIND HUMBER BOY B

Noah's mum: After the court case, I thought about leaving Hull. It was too much, walking past Noah's old school, going to the same shops and having to put up with the pity of strangers. But now I think it helps, that he was here, that he is somehow still here. The lovely woman at the corner shop has put up one of my posters about the fundraising event at the church, and seeing how people care makes such a difference. I was living a life, as best I could, before HBB was free. Now the world seems an awful place, knowing he's out there. But I won't forget the kindness of people in Hull. In case I don't get another chance, let me say thank you.

Nazma Patel: My mum was happy to do it. She doesn't like the Internet, but I tell her about your site and we are hoping you get some results from it. She will never forget that day, as she was one of the last people to see Noah. It haunts her that she didn't stop him running off with those boys.

Noah's mum: Tell your mum that she couldn't have known what was going to happen. She isn't one of the people who should have intervened. And there are plenty who should have.

35
Cate

Paul grasped his ribs, he thought it was so funny. "So women can't be vigilantes. He actually said that? Christ, that's good. Suggest your French bloke spends a week in this office and we'll show him otherwise."

"He must think all women care about is getting a man and having babies. It's like he's living in the 1950s."

But rather than focusing on what Cate was saying, Paul had suddenly noticed the green silk blouse she was wearing and a look appeared on his face that suggested the penny had dropped.

"But that's not why you're pissed off, is it? Not really. It's because Olivier wasn't struck dumb by your fantastic outfit and the fact that you look beautiful."

Cate pulled a face, "He didn't even look up when I entered the room."

"I knew it!" Paul started laughing again, "So much for your feminist outrage. Maybe you aren't so evolved from those fifties housewives after all."

"Sod off, Paul."

He looked triumphant. "See? You really like this man."

"I have work to do, Paul." Her phone vibrated on the desk, but she pointedly ignored it, sitting back in her seat and turning to her laptop screen. The phone stopped vibrating, then pinged to say a message had been received. She didn't even glance at it, pretending that she was engrossed in the screen of her computer.

"I take it that's the very devil of whom we speak?"

She continued to stare at the screen, but Paul could see her face in the reflection. She looked upset and angry, a fatal combination for Cate who would cut off her own nose to spite her face.

"He's called four times, but I'm not picking up. He wants to take me out tonight."

Paul sighed and gave her a quick hug, kissing her cheek. "Darling girl, it is he who wants to pick *you* up, you just have to settle your fiery temper enough to let him."

"Even though he's a dickhead?"

"We all have our crosses to bear, and I grant you he is a sexist Frenchman, but if he is half as sexy as you describe then I think that is a flaw that should be overlooked. Now do I have to send a reply for you, or are you going to be good and do what you're told for once? Go to dinner, Cate. Give the poor man a chance!"

"You're being very attentive," Cate said, as Olivier poured her a glass of wine, red as rubies in a glistening glass. It tasted of plums and caramel.

Olivier looked surprised. "But of course."

"Different from in the meeting this morning," she said, hearing herself how sulky she sounded and hating herself for it. "You were a bit cool with me."

"Cate," Olivier looked perplexed, "I had a very nice time with you at the ski centre, and I am happy to be with you now, but please understand, at work I am a very different man."

"That seems odd to me. I mean, I'm the same wherever I am. Why do you need to act different?"

"It is the way it is, for me. And Cate, we agreed that our friendship must be a separate thing. When it is me and you, whether we slide on ice inside plastic tyres or drink wine, we never speak of Ben. But at work, we must be our professional selves."

"But I can't cut myself in half that way."

"As you English like to say, there can be no buts."

She bit her lip, frustrated. But then she decided that Olivier was wrong; Penny had been friendly, so had Steve. And she was damn sure that Ged was his real self at the meeting, he was grumpy but no actor. The wine loosened her tongue.

"You were a total dick this morning. All that nonsense about women not being vigilantes."

There. She'd said it. She gulped more wine and looked into the burgundy depths, thinking she might have blown the romance before it had even begun.

Olivier looked agitated then amused. "So you say. But I am police, and you are probation, so it is natural that you think this. We see things differently in these roles. But here, now, we are not these things – police, probation. You are a beautiful and funny and slightly strange woman and I am a man who lives in a mediocre hotel on a roundabout and is rubbish at ringoing."

She lifted her glass and touched his. "I'll drink to that. But I don't know what makes me strange."

"Perhaps this is a translation error. I mean to say, unusual. I would like to say one thing, and then we can close this subject. You may think I am a dick, but the police are very necessary in managing this case and we cannot all see Ben in the same way. But without you, without you to see beyond the evil murderer that we police see, then there would be no point at all. We will keep Ben safe, but you will save his soul."

And saying this, he leaned across the table and kissed her, once, on the temple. In that moment she felt every inch the 1950s housewife who only cared about what her man thought of her. Fortunately, the waiter soon appeared with the food and the moment was broken.

36
Ben

I wake to the sound of angry buzzing and the constant drilling noise sends me straight back to the prison, to the shrill cry of a wing alarm, the sign that there's a fight or an accident, and I sit upright in panic before remembering that I am free. There is silence in the flat, and my heart steadies.

I fall back on the bed in relief, gazing at the white ceiling where the paint sticks in clumps. Mr May in the painting and decorating workshop at Swinfen wouldn't have stood for that, he'd have demanded it was done again, with a roller for a smoother finish.

Buzz. Buzzzz.

This time the noise carries on, loud and insistent, clearly here, inside my flat. It's the doorbell. Someone wants me.

In the prison there was constant noise, doors got opened and shut, but I was never the one with the keys or the responsibility, but here no-one else is going to check what's wrong. I pad to the door, shivering in prison boxers and my Superman T-shirt.

"Hello?"

My voice is weedy, whoever is standing on the other side of the door certainly can't hear it. Only me, as if I'm greeting myself – free and newly named and pathetic. With that thought I steel my nerves and open the door.

The navy uniform is the first shock, so is the man's stern face, his gritty eyes that already judge me. I think straight away it must be the police. The police officer who came when Noah's blood was still on my T-shirt, he looked like this. But this is a different man, older and greyer, a different uniform. I think I recognise him, but I can't be sure if my mind is just playing tricks again.

"Hello?"

"Here to read your meter, mate."

Mate. Other boys in prison called me mate, but they usually weren't friends. It was a word that meant they wanted something: cigs, a phone-card, a magazine.

The man looks me up and down with an interest that makes my skin crawl, then says, "You going to show me where it is, or do I have to guess?"

Not knowing what it is I'm supposed to do, I stand aside and let the man into the flat.

"In the kitchen, is it?"

He strides through the flat into the tiny space. He looks at the worktop, along which is a neat line of tins: tomato soup, carrots, new potatoes. Things I can heat and eat, cooking being a skill no-one ever taught me. There's a second line on the other worktop: bread, jam, a box of cornflakes. The man takes his time as he considers the two lines, and I know he's seeing something wrong, though I'm not sure what. In prison we all kept our belongings in a line along the window ledge.

Then he turns and on his face is a cruel smirk. He has worked me out, I'm weak, I'm a freak. I think then that I'm not paranoid: this man knows who I am.

"Bit OCD are you? Okay, mate. So where is it?"

I can't hide my ignorance any longer but I try not to show my fear.

"I don't know."

He gives a long sigh and starts opening cupboards, finding them all empty, but still seeming to take a moment to look inside each one.

"You just moved in?"

I pause, not sure how much to say.

"Um, yes. Last week."

The man finds a box inside one cupboard, boarded to the wall. He takes the pen from his chest pocket and peers into the box, writing down the number on the dial. What it means, I don't know. I'm just hoping he'll go away soon though he seems in no hurry.

"Nice flat. Good view of the marina. Wish I had a view like this."

He walks back into the sitting room and goes to look out of the window. I can feel my hands flex to fists, the tension inside, from needing to get the man to go away, not knowing how to make that happen. He turns from the window so the sun is behind him; his face is just a dark shape.

"Okay, that's it, then?" I ask, the desperation coming through in my voice.

The man stands still, the dark shape of his mouth moves.

"You on benefits? Income support, is it?"

Is this part of the form that he's filling out, do I have to answer? But I'm used to answering questions, doing as I'm told. I just want the man to leave, I'm afraid of what will happen if he stays.

"Jobseekers allowance."

"No wonder you kids can't be arsed to work when the government pays for places like this."

He gives a whistle and I know I've made him angry but I don't know what I can do to fix that.

"I need you to leave now. I, um, I'm expecting someone."

He hesitates, I think he's going to refuse. Then he moves towards me. "Next time, have the meter reading ready. Okay?"

I nod, though he doesn't say when next time will be or how I should take the meter reading.

Finally, he leaves and I close the door, press my back against it, feel my heart thudding in my chest and a tingle all along both arms like there's an electric current running through me, the only thing keeping me upright.

The flat feels different after the man has gone. Like it's been invaded, it isn't a safe place any more, and I'm stung at how easily my few purchases in the kitchen gave me away. I'm doing things wrong all the time, but I've no idea how to do them differently.

I look around the flat, and try to see what he saw. It's bare, that's the first thing. I assume that other people have phones and computers and lots of belongings, but I wouldn't know where to start. Does a computer just connect, or would I need help? And who would help me?

I'm a foreigner in my own land with no family to guide me. I can't cook, can't even shop. I see buses going to who-knows-where but I've no idea how much they'd cost or what kind of ticket to ask for. I'm useless. I slide to the ground, back still against the door, and weep for the prison, wishing I was once again locked within its safe walls.

Later, it's hunger that forces me to snap out of it, but once I'm out next to the docks, under the sky and its dizzying vastness, I long to be back in the flat. Not at home anywhere. I know I have to push through this, if I'm going to make a life for myself I have to at least try. I go to the Spar, but there's no sign of Shirl. I buy a can of coke and a chocolate bar, then head for the safety of the aquarium.

Leon barely looks up from his paper as I walk in for my shift. "Hello, son."

"Shall I clean out the river fish? The glass was looking a bit smeared yesterday."

"Aye, alright. I know you like them sullen buggers."

I do like them, I like that the tank is at the back of the aquarium too. I fetch the steps and the cleaning wipes, they have to be used almost dry and it makes it hard to do a good job, but with patience the glass will come up well.

The aquarium is almost empty and I make my way along corridors of fish, heading to the carp tank.

In front of the tank is a bench and I sit down while I sort out the wipes, spraying them lightly with water before I start. I'm surprised to hear a man's voice behind me. I tell myself that it's okay, that it's just a visitor and I need to stop being so nervy, and fix my attention on the tank in front of me. I start in the far corner, working slowly in hypnotic circles, watching the fish who haven't even noticed me, listening to the filters pumping oxygen or cleaning the water or whatever it is they do, a sparkling sound, a thrum in the background. The fish seem happy enough in their glass prison. Or unaware. It's the carp tank, I don't know why the bench is here, because these lumbering fish are grey and flat and move slowly around their space, far less interesting than any other tank, at least to most people.

The voice comes closer, then quick feet. A boy, he looks about four, is running down the corridor; his dad is walking several feet behind. The boy taps his fingers on this tank, attracted by the colourful darts of other fish, or the creepy salamander. But no-one is interested in carp, except me. Even the fish are oblivious to each other, seemingly unaware as they bump sides, as if each fish only exists for itself, maybe not even as much as that. Mouths open and close, funnel-like as they suck up the floating debris.

The boy is about ten feet away, gaping at the tank where the salamander lives. I can see it above the water-line, hunched on a log, with a black oily body and yellow markings it looks like some alien from outer space. Its quivering eyes seem to be considering the boy as if it too is stunned by the strangeness of the other. The dad reads aloud the information on the card next to the tank, talking softly, but the boy seems to be only half-listening. I don't listen either, just to the tone. Educating, but kind. Gentle and instructive. This is what it is, then, what a father is like with a son. Giving information, asking questions, pointing things out.

My dad didn't take me to museums, his visits were never announced and were always when Stuart was at sea, as if he was monitoring things and knew when it was safe to come around. Mum would be pleased enough to see him, so long as he had something to give. A twenty pound note or a gift for me. He'd get it wrong, usually, a gift that was too young for me or that broke within five minutes. But still, at least he tried.

Unlike, Stuart. I doubt Stuart knows anything about salamanders, and even if he does he wouldn't tell me. The story he sold to the papers after the trial, tales of terrible and odd things I did as a boy, they were things I couldn't remember. The tag line was: *I wish my step-son had never been born.* My own dad simply disappeared. I haven't seen him in eight years, not since my birthday before Noah died. Dad never came to the trial, so at least he never heard all those things they said about me.

Adam had a different barrister to me, and he made it seem to be all my fault, but I was the youngest so how can that be? So skinny and small, how could I be the evil child the papers said I was? My barrister must have agreed because he never even tried to defend me, not properly. He never shouted, never got emotional. It was as though he'd already lost his case.

The glass is shiny and smear-free. I move my steps and start to work the glass at the other side. The carp continue moving around each other as if not knowing that they are the same thing, relatives or friends. What they look most is bored. One faces me in the tank, opens it mouth showing me a dark disc of oblivion. I wish I was a carp. I can do boredom, I've done it for eight years. I could live in that tank and feel safe, and not have to worry about someone recognising me or working out who I am, seeing the evil in my eyes or on my skin.

The boy is at the next tank now, looking at the bulging-eyed frog. His dad stands behind him, a possessive hand on his shoulder, and I wonder if that's because of me.

140

"He's ugly, isn't he?" says the boy, and at first I think he's talking about me.

"He's not ugly," says the dad. "He's cool. Different. Come on, Noah."

And then I have to grip the step-ladder, the world tilts, because of that name, Noah. The coincidence of it, because it's not my Noah, my friend from the other side of the estate, the boy who fell from the Humber Bridge.

I have this strong need to get out. I can't stay anymore, not with the carp, not with the boy whose name is also Noah. I need air or I might be sick.

I run past Leon, who is eating a sandwich, it smells fishy like tuna and makes my mouth fill with bile. "Ben? Are you alright?"

But I don't stop, don't speak. I have to leave.

I stop outside of the aquarium and heave, hands on knees, but nothing comes. I take a deep swig of air.

Across from where I'm standing there's a park, next to an ice cream van, both under the shadow of the Orwell Bridge. It isn't like the Humber Bridge, which towers above, but it's still high and formidable enough that if someone was to fall over the side they'd probably die. Which is why I don't look at the water or up at the bridge. What I look at is the park, the two children who are playing, watched by their mother. It's not like a park I've ever been to before, with a swing and a slide, a roundabout maybe. No, this park is something special. There's a wooden pirate ship with rope rigging set in blue gravel to represent the sea. In the gravel are wooden posts that the children use to hop across, from the safety of shore to the ship, avoiding water.

Noah. If he'd only found a stepping stone, a boat, a rope. Everything would have been different for all three of us.

The mother is helping one of the children – a girl – climb the rigging. I see then that the children are twins, the same size with the same blond curly hair though different as they are boy and girl. I don't know anything about twins, the mechanics of it, but I can't stop staring at the two children and wondering how a boy and girl can be so alike when I realise that the mother has seen me. In that second I know what she sees, a weirdo in a hoodie, a lout who doesn't belong. She sees my strangeness just like the meter man did, like it's stamped on my forehead. She calls to her children, clutches their hands and glances my way, worried. I'm too old to be hanging out on a kid's playground. She is trying to work out why I'm here, if I'm a junkie or a paedo.

A shot of anger twists my gut. Maybe I just want an ice cream. Am I really that strange? I haven't got horns. The man in the van has started to smoke, the smell of cigarette drifts my way, and when the children who are being tugged away resist, ask for ice creams, the mother shakes her head, looking disgustedly at the van. I can see she objects to the smoking, that she's thinking the man is unhygienic or whatever, but I wouldn't care about that. I'd love an ice cream but I'm afraid that getting one will make me look stranger than I already do. The sun, which oppressed me in town, feels delicious here by the water, a second layer over my hoodie and jeans. I pull my hood back and run my hand over my scalp, the hair is growing now, I can't feel my skin or the bony nodules anymore. It feels soft.

There's a breath, feet pounding the pavement behind me and I cower, twisting my head as the blow falls. But there is no blow, it's just a jogger running past. No-one will hurt me, I keep telling myself. No-one knows who I am or what I did. Maybe the mother just had to get her kids home for a nap. I'm paranoid, that's all. The jogger disappears up the track to the top of the bridge, I hear his panting breaths getting farther away.

Now the jogger and the kids have gone I'm alone, apart from the ice cream van, but I can't see the man inside anymore.

I'm alone, but that doesn't bother me. I climb up onto the pirate ship. As if it can save me.

37
The Day Of

Ashley was slumped at the edge of the back row, his torch in his pocket, enjoying the opening scenes of *The Devil's Playground* in which the young rich couple decide to set up a camera in their own home. The boyfriend doesn't believe in demons or ghosts, but the girl knows better and so does Ashley. Skilled as he is in interpreting films, he knows the home movie idea is a ruse to spook out the punters, but he'll go along with it, and enjoy whatever evil force is unleashed.

Getting the job at the Palladium was a coup for Ashley, it gave him a bit of cash, plus he got to see all the latest films. Another bonus was Michaela, the foxy manager. She seemed to like him too even though she was ten years older and already had a kid. When she heard about the teacher's strike she'd asked if he wanted to do an extra shift, and though he should be revising for his A Levels, *The Devil's Playground* had just opened in Screen 3 and that was enough to swing it. I mean, he'd been waiting years for that film and God knows what took them so long, it wasn't the set, that was just someone's house and a hand-held camera, even the blood looked fake. Must be some cool effects on the way. Besides, it almost counts as studying when one of your A Levels is Media Studies, and Ashley had plans to be a film director, so this was all research. And he was being paid to do it.

Ashley chuckles to himself as three hunched figures run up the aisle and sneak into the third row, thinking they haven't been seen. But he's in a good mood and doesn't want the hassle of chasing them out, not when the film is just getting going. Let them enjoy it, even if it scares the shit out of them.

It's no skin off Ashley's nose.

38
Now

FACEBOOK: FIND HUMBER BOY B

NickyP: This morning on GMTV, Lorraine Kelly was talking about kids these days seeing too much stuff that they shouldn't and they mentioned Noah's case. Did you see it?

Noah's mum: They asked me to be on the sofa. But I can't blame a horror film for what that evil child did to my son. Normal people wouldn't be influenced, no matter how many films they saw.

NickyP: I agree. But maybe it was a trigger? The film sounded really creepy, and it was about a young couple who did a Ouija board, unleashed an evil spirit. They said that Humber Boy B was into that spooky shit, that he'd conjured the Devil that day.

Noah's mum: I believe the Devil was on the bridge with them. I think God was looking away.

Silent Friend: Let's not make excuses for human evil. It's time for action.

39
Cate

Cate awoke on Sunday morning, having dreamt that she and Liz were playing by a large bridge, and that Liz had fallen in. Cate had jumped in to save her, but gave up quickly, before she'd even got her hair wet. She swam to the shore and let her sister drown.

She hadn't thought about Liz in years, but the news that she'd been in touch with their mother had awoken thoughts, shreds of memories. Plus, you didn't need to be Freud to know that the dream was triggered by her dealings with Ben, reading Roger Palmer's terrible description of Noah falling from the bridge, but also the statements of other people who saw the boys that day, like the joggers who ran past, the drivers who were too rushed to stop. There were so many moments when things may have taken a different turn, single moments that added up to a boy in the water. If the guy who was working at the Palladium had been more conscientious and chucked them out, if Mrs Patel had called the police about their shoplifting. If the teachers' strike hadn't happened.

Cate groaned, rolled onto her side and turned to the window, blinking at the sun that was streaming through the gaps in the curtains. It was a beautiful day and she promised herself she wasn't going to think about work.

She got out of bed and opened the curtains to let in the sunshine. Amelia was still asleep, so she went downstairs to make a coffee. What she was itching to do was to go to the office, and continue to read through the pile of witness statements, to obsess and delve and think about the case. But it was Sunday, a day off, and these last days of September were turning into a mini-heatwave. She would take Amelia to Felixstowe, enjoy the beach before the weather broke.

"Up you get, Amelia! Let's not waste the day in bed. Chop chop," she called from the bottom of the stairs.

Before she'd become a mother, Cate had always disliked Sundays. When she was growing up she hated the boredom. Sunday never had the promise of Saturday, and she and Liz would quickly run out of things to do, especially if it was raining so they couldn't skate or bike in the street. They'd soon squabble over what to watch on TV until Mum emerged from her bedroom, yelling at them to be quiet. If Dad spent a weekend at home things were different, they would have to participate in rituals like going to church (if it was Easter or Christmas), the family walk in the park, roast beef for dinner, and the Sunday serial. She was only seven when she knew what her mother refused to acknowledge – that family was a show they put on. And the audience was her father.

Cate sighed, thinking about her mother. She felt sorry for her, really. Even when she was just seven years old she seemed to understand more than her mother, who was always trying to pretend they were a happy family. If she confronted the truth the whole charade of their marriage would be exposed, and she'd have been afraid that if Dad actually left she wouldn't cope. Coping was something she didn't do well, and alcohol was her way of not confronting things, blunting the edges of reality.

But it had happened anyway, the family had split and her mother was one of the victims. Cate could only acknowledge this when they were apart though. When they were in the same room it only led to arguments.

Amelia came down the stairs like a princess who had just woken from a hundred-year sleep, dressed in her *Frozen* nightdress and stretching both arms above her head. On

147

impulse, Cate grabbed her and gave her a huge hug, smacking her on the cheek with a fat kiss.

"Whoa, Mum. You're in a good mood."

"Good morning, gorgeous girl. Go and eat breakfast while I pack a picnic. We're going to the beach."

The September sun was pleasant as they found a spot near the water. Amelia had brought her loom bands kit and she began twisting the coloured plastic into an intricate shape as Cate settled into reading a book. The world felt warm and peaceful. Like the calm before a storm.

40
Ben

"Hello… "

He stands in front of me and calls me by the name that died with Noah. On his back is an orange rucksack.

I don't move, only just manage to call him by his, the only name he's ever had.

"Adam."

Adam, my brother. Humber Boy A. He was four years older but not necessarily more culpable. Humber Boy A, who said with a stutter I didn't know he had that his younger brother made him, suggested, lifted, pushed. Humber Boy A whose father, Stuart, bought him a smart shirt.

It comes back in a tumble just hearing him say my name. Adam had sat with his head bowed while Stuart said that all of our family problems were my fault. Adam had always looked out for me before, and he was there on the bridge. He knew the truth, yet he let Stuart make me out to be a runt, the half-brother from a foreign and inscrutable source. He even went as far as to say I was wrong in the head, and the psychiatrists went some way to agreeing, though not far enough to keep me out of prison.

I was just ten, sat in my stained T-shirt with no-one to speak for me, watching as the court artist sketched what she thought a murderer looked like. After just two hours of deliberating the jury agreed.

But Adam, he wasn't a killer. No, he was guilty of

compliance, guilty of covering, but not guilty of what really mattered. To the count of murder how do you find Humber Boy A? Not Guilty. He got just four years in prison and he got to keep his name.

"How did you find me?"

He stands, just a yard in front of me. And still I don't stand aside to let him in.

"Google Earth."

It's my fault, I put my address on my card to Mum, the one I'd been told never to send, the one she hadn't replied to anyway.

Adam shifts position, looks bored. He was always good at that.

"Come on then and let us in, our kid."

He looks uncertain for a moment, as if it suddenly occurs to him that I might not want him there, and I don't recognise him in that moment, but then he firms up his jaw and his shoulders and that's the Adam I knew, no-one would mess with him, the brother I was so proud of. He looks just like Stuart.

Adam follows me into the lounge and, as I've noticed everyone always does, he walks straight to the window.

"You jammy bastard. That's some view."

"It is."

"How d'you feel looking out on all that water? And that there bridge."

His accent is so obviously Hull that it makes me feel weak inside, the way he says water like 'what-ha', you with a deep 'oo', it takes me back to our boyhood, and I think how I no longer sound like that. My voice has been neutralised by years of moving around, and my own will, straightened out so I no longer says 'a' as in apple, not when I'm saying 'bath' or 'laugh' anyway. My 'a's' are like 'ahs' and I no longer have a problem with 'u'. But I haven't said enough for him to know that yet. I can't answer his last question.

He starts checking out the room, picking up my book from

the floor. He reads the spine. It was a leaving gift from Roy, it's Dante's *Inferno*, half the page in Italian, half in English. He tosses it back onto the floor, giving me a narrow glance that looks like envy but it can't be that. Nobody would want my life.

"You gonna get me a drink or summat? It's a long drive, you know, from Hull."

He doesn't say he arrived yesterday, though I know now it was him I saw in the library. I don't ask him where he spent the night. "You've got a car?"

He walks towards me and gently taps my chest with the back of his hand. "How else you think I got here, flew? Now, when are you gonna get us a bloody drink? I'm parched."

He follows me to the galley kitchen and watches as I open the litre bottle of Spar Cola.

"Got any brewskies?"

I shake my head. It never occurred to me to buy any beer, and anyway it would be expensive.

Ignoring the glass, Adam reaches for the bottle, twists the top and drinks it down even as the foam fizzes around his lips. I watch him drink my coke until the bottle constricts, thinking pathetically that I have nothing else in the flat except the water in the tap and I don't feel up to another trip to the Spar just yet. Even though Shirl is friendly I still have to steel myself each time I walk into a shop. Adam sucks down air with the last of the bubbles. When the bottle is done he pulls it free and burps then grins at me.

"Any grub?"

All I have is some sliced white bread and marmite, but even that feels precious to me, so I hesitate. He's my brother, and this isn't about bread, it's about the trial. I don't want to give him anything of mine, I feel he's taken too much already. In the silence I can feel him weighing me up and finally I look at him directly.

I haven't seen him in eight years, but he's so familiar and I realise it's because he's looking at me in the same way Stuart used to. Then I see that his expression is Stuart's but his face is all Mum. And mine. We all have it, the oval face, the sky-blue eyes, the look that may be a result of living on the east coast where the Vikings once landed. "We're descended from them," Mum would say. "We're tough, us. Whatever life throws at us we keep buggering on." She liked the idea of us being Vikings, and she certainly liked a fight so there may be some truth in it. I'm shorter than Adam, though, and that's not like a Viking, and I have white-blond hair like my dad whereas Adam's hair is dark. You'd think my smallness would have helped me in court, that the jury might think the older and bigger boy was more responsible.

Adam wanders back into the lounge, looking again out onto the Orwell River, and then turns to face me. "You've hardly got owt. Where's the stuff the prison give, to help you out and that?"

"Did they help you?" I countered.

Adam reddened then looked down at the carpet.

"I got nowt, not a posh flat like this. I had ta go live with our mam."

This stings, sharp. He was allowed back to Hull and Mum took him in. Everything was different for him, the trial, the sentence, the way Mum responded. Then another thought arrives, as deep as a belly blow.

"Are you still living with her?" Is that why she wouldn't even consider moving to Suffolk with me?

He shrugs as if it's of no consequence. "Sometimes. When I'm not with our lass."

I remember his letter then. "Is that your girlfriend WHO KNOWS? What right did you have to tell her when there's a Facebook campaign to find me?" It's only when I hear my voice, the sharpness in it, that I realise how angry I am. He's in Hull, with Mum. He has a girlfriend.

He seems surprised by my anger. "I didn't tell her nowt, our kid. She was there. I couldn't say in the letter, didn't think that would be smart, but I'm with Cheryl. From the bridge."

The information drips slowly through.

"Roger Palmer's daughter?

It doesn't make sense to me that he could be with her. Not when she was so involved with what happened. He's watching my face and seems to understand my confusion.

"You remember how we saw her, in court? After she'd been in the witness box she was allowed to sit with us and we all had a drink and summat to eat. Remember?"

I think back, to sitting in the waiting area, shielded from the press. Cheryl was there, a prosecution witness because she saw us that day, first outside the shop and then at the river. But she'd already testified so she was allowed to wait in the room with us, we were all given snacks and my social worker went to the vending machine and bought us all some sweets. We may all be involved in a murder trial but we were kids too, and we argued over who got the mints and who got the chocolate.

Two defendants and a prosecution witness in the same room, sharing a packet of Polos and Maltesers but no-one seemed to think it an issue. Cheryl broke ranks, she screwed a letter into a ball and when she passed, seemingly to go to the toilet, she threw it into my lap.

She'd used our names, because she knew them, even though no-one was allowed to say them in court. I still know the letter by heart:

You're going to prison, my dad says there's no getting away with it. I want you to write to me, wherever you go. I'm putting my address at the end of the letter because I need to know what happened after I left the bridge. Noah was alright, I liked him even though he was a bit posh. And I'm sorry he's dead. Are you? Why haven't they asked you that?

I screwed her letter up, put it in the bin.

"How did she know where you were?"

There are several secure units in the north, he wouldn't have been easy to find. Then the penny drops, Adam must have taken the letter from the bin, smoothed out the crumples.

"You wrote to her?"

"Well, you know how it was." He shifts from one foot to the other. "I mean, I was lonely and no-one came to visit much – you know our mam's not brilliant at letters. And Cheryl knew what had happened, her being there and that. I wasn't allowed to write to you but no-one told us not to write to her, so it just kept pouring out. And then, she visited us. By the time I got released, we were in love."

"Oh, for fuck's sake!" I can't help it, the words come out without permission. I don't know why him being in love with Cheryl bothers me so much, but it does. That letter was for me, not for him. Something else he stole from me.

He shrugs again, a gesture I've already deduced has become his response when he doesn't know what to say.

"One thing led to another."

"One thing led to a fucking other! How is that even possible? She knows who we are. She was there, she was part of it."

He held both hands up as if in submission. "We were children. It were ages ago."

As if that makes any difference. I look to the floor, the weight of it all suddenly pulling me down.

"Look, our kid, you need to know it was Cheryl who told me to come down and find you. She wants to see you too."

"So you're the welcome party?" The idea is unsettling. Who else will come knocking on my door? Adam looks like he doesn't get what I mean. "I said I'd call her when I got here. Tell her it's safe."

41
The Day Of

Noah walked quickly out of the side door of the Palladium, his eyes sparkling like hot coals. "Let's go do it." As if fear hadn't frozen him but woken him up.

"Do what, idiot?" Adam said, following Noah down the passage but sounding wary. His face was still pale, and his heart hadn't quite found its rhythm yet. The film had been scary, not that he'd admit that. "Buy us a house in the woods and conjure up some Devil shite?"

"Not that, the Ouija board. We could use the dining table and I've got a tape recorder to catch anything that speaks. My mum won't be back for hours." Noah was speaking fast, words strung together by nervous excitement, tripping over his shoelace which had come undone yet again. He knelt and re-tied it, a double knot like his mum had taught him.

To get back to the estate the boys would have to walk in front of the Palladium, where Ashley was taking a five-minute cigarette break. Seeing him, Adam grabbed Ben by the collar of his T-shirt, yanking him away from the cinema entrance. "Let's frame, that's the lad who checks tickets. Scarper!"

Outside his home, Noah picked up a stone, or what looked like one, and turned it over, sliding his fingers along the back so it opened, revealing a key.

"That's fucking cool," said Adam, taking the plastic stone from Noah and tapping it, sliding the key safe to examine it.

"No burglar would suss it wasn't real."

Noah pushed out his chest and said proudly, "My mum got it from the Internet. She thinks of everything."

Only then did he pause, the key in his fingers but not yet ready to open the door.

"No mess, though. She'd go crazy if she caught us."

"It's okay, Noah," Ben reassured his friend. "We'll be careful."

"But we're conjuring the Devil," said Adam, waggling his fingers. "Owt might happen."

Inside the house were other signs of just how clever Noah's mum was. There was a wipe-clean board that had the days of the week on it, and beside them menus for each day. Ben read the meals in wonder, vegetable lasagne, chops, fish. His mouth watered at the thought, even though some of the meals he didn't know. What was gumbo? What was fajitas?

Noah saw him reading the weekly menu. "And she works, full-time," he said, enjoying showing off and though Ben didn't like him for it he was fascinated too, by this insight into what normal families did.

"What about your dad?"

"Oh, he's at the garage. He'll be home later, probably."

Adam started to root around in the fridge, and though Noah tried to stop him, no way was Adam going to resist the slices of ham, the fresh juice. In the end, Noah gave in and all three boys started to graze, grabbing juicy strawberries, Greek yoghurt and breaking brie with their fingers. Ben wasn't sure he liked the brie but he ate it anyway, just because it was different and new. There was bread too, so they had a makeshift picnic, munching as they stood, handing round the carton of juice until it was empty.

With full stomachs and feeling sleepy, the boys pulled the curtains closed in the lounge and sat cross-legged with knees touching, a triangle around the Fisher Price tape recorder that they placed on the carpet in front of them.

"It's all I have," said Noah. "I mean, I have a CD player but it doesn't record. And this has a mike, look." He picks up the white plastic microphone, and the other boys laugh at it, even when the sky darkens and the room becomes quieter.

"What if summat happens?" asks Ben, thinking about the film, about the blood and pain that followed the conjuring.

"Scared, our kid?" taunted Adam. "Come on, I'll go first. Give us a pen, so I can work out what to say. Backwards, like they did in the film."

And he wrote on the jotter: *come to devil the ask we.*

The boys began to chant, saying the line again and again until they felt dizzy and hoarse and the sound of the letterbox made them all scream. But it wasn't the Devil, only a flyer for the new Morrisons.

On his way to the loo, Ben saw something he couldn't walk past without exploring: Noah's bedroom. The door was ajar as if to invite him in. Although he'd called at Noah's house several times over the past few weeks they had stayed in the garden or played in the sitting room, where Noah's mum kept a giant box of Lego, so Ben hadn't seen the bedroom. Now he stood in the doorway, unable to fathom why Noah would ever play outside when he owned such amazing things, the spoils of a childhood Ben had never had. Lego pieces, assembled and displayed on shelves, a Scalextric set on the floor, cars scattered around as if they weren't precious. The bed even had a Hull Rovers duvet cover and pillow. Tacked above the bed, given the proudest space, was a red and white Hull Rovers scarf.

Ben stepped forward, his hands itching to touch all of Noah's possessions, clenching into fists as he thought of his own room, the stained duvet without a cover, the broken toys that Adam had passed down, the football that had a puncture. Noah had all this and he was still a whinger. Poor little rich kid. And that was when he decided, if Noah wanted to see the

Devil then he bloody well could.

Downstairs, Adam and Noah were bent over the table but it was only when Ben joined them that the glass started to move. Spelling out H-E-L-L-O. Then another word. D-I-E.

"Who's going to die?" Adam asked the glass, stifling a giggle, but looking strange all the same. Ben bit his lip, hiding how much he was enjoying seeing the others so scared and knowing he was causing it. It was a fun game.

O-N-E.

"One of us?" said Adam. There was no giggle to suppress now, he gave Ben a thump on the chest. "Are you pushing the glass, our kid?"

"No." And as he said this Ben realised it was true. The glass was moving against the pressure from his fingers.

Noah looked like he was going to shit his pants, and it was all Ben could do to keep his finger on the small shot glass, it moved so swiftly around the letters to make the final word.

M-U-R-D-E-R.

The boys all pulled back from the glass as though it was hot, and it fell on its side, rolling over the letters and stopping, completely still, over one letter.

The letter N.

42
Now

FACEBOOK: FIND HUMBER BOY B

Silent Friend: I've had word of where he is. Tomorrow I'll know for sure.

Noah's mum: I don't know who you are, but you sound like you're on our side. Thank you. I just want a chance to speak to him, I have just one question to ask him. Do you think that would be possible?

Silent Friend: He's had the chance to explain himself. It may be too late for that.

Noah's mum: It's what I want. To look him in the eye and hear what he has to say. I don't want any more violence.

Silent Friend: I'll see what I can do, Jessica.

43
Cate

Cate and Amelia tumbled indoors tramping sand into the carpet, Amelia sticky and smiley, Cate sporting pink skin on both shoulders where she'd neglected sunscreen, assuming no-one would burn in September, not even a redhead. She never learned.

Amelia saw the flashing light on the answerphone and pressed it:

"It's me. Mum will have told you I called. I'd rather have spoken with you but I didn't have your number. I've called a few times, but you're always out.

"Look, I'm coming to Ipswich in a week. Can we meet? I'm staying at the Great White Horse. I hope it's not the dive it was when we were teenagers. Anyway, come see me Cate. We have a lot to talk about."

Amelia cocked her head to one side and spoke as if to the machine, "Who's that?"

"It's Liz. My sister."

After pressing re-dial, Cate discovered that the number Liz had called from was ex-directory, so Cate had no way of returning the call even if she'd wanted to. Amelia trailed after her as she walked into the kitchen to unpack the remnants of their day.

"Why don't we ever see her? Does she have any children? They'd be my cousins."

Of course the questions would start, Cate didn't blame

Amelia for this. She just wished she had some answers for her.

"I don't know, love. Liz left home when she was seventeen. She just packed a bag and went, and I haven't seen her since."

Amelia jumped up on the kitchen counter and for once Cate didn't stop her. Amelia grabbed the half-empty bag of marshmallows that they toasted at the beach and sucked one thoughtfully. "If Chloe left, I'd try and find her. I'd be like Anna in *Frozen*, I'd search everywhere."

Cate scrubbed at the cutlery and tipped the charred barbeque in the bin, going through the motions of clearing up while her head was full of Liz. Had she done enough to find her? Did she really not know why Liz had left? Nagging, niggling thoughts that she'd kept supressed for years now woken and moving around in her mind. The pain, too, of losing Liz began to throb under the scab that Cate thought was healed long ago.

"Tell me what happened in the second film, Amelia. Did the sisters live happily ever after?"

Amelia had a brain like a movie reel, scene by scene in chronological detail and she was unable to edit. As she started to tell the story of the two sisters, separated but then re-united, Cate listened closely, soothed as the sweet sound of her daughter's voice tumbled over her.

She waited until she was sure Amelia was asleep before she called her mother, having administered a glass of Chardonnay and a strict warning to herself not to shout.

"Mum, it's Cate. You gave Liz my number."

She could hear the sigh down the phone and knew exactly how her mother would have pursed her lips, defending herself against any suggestion of wrongdoing.

"Well, you want to see her, don't you, Catherine? She is your sister."

Suddenly taken over, not by the alcohol or her own self-warning, she found she was simply too tired to argue. Too

161

sad. "Did we let her down, Mum? Did we try hard enough to find her?"

There was silence on the other end, though Cate could hear the chink of glass. It seemed both women were armed with their tonic of choice.

Cate asked gently, "Are you drinking again, Mum?"

"No. It's just water."

Cate wished with all her heart that this were true. That Liz coming back into their lives was a good thing, that it might even heal their mother.

"I tried my best to be a good mother. I gave you all the love I could. Maybe it just wasn't enough."

Cate washed her glass and put it away. She brushed her teeth and went to Amelia's room, pausing before she switched off the light to watch her daughter sleep, resisting the urge to kiss her because Amelia was the lightest of sleepers, unlike Cate who could sleep through an earthquake. She had slept through Liz packing her bags and leaving. She had slept through her parents' rows.

The phone call felt like a watershed, it was a rare thing for her mother to use the word 'love'. But also, Cate had heard a partial apology in her words, though she knew the blame had to be her dad's too. Whatever had happened, it was the whole family that was rotten, not just one individual. Cate – or Catherine as she was back when she was a child – and her sister were reminders that her parents had once loved each other and earned the status of 'family', but her clearest memory was their simple lack of interest in her. She was discouraged from having friends over and remembered her mum saying things like, "Well, it's a bit inconvenient at the moment, dear. Maybe another time?" Finally, Cate stopped asking. And as long as she was doing well at school, her mum didn't see the point of going to parents' evenings. Though they weren't poor, Cate often went to school without lunch money, her shoes would be too tight before she got a new

162

pair and her school uniform too small before it was replaced. Low-level neglect, a simple lack of interest.

Cate had actively sought her father's love but he was always busy, more interested in work than family, always on the phone or at meetings, occupied with the shadowy world of business. Whenever teachers or other kids asked her what her dad did she struggled to answer.

"I'm a manager," was all she ever got out of him, simply stated without even looking up from *The Telegraph*. It was an inadequate answer, but she didn't want to push further in case she was told to give him some peace and go to her room. Just to sit silently by his side felt like a victory.

But Dad never ignored Liz. If she came into the room, he would put the paper down just to look at her. And he would read Liz a story before she went to bed, lying on the duvet next to her, in a way he never did with Cate.

No wonder then that, by the time she was a teenager, Cate slid from favour and sought the company of those who at least noticed her. Dad was no longer bothering to excuse his more frequent absences and her mother was drinking even more; Cate would arrive home late to find her mother collapsed on the sofa.

She longed to escape, longed to be loved. She was just eighteen and in the final year at sixth form she met Tim, during a weekend shift at the Great White Horse. At first she was afraid to trust him but the more she resisted, the more he persisted, and she started to think that she was safe. She convinced herself that finally here was someone who loved her. How wrong she was.

Amelia's sleep was deep, her eyes were moving to whatever dream was playing in her brain, maybe happy thoughts from their day at the beach. Cate turned off the light and went back downstairs, wishing there was someone there to talk to.

44
Ben

I'm hiding and I know it, staying in bed to avoid leaving the bedroom and having to face my brother. I can hear Adam moving around, banging the cupboard door in the kitchen, clearing his throat noisily, and I can't bear it, this proximity to him. My thoughts are jumbled with how they let him go back home. None of that is his fault, but was it really all mine?

I think back to the trial, how he looked so pathetic, so stupid and gullible. The jury bought it. Maybe that isn't his fault either, he was just playing a cleverer game than me. I simply told the truth, thinking that was what mattered. Hearing him moving around, opening up the window, yawning, I realise that if I allow any of my feelings to surface I'll end up lashing out and what I learned in prison is that it's best to keep any strong feelings inside, where you can control them. If I see his face for too long I just might do something I'll regret and lose everything. I have to get out of the flat.

It's a swift walk from my bedroom, into the lounge, out to the door. "I'll go get some milk," I say, grabbing my hoodie and some change from the table. The words are like bullets from a machine gun, no pausing space for him to say he'll come with me.

He just yawns again, rubs his eyes, and says, "And some beer. For later."

Later. How long is he planning to stay? But I don't feel up to asking him right now, or hearing his answer, I grab my key and leave. It's only as the door closes shut behind me that I think how wrong it is, that he's in my flat and I'm on the outside.

I take the stairs in long strides, so my chest hurts by the time I'm out of the building and into the glare of the sun. Blink, stagger, and think about which direction to walk. *Slow, Ben, go slow. The quicker you go the sooner you'll have to see Adam again.* But he's in my flat, somehow soiling it and I hurry just the same.

Shirl is on the till and she smiles when she sees me, but I'm so nervy I can hardly look at her. "You alright, love?" she says and I feel she can see inside me, that everyone knows what the problem is. It's all going to collapse, the whole charade, leaving me exposed as the kid who killed a kid, as Humber Boy B. And then I'll be dead anyway.

I walk back to the flat, holding the milk in one hand, a four pack of Spar lager in the other, and a thought jangling in my head. *If Cate finds out Adam's in the flat I'll be in breach of my parole, I'll get returned to prison. But at least there I'll be safe.*

When I return I see that Adam has made himself at home. On the arm of the sofa is a pile of clothes, jeans and T-shirts, and on the floor is his unzipped orange rucksack, underwear spilling out. He has enough for a long stay. There's a wash bag too, and he sees me gaping at it all.

"I just nipped to the car while you were gone. Got the rest of us stuff."

Then Adam looks back to his lap and I see he has an iPad there, black and sleek, colourful pictures and words on the screen. I can't swallow my jealousy fast enough so the words come out like stones.

"Where did you get that?"

He moves his finger over the rim, shifting it so I can't see the screen. "Got it when it was on sale. Argos."

"Pricey, though, aren't they?"

He looks up at that, at my bitter tone, and I see something cross his eyes that seems like naked honesty but becomes replaced with a more calculated expression. I know what he says next will be a lie.

"Like I said, it was on sale. And I'd some brass put by."

I wonder if Mum bought it for him. Or Stuart. Am I going crazy, thinking like this, driving myself mad? Even though life and all my experience has already taught me how unfair the world is?

"So what's that page you're looking at?"

Because I'm curious, I edge closer, and before he has time to remove it I see a blue and white screen, words and pictures. The header says:

FACEBOOK: FIND HUMBER BOY B

"Us," he says, looking embarrassed. "Well, to be fair, you. Looks like someone knows where you are, our kid."

We read it together, the messages from Noah's mum, the photos.

"Who the fuck is Silent Friend?" Adam asks, casting me a sideways look as if I would know. "Who knows where you are, other than me?"

As I think about his question I feel chilly, a shiver that starts inside and ends up on the surface of my skin. Silent Friend could be anyone, but whoever it is he knows my flat is by the marina. It could be the boiler man from yesterday who seemed familiar, it could be Shirl from the Spar, hell, it could be Leon. It could even be Adam himself who was in Ipswich a whole day before he appeared at my door.

I hand him his beer and he says, "Cheers, bro. Oh, meant to say. Cheryl just sent us a text. She's on the train."

"To Ipswich?"

"Well, duh. She wants to see you, our kid. I told you that."

I don't even know how to respond to this. Cheryl, whom I last saw at the trial. Whose dad tried to save Noah but failed.

"No way. I can't see her."

Adam sighs, exasperated with me that I can't see what is blindingly obvious to him. "What happened on the Humber Bridge, it changed Cheryl's life. And my feelings for her, they're strong because she understands. Christ, someone died. You can't get closer than that."

I'm totally confused now. Cheryl was a prosecution witness, part of the Crown's case against us, yet he's talking about Noah's death like it was some act of union between them, something binding. But it tore my world apart, ripped me from all I knew and was. Isn't he sorry, for what we did? He seems too wrapped up in his love life.

"Because I can tell Cheryl everything, anything. But there's a piece missing and it's you. She needs to see you again."

"Fuck that."

It's as if he can't even hear me, he's already gathering his keys and phone from the table. "Her train arrives in twenty minutes. So I'm going to fetch her, sharpish. Can't leave our lass standing waiting, she'd swing for us."

I watch him head for the door. He's gone, I can hear the lift making its mechanical descent down to his car. In a panicked split-second decision I run from the flat and take the stairs, two at a time, trying to beat him to the bottom. If I have to meet Cheryl, it's better that it happens on neutral ground.

I'm sweating when I slide into the passenger seat of Adam's Mazda. It feels wrong getting into a car driven by Adam, the last thing I saw him steer was Noah's scooter and he was none too clever at that. He surprises me, though, he's gentle with the gearbox, easy on the brakes and I feel safe. He's careful and composed as he drives us out of the marina and onto the inner ring road, navigating double roundabouts easily. I think that this was an Adam I knew too, one I saw every now and then when things were going well and Stuart was back with Mum and there was food in the house. He used to be calm then, in control. 'Little Man', Mum used to say, and he liked that.

The car smells of mint and it's immaculate. I can see where he's polished the plastic, the carefully chosen rosary beads hanging from the mirror. Lads in prison had rosary beads, a few years back they were the fad. But then that got old and in came the WWJD bracelets and then it was fluorescent loom bands. But Adam didn't see those later phases, he was released four years earlier than me.

"Fuck. I'm in the wrong lane for the station."

Adam tenses as we get closer to Cheryl, his breathing becomes jerky, but he still drives with confidence, cutting up the slower cars to change into the right lane and following the sign. He seems to know his way around better than me.

"Have you been to Ipswich before?" I ask, seeing if he'll tell me the truth now we have broken the ice.

"Nah."

"You look like you know where you're going."

Then he taps his chest pocket where he keeps his mobile. "Sat nav. Fucking brilliant."

Another sting of jealousy, that he has a second gadget I know nothing about. Adam has re-entered the world and embraced it, I've just spent my time in an aquarium and my only friends are an old man and his wife.

"Was it hard for you when you got released? At first, I mean?" I don't want to sound pathetic, like I'm saying I'm struggling or anything, but my curiosity is too much.

We take the roundabout by the cinema, then get into the one way system where a red light stops us. He starts tapping the steering wheel and I don't think he's going to answer me, but then he says, "Some lads on the estate jumped us one night, down Hessle Road. Broke us arm. After that, nowt much. Some shouting, dog shit through front door. But no more broken arms. People just got used to us being back."

"You returned to Hull and people just got used to it?" I can hardly believe what I'm hearing and I wonder if it could be like that for me too. No-one died of a broken arm, and if things calm down after…

He gives me a sideways glance then turns his attention to the lights that are now amber, then green. "Don't go thinking you can go back, our kid. Summat bad would happen," he says, putting his foot on the accelerator. "You're a convicted killer."

Ipswich train station is buzzing with taxis, people with briefcases, it's busy and confusing and no less disconcerting because I've been here before. A delicate blonde teenager stands in front of the building, hands clasped in front of her like a schoolgirl, holding a small white sports bag. She stands out, her golden hair, her poise. She seems to know exactly what she is waiting for and when it will arrive. It's only when Adam pulls the car directly in front of her that I recognise her as the girl from the bridge. In a line-up of ten girls I wouldn't have known her for the polite gymnast who spoke so nervously at the trial, though she still looks like a dancer. She opens the car door in one graceful arc and slides in behind me, into the back seat.

"God, it was mafting on the train." She doesn't look hot at all. Her thin summer dress is perfect, considering she's travelled five hours by train. "Turn that AC up before I faint."

Adam obeys, and she leans between us and kisses his cheek, making him blush and smile, like a lovesick puppy. The air conditioning belts out icy blasts.

"This should cool you down, babe."

She doesn't even acknowledge me and soon the car is moving again, overtaking and smoothly swooping around the docklands and back to my flat. No-one speaks, there's just the sound of cool air pumping through the vents but I can smell her, fruit like tangerine or orange scenting her skin. Adam is still red-faced and I can feel that with every concentrated move he is thinking about the girl in the back seat, who I can't see and daren't turn to speak to.

The journey feels longer than it was coming and finally we're parked at the marina and heading towards my flat.

I take the stairs, but they beat me to the top by taking the lift, waiting as I get the key from my pocket and lead them into the flat. Only then, in the lounge with the big window, the three of us so close together, breathing heavily from the exertion, does the tension break.

"You're still skinny," she tells me, even though I'm wearing baggy jeans, and I see again the girl who bossed Adam around that day. The girl who was the first to say that Noah should suffer, though not the last.

She takes her shoes off and stands barefoot, her dress skimming her knees.

"You still look like a dancer, Cheryl."

She smiles at this and stretches down to touch her palms to the floor. I catch Adam scowling at me and even though I have very limited experience of love I can see that he's really into her. She stretches up, notices Adam and moves to press against him. "I haven't said hello properly."

And then they kiss. I have to look away because I can see the pink tip of her tongue flicking Adam's teeth. I look away, down to the marina glinting below.

Cheryl wanders around the lounge, touching the sofa, lifting a pizza delivery leaflet that got posted in my box. There's not much to see. "Voila, chez moi," I say, without thinking.

She looks at me with an expression that could be contempt, could be naked curiosity.

"You know French?"

"A bit." I don't tell her that I have a GCSE A* in the subject. "I've just been to an eight-year boarding school is all."

"With bars," she adds, unnecessarily.

"Yeah. Not much to do except study."

Which isn't true. There was weight lifting, drugs, sex, which I tried, but didn't like. Looks like I might be heterosexual, though I haven't had a chance to test the theory. So, for me it ended up being study. It wasn't exactly a rounded

170

education, but it had some advantages.

I've read all of Shakespeare's plays, Marlowe, Webster. I've read Dante and Goethe. I'm also fairly up to speed on American crime novels of the twentieth century. And I could order a meal in a French restaurant, not that I'll ever need to as convicted killers can't travel, not while they're on life licence anyway.

The flat is shrinking, with both of them there. Adam sits on the sofa, pulling Cheryl down next to him.

"Can I get you guys anything?" I say, needing a reason to escape.

Cheryl looks up and nods. "I'd love summat to drink."

"I have beer or milk. Or water."

"Water for me, ta."

In the kitchen I run the tap until it's cold, listening to the water hitting the steel, and not hearing Cheryl come up behind me.

"So. How does it feel?" she asks, and her voice isn't light or friendly anymore. It's taunting.

"What?"

"To have done your time. To be free."

I know I'll never be free, not really, but I don't think this is what she means. "It's different. From prison, but also from what I remember. Scary."

I hadn't known I was going to admit this, but the way she's looking at me, assessing me, makes me nervous and I want her to soften again, to be the dancer with the beautiful body. I want to see her smile at me like she does at Adam, I can't get the thought of her pink tongue out of my mind.

"Yeah. Well, better scared than dead."

She means Noah. And between us is a silence within which a boy's red trainer falls to the river below. When she speaks again her voice sounds slow and threatening, and I look over her shoulder for Adam to help me but he's not there.

"It changed everything, that day on the Humber Bridge. It changed my life. My dad never returned to work, he got signed off sick. Did you know that? He was home all day, there was never any peace from him and his misery."

I don't want to hear this, I'm not ready to.

I press the glass of water into her palm and walk back into the front room.

Adam is sprawled on the sofa tapping something into his iPad. He shifts so I can't see the screen, and I'm too proud to ask, but I wonder what he's doing. Cheryl joins us, asks where she should put her bag. Her white sports bag is small and can't hold more than a purse and toothbrush. This gives me hope that they'll leave soon.

"We'll take your bed tonight, our kid. Two of us won't fit on this sofa."

I'm being taken over, by Adam, by Cheryl, by the past.

45
The Day Of

Cheryl sits shivering in her swimsuit at the muddy edge of the river, knees to her chin because her stomach still hurts. She sees the three boys appear over the bank, coming from the direction of Gypsyville. They're farther along the tow-path, and haven't seen her down by the water.

She's feeling invisible today, her dad isn't watching her, he's too busy piercing a wriggling maggot as bait. She thinks of all the years after her mum left when she longed to be invisible, like she is now, but now that her dad is ignoring her she hates it. How can he just act like nothing's happened when Jessica has dumped him, and their chance of being a normal family has gone? Cheryl thinks Jessica was her dad's last chance. Her mother left, and there's been no-one since. He was lucky to get Jessica, is a fool to just let her slip away while he tries to catch a fucking fish.

The wind picks up, but Cheryl doesn't put her clothes back on over her swimsuit, she just grabs her towel and wraps it around her waist, telling herself she's an Egyptian princess, Cleopatra moving through the reeds.

Her dad is like a garden gnome, bent over his rod, his green tent around him. He might even be asleep. She doesn't even bother telling him that she's going, she just walks away.

The boys are sat in a line on the hump of the hill.

"You lads look like the three wise monkeys. Not." Cheryl

173

laughs at her own joke, standing in front of them, aware that they are looking at her swimsuit. It's tight on top and her boobs are bulging round the sides. She puts her hands on her waist to re-adjust the towel.

"So," says Cheryl, kicking the sole of Noah's red trainer with her bare foot because she can't stop herself from taunting him. "Where's your mam?"

Noah's eyes widened at the question, as if just realising that he'd lost her. "In London. For the strike."

"And she left you on your own?" Cheryl kicks the shoe again, but softer this time.

"She sorted for me to go round Ben's." He looks at his friend then, and there's a spark of resentment. "His mum is supposed to be looking after me but she's sick."

"Sick in the head," said Adam, bitterly. "She can't even look after herself right now."

"You know she gets migraines," Ben muttered. He didn't say that this was always after downing a bottle of spirits.

Noah pulled his legs up, knees to his chin, and stared out towards the water. "Mum didn't want to leave me. There was nowt she could do about it, 'cos it's the teacher's strike today. She had to go to London, she's a union rep."

Cheryl knew this, of course. She also knew that her dad should be there too, if he hadn't rowed with Jess last night. And here he was, the precious son who couldn't possibly cope if Jess had left Dave like she'd promised, who couldn't stand to live with Cheryl and her dad.

Noah was the reason Jess had ended things, the reason Cheryl had lost her chance at having a family. Those few months when Jessica was around everything changed. Jessica had cooked and cleaned and kissed her dad, and he in turn had started to treat Cheryl like a normal daughter.

She couldn't go back to the way things had been before then. She would rather die.

Noah quivered at the chill that wrapped around him. Cheryl

stared at him as if to memorise his face, thinking how pathetic he was to be so shivery and weak when she was only wearing a swimsuit and towel.

"What's a union rep when it's at home anyway?" Adam asked.

Cheryl put on a superior voice, "It means she voted on the strike, so she has to go to London and spend the day holding a poster. My dad didn't want to go because he didn't want to see the slut." This final insult she spat at Noah, since Jessica wasn't here.

Noah frowned, bit his lip.

"Do you know who my dad is?" Cheryl asked, curious to discover what the boy knew.

Noah nodded, without looking up. "Course. He works with my mum, they teach together."

That's not all they do together, Cheryl wanted to say, but what would be the point because that was over now and Jess wouldn't be moving in. It would just be her and her dad, forever and ever. And it was Noah's fault.

"He's over there now," Cheryl jerked her thumb behind her. "Fishing. He doesn't even know I'm here. He's got a bucket of ugly fish and that's all he cares about."

"Has he?" Noah's face lit up, as if getting a fish was the most important thing in the world. Then he hesitated, realising that this strange girl did not seem to like him. "Think you could get one? To look at, like."

"If I wanted to." Cheryl enjoyed withholding something the boy seemed to want so desperately.

"Will you get us one?" he begged. "Please."

Cheryl disappeared in the gap in the hedge, glad to have a mission even if it was a slimy one, and returned moments later heaving the weight of a large grey bucket.

"Hasta got one?" Noah pushed himself to standing, and Ben too pressed forward, both boys crowded round her. Adam, pretending to be cool, looked over Cheryl's shoulder, at the fish, then at her breasts. All four children were circled around the bucket as their heads were pelted with regular drops of rain.

"That one's huge!" Noah crowed.

"What is it?" Ben said.

"A carp, stupid," Cheryl told him.

"But it's not moving."

"It is," Noah said, poking a finger into the brown water and touching its head. Then he said, "Oh, that's just the water. The fish is dead."

"It's just sleepy," Cheryl said, in a voice of authority. "Don't poke it!"

"There's blood."

"Fish don't bleed."

"What's that, then? It's horrible."

They were silent then, all staring at the large fish wedged amongst the small ones in the bucket of dark water.

"Are you going to have it for your tea?" Ben asked Cheryl, in wonder. The fish didn't look like the type Stuart brought back with him.

"Dad'll want us to have it for us tea." Cheryl said, suddenly tipping the bucket up so the fish flopped out onto the grass, then righting the bucket so the other fish were saved. "But that's his tough shit."

And with both feet, bare and pale, she jumped on the fish so its guts spurted out in a white and red mass on the ground.

"No!" cried Noah, his hands over his eyes as if he couldn't bear the destruction of such a blameless creature.

"That's so gross," said Adam, with a grimace. But when Cheryl looked at him he changed his expression and grinned. He held out his hand for Cheryl, steadying her as she wiped her feet clean on the grass, her towel slipping its knot at her waist. She took his hand and she led him up the bank like she was a queen, regally taking a seat in the undergrowth and pulling Adam down beside her, her towel slipping from her waist.

The two younger boys stood over the body of the ruined fish, until Noah couldn't take it any longer. He collected the fish in his arms, like it was a broken toy, as if this gesture would make it start to live again.

46
Now

FACEBOOK: FIND HUMBER BOY B

Noah's mum: My church have been raising a collection, they have £15,000, and they've asked what I would like it used for. Something in Noah's name.

It took Dave and me a long time to decide, and we thought about what Noah would have enjoyed. He loved football, of course, so we toyed with that idea but, finally, we've decided on a skate park. He had his scooter with him the day he died, and he loved scootering around the estate. Lots of local kids still do, and I'd like them to have a safe and fun place to go. So the money will build a skate park on the waste land (brown field) that's just beside the entrance to the Humber Bridge, next to the viewing area. The café is all closed up now, but a skate park would make it more attractive for a local business, so maybe the whole area will become a nice place to visit.

We looked at the location yesterday, with the fundraising team from church, and I was sad to be there. I always am. But I think the skate park will help this.

I want to go to the Humber Bridge and see children playing, having fun. Something good that will live on long after we've gone and joined Noah in heaven.

Silent Friend: That £15,000 could be used as a reward, Jessica, which would be a better way to spend the money.

Dave: We don't know who you are, but that is church money, for healing. It's not blood money.

Silent Friend: But it should be. £15,000 would be a small price to pay to see Humber Boy B dead.

47
Cate

Cate could see that Ben was agitated, even more than usual. There was a battle going on behind his eyes, one she recognised from personal experience as the weighing up of whether to talk or keep something inside.

"Ben, I want you to listen to what I'm about to say because it's important. In this room, like nowhere else in your life, you have to talk. And I know that's much easier for me to say than for you to do, believe me, but I can tell that something is wrong. So I want you to take a very deep breath and tell me. What's the problem?"

"It wasn't my fault," he begins and she feels the wariness creeping inside. So many conversations in this room started with that very sentence.

"It's not my fault he's here. I didn't invite him, I've not seen him since the trial."

"Who are we talking about, Ben?"

"My brother, Adam. Humber Boy A is in Ipswich. In my flat."

Paul whistled, pointed his pencil at his forehead as though it was a gun and pulled his thumb like the trigger.

"Great. This is all we need at three o'clock on a Friday afternoon."

Cate, having rapidly terminated her session with Ben with a warning that she needed to pass on what he had told her, was now stood in Paul's office, her hands placed on his desk as she leaned forward to hear what her manager would advise. "You think I need to recall him?"

Paul slumped in his chair. "Parole condition of non-contact?"

"No direct or indirect contact with victim's family. No entry to Humberside."

"But nothing about co-d?"

"Not on the licence. But they've always been kept apart."

"I should bloody hope so. If they'd been kept apart on that day maybe that poor kid wouldn't have ended up floating in the Humber. Right, so we don't need to recall."

Cate saw that Paul was relieved, recall could be a lengthy process and the weekend was almost upon them. But she wasn't willing to let go of the option that easily.

"What about for Ben's own protection? The postings on Facebook from Silent Friend are getting more threatening. The last one said Humber Boy B should be dead. The posts suggest he knows where Ben is, and now the brother shows up. Something's very wrong."

"Agreed. We do need the co-d gone from the flat, preferably from Suffolk, pronto. Got it?"

"That's it?" Cate released the desk, the edge of which she had been gripping in her hands since she walked in. "No recall."

"Not unless the brother won't leave. But since I have tickets for Peter Grimes at Snape Maltings tonight, I know you'll make sure he does."

Cate drove straight to the marina, but when the door to Ben's flat is opened it isn't him standing there, it's a girl of about twenty, lean and leggy with a damp ponytail of blonde hair, and wearing only a towel.

Cate feels her jaw drop and steps back to check she's at the right flat.

"Yes?" the girl asks, and Cate can hear the north in her

voice, even with this one word.

"I'm looking for Ben. Is he here?"

The girl opens the door wider and stands back, one hand on her hip, "Well where else would he be?"

Seeing Ben and Adam sat together on the sofa it is obvious they are brothers. She knows they have different dads, and Ben is blond where Adam is dark, but they have the same facial shape, the same sharp cheekbones, the same blue eyes. Adam is significantly more confident, though; Ben gazes at the floor. But Cate doesn't know who the girl is, and she can't speak openly until she does.

"This is my probation officer," says Ben, directing his words to the ground, "and this is my brother Adam and his girlfriend. She knows." Here he looks up, saying this with feeling, glancing at Cheryl who is perched on the arm of the sofa next to Adam, still wearing just a towel.

Cate hesitates. Whatever this girl knows, it may not be the whole story. And if she knows then how many others do too?

"Do you want to go get dressed?" she says, not hiding her tone of disapproval.

"I'm alright, ta."

Though the girl had clearly just got out of the shower, she had no intention of going anywhere, and this made Cate nervous. She could see the girl wasn't moving.

"These are sensitive times, Adam. There are a lot of people looking for Ben right now, and you being here would make it easier to put two and two together."

Adam looks at his girlfriend before he speaks. "Is there a law that says I can't be here?"

"No law. Just common sense."

Ben clears his throat, his voice is unexpectedly firm. "The thing is, Adam, I'm not used to being around people like this. It's stressing me out. I need some space, to suss out how to live."

Adam looks surprised, then angry. "You asking me to leave, our kid?"

Ben bites his lip, looks towards the window whilst he gathers his strength. Then he says clearly, looking his brother squarely in the face, "No, Adam. I'm telling you."

Cate wants to cheer, but she settles for a satisfied smile. There is hope for Ben, after all.

48
Ben

Adam presses the horn, hard. The Mazda is already juddering, Adam's hand is on the handbrake ready to release it. "Come on, Cheryl. It'll be gone midnight when we get back home as it is."

But she doesn't move, she just stands near the car, stretching her arms to the evening sky and rolling her shoulders as if she is about to exercise or dance.

"I'm not coming."

I'm as surprised by this as Adam, I gape at her and wonder what game she's playing now.

"If that's okay with you?" she says, turning to me, smiling sweetly like she did at Adam when he turned the air conditioning on yesterday. I feel like I'm being played, but for the life of me I can't think why. I have nothing more to give.

"It's a long journey and I've only just arrived."

She says it like coming to Ipswich is a holiday. I don't know how to respond, because she's trouble and she needs to go, of course she does, but at the same time the thought of being alone with Cheryl makes the skin on the back of my neck tingle.

The Mazda dies and Adam gets out of the car and walks towards us, his hands open as if begging.

"Come on, lass. Don't fuck around. We don't want to get our kid in trouble."

She steps forward, so I think she's agreeing, kisses Adam on the mouth until his eyes close tight and his hands drop helplessly to his sides. Then she pulls away from him, leaving him standing there like a puppet without strings.

She still doesn't move towards the car. "His probation officer said you have to go, Adam. But she didn't say I have to."

Adam looks at me, demanding I take his side in this, even though we can both see where the real power lies.

"And what do you have to say about this, our kid?" He's angry, he's hardly spoken to me since I ordered him to leave. After Cate left, with instructions that he should leave Suffolk straight away, he packed his orange bag in a fury. Though the fury has evaporated his eyes are so much like Stuart's that it's all I can do not to cower away and leave Cheryl to sort it out between them. But my days of cowering are over, so I stay.

Standing in the evening gloom, his body caved and his face downcast, I see the brother who let me down. The brother who blamed me for everything.

"Fuck you, Adam. Cheryl can stay if she wants."

Anger turns to energy, turns to power, and he moves forward, jabs his fist up like he wants to hit me, though his face is slack and his eyes are wet.

Cheryl steps forward again, she puts a hand on his shoulder and pulls herself up so her mouth is against his ear, whispering something.

When she turns back to me I see the determination on her face, the same look I remember from the bridge. Adam, finally defeated, goes to his car. He must see that look of Cheryl's too. There's no point in arguing.

We stand together, Cheryl and I, by the water and watching as Adam does a clumsy three-point turn that takes his wheel dangerously close to the edge of the marina. Then he floors the car and is gone, tyres skidding on the pavement and hot fumes where the car once was. I feel his pain like a slap, as I always did when Adam was hurt by someone he loved.

Cheryl choosing to stay with me must feel as bad as when Stuart left that day. He's my brother, and I ache for him, but it doesn't hurt enough for me to turn her away. Although I know he's hurting I have a growing anger inside at what he did to me. What he put me through.

It's gone forever, the relationship we used to have back when Adam taught me how to skim stones and how to build a go-kart from the old pram in our shed.

Adam is gone. And I'm alone with the girl from the bridge.

49
The Day Of

"You're nithered, lass. Come here and let me warm yer up."

Adam moves so Cheryl is snuggled in closer to him, and puts an arm around her bare shoulder. She should really go back to her dad and get her clothes, but he can't stand to let her go just yet and being so close to her when she's only wearing a swimsuit is a thrill he's never felt before.

Cheryl rests her head on his shoulder, wincing as yet another stab of pain hits her in the lower abdomen. "So, where have you lot been, anyway?"

The three boys look at each other, two pairs of eyes large and startled but Noah's, still holding the dead fish, spark to life.

"We saw a horror film and then we conjured the Devil," he babbles, his voice loud and high, revealing how very young and frightened he is, but also how excited. "We did a Ouija board and it worked."

Cheryl pulled a face at the little brat. "What are you even talking about? Who believes in the Devil anyway?"

"I do," said Noah, serious now. "If you believe in God you have to believe in the Devil too. My mum says."

His mum, oh yeah, Jessica. Dad's ex-lover who wears a cross around her neck but still shows her red camisole at the top of her open-necked blouse. Cheryl had known about the affair for months, had seen Jessica playing house with her dad, ignoring her wedding vows. Cheryl knew exactly how much Jessica believed in God and the Devil. All that was bullshit, Cheryl knew it now, all of it was a lie because Jessica had let her and her dad down. Everybody would fuck you over in the end, given the chance.

Cheryl looked at the earnest boy and saw Jessica in his eyes and chin.

"You're an idiot," she told him. "There's no Devil or God."

"You're wrong," he stood his ground, his dark eyes unsettling in the way they didn't move from her face. "The Devil spoke to us."

"Oh yeah? And said what?"

Noah hesitated, feeling them all waiting for him to answer.

"The Devil said… he said… that something is going to happen today. Someone is going to die." He couldn't bring himself to say the word 'murder' that the glass had spelt out.

"Well there you go," said Cheryl, pointing a finger at the fish. "That's your dead thing. Now what about resurrection and all that bullshit? If you can speak to the Devil, prove it."

"No," said Noah, his lip wobbling and his eyes drowned with hot tears, "It stopped at the letter N. I think it meant me." He looked at the fish in his arms. There was blood around the gills, which gaped, revealing pink flesh. The fish had round eyes, a hollow mouth.

He was used to its weight now, the slippery grey skin.

"What should I do?" he asked, helplessly. The tears fell down his cheeks, landing on the tarmac.

"You're the Devil worshipper," Cheryl told him sharply. "You tell me."

"We could save it," said Ben, suddenly desperate to help his friend, guilt nibbling uncomfortably for the distress he'd caused. But he didn't push the glass in the end. It must have been Adam. "Let's throw it back in the water. Try and shock it back to life. I saw this hospital programme last week and this lad had been dead for like, six minutes or something, but they gave him a shock and he started to breathe again."

Noah's face lit from inside with happiness, as if Ben's

suggestion would remove the curse of the Ouija board. "Let's try it."

"From up there," said Cheryl, pointing up to the Humber Bridge. "To show the Devil we're not scared."

Because she wasn't. Not now the life she'd prayed for was never going to happen. She was untouchable in her anger.

50
Now

FACEBOOK: FIND HUMBER BOY B

Noah's mum: I've been getting private messages to say that HBB may be in the East of England. I would like it on public record that whilst I agree that this EVIL MONSTER needs to be locked away, I don't, and never have, supported violence.
Silent Friend: Really?
Noah's mum: As God is my witness. I don't want him dead. I want him to live with the consequences.
Silent Friend: Jessica, you are a better person than me. You always have been.

51
Cate

Paul was reading the latest Facebook postings over Cate's shoulder. "Fuck me, private messages? This is not sounding good. Do you think it's connected to the brother arriving?"

"Could be. And it gets worse. When I got to the flat the brother had brought his girlfriend. She was a real piece of work, sitting around half-naked. It was fairly clear that she was getting a kick from being there and she could have told anyone about Ben. It's like a runaway train we have no way of stopping."

"I think you need to arrange an emergency Risk Management meeting." He cleared his throat knowingly. "Which means you'll have to call Olivier, which I'm assuming won't be a hardship. I see you've done something with your hair."

Cate ran a hand over her sleek, auburn bob, which had been straightened and treated. "Why does everyone think that if a woman changes something about her appearance it has to be because of a bloke?"

"So, it's nothing to do with Olivier?"

"Of course it bloody is. He comes from a country were women spend ten percent of their salary at the beauticians."

"Well, you look great, hon. And change is always good," Paul added, cautiously. "Do I take it that the sexist French dickhead is treating you okay?"

"He is when we're on dates. Attentive, charming." Cate

191

shrugged her shoulder, flicking her new haircut so it sat neatly to one side. "But in meetings he's still a dickhead."

"Hopefully you don't tell him that?"

"Only in my mind," said Cate, smiling.

When Paul left, Cate turned her attention back to her lifer. Humber Boy B was causing her sleepless nights, and she wasn't sure what she could do to fix it. His placement felt compromised; he should never have sent the card to his mum, never have let Adam into his flat, and the cocky girlfriend just added to the problem.

"But we're brothers," Ben had protested. "I couldn't just turn him away. We're joined by blood. You know?"

She didn't know if he had meant their shared DNA or Noah's blood that had been spilt. And she doubted that siblings had the strong bond he suggested. Cate couldn't think of anyone she knew who was truly close to their siblings once they were adults. A shared childhood didn't always establish a bond in later life; it might actually guarantee the opposite.

Of course Cate was biased.

Liz had left that message about wanting to meet, and she'd chosen the pub where Cate had worked back then. Liz would be thirty-three now, but there was no way of answering Amelia's questions about if she had children, if she was happily married. Had Liz managed that feat, a relationship that could endure the bad weather life throws at love, while Cate had failed? But all of these questions came to nothing against the one simple fact: Cate did not want to see Liz.

Not to satisfy her curiosity on these questions, not to hear why she was now trying to get in touch and most of all not to hear why she had left in the first place. She was too afraid.

But, the old scar was puckering at the edges.

Ben's case, though just one of her groaning workload, was forcing her to ask questions: how can a ten-year-old boy commit murder, and his older brother avoid conviction? She had to know, in order to help Ben, but also for her own sanity, what exactly happened on that bridge? A dark place, one she couldn't get Ben to visit just now, not while so much was happening around him.

Cate felt the pressing need to escape these questions. The September sun was shining and Amelia was with Tim all weekend. Olivier's number was a temptation, a lighter option, though her fingers slipped on the keys as she scrolled through her contacts and waited for him to pick up.

"I was just wondering if the Novotel was so swanky that you didn't want to see any more of Suffolk?"

There was a beat, a laugh, then Olivier said, "Wonderful though the blue carpet and grey bedding is, it does get monotonous. Even the room information, I have noticed, is returned to exactly the same spot on the dresser. I assumed the chambermaid must use a mark, so I checked. I am pleased to say it is purely her own skill."

"That sounds very impressive. Maybe I should leave you to ponder your room some more?"

"Please, no. I already know it so well it is in my dreams. And from the window I can see a roundabout, where I have looked for so long I am now familiar with the cars each day. Save me, Cate."

Cate smiled. "Be waiting in your hotel lobby first thing tomorrow morning. And watch for me coming round the roundabout."

"Sounds wonderful."

"And then I'll show you why locals call this Ipo-rock-city."

"Mini-golf? First ringos and then this. Are there no art galleries or museums?"

Cate supressed the urge to laugh as Olivier looked in confusion at the array of plastic bridges and tunnels, the mini-rivers that snaked around flags. He was dressed in red trousers, a check shirt and brown brogues, a look so very French that if he was any less relaxed in his skin it would be a cliché.

"Sorry, Olivier. Sadly, probation salary doesn't stretch to membership of a proper club."

Olivier looked at the child-sized golf club, with its blue plastic putter, and strode towards the first hole which was strategically placed between the legs of a plastic zebra.

"The only mystery is why Novotel is half-empty, when Ipswich has so many tourist attractions magnifiques."

Cate chipped her ball past Olivier's and it clunked satisfyingly into the hole.

"Ah!" said Olivier, "Now I understand. We are here so you can whip my butt." The American expression sounded all wrong in a French accent, and Cate didn't stop herself from laughing this time, even if it was at Olivier's expense. She was enjoying herself.

They walked together over the mini-bridge that if played wrong would result in the ball being lost into a well some twenty centimetres deep.

"I used to come here a lot," she confided, after chipping the ball into the hole in just two shots. "My dad would bring me and my sister."

Olivier moved closer to her. "I can imagine you as a girl. Goofy teeth, bad hair. But very pretty eyes. But you know, Cate, what you are telling me means that you are a cheat. You have an unfair advantage today, as you know the course."

Cate looked him over. "I can imagine you as a child, too. The neatest room, the smartest clothes. Teacher's pet. Maybe it's time someone wiped the smugness from your handsome face."

Later, they walked into town and found a Turkish restaurant with pretty turquoise walls and pink velvet chairs. Cate felt Amelia would approve that she was choosing things because they were fun, colourful. She clinked glasses with Olivier and they shared a plate of vine leaves, olives and delicious salted cheese. She knew that when she saw Olivier next would be at the emergency meeting on Monday morning and he would be back to his sombre working persona, so she wanted to enjoy him being relaxed and soak up every minute of their weekend together.

52
Ben

The orange sun sinks in the distance, dying rays gleam off the girders of the Orwell Bridge. I stretch my hands across the plush of the grey sofa, reclaiming it with my fingers. It's all mine now that Adam isn't here. When I bring my hands together in my lap they are clammy, cold. I am shaking.

I'm relieved Adam is gone but also sad that so much was left unsaid. Eight years of hiding who I really was and here had been the one person who really knew what had happened that day on the Humber Bridge, and we didn't even talk about it. Neither of us mentioned the trial, the lies, the secret we kept.

Now that Adam is gone there is no-one to really talk to and my loneliness feels as complete as a wall in front of my face.

The sun is now fully lost, the sky inky, lit up by a few solitary stars. Dying planets, a teacher once told me. But what is the use, all this knowledge crammed in my brain, the exams I studied for, certificates gained, it still boils down to being alone, just me and my conscience.

"Can't you sleep, Ben?"

Cheryl is in the doorway of my lounge, tussle-haired and wearing only a T-shirt. It's my Superman T-shirt, she took it from my chest of drawers without asking.

"No."

She sits next to me and the T-shirt rides up her leg.

"Me either."

Two of us, silent and awake, watching the sky. I want to ask why she's here, why she didn't leave with Adam, but something stops me. I'd rather pretend that she's simply here because she wants to be with me. She slides her hand in mine and rests her head against my shoulder, a gesture so intimate that I hold my breath in case any movement scares her away.

Eventually I must fall asleep on the sofa, because when I wake Cheryl is gone. It's early, just past eight, and I walk around the flat to check if she's gone for good but her white sports bag is still by the door and her wash stuff is in the bathroom. Wherever she is, she'll be back.

I go to the bedroom, looking for my jeans, but poking out from under my bed is my canvas bag. Pulling it free I can tell she's opened it, it's not sealed as carefully as I would have left it, and the letters inside are jumbled. Cheryl has peered inside my very soul, without permission.

The door slams, making me jump guiltily even though this is my bedroom, these are my letters. I look up as Cheryl walks into the room, still wearing my Superman T-shirt but with black leggings and black pumps, looking cooler than I ever did in it. She sees me holding my bag of memories but doesn't react, as if she has done nothing wrong. I think then that this is a girl who never believes she is in the wrong, that she never thinks she may be responsible.

She hands me a box.

"Present for you," she says.

It's a narrow box, black with white writing. It says Vans on the side, the make Kevin said I could never afford. I open the box and see a pair of red trainers, almost identical to the shoes Noah wore that day on the bridge.

"Like them?" she asks, innocently.

And I do, though I think I shouldn't.

"Don't lose them," she says. And I think of the trainer

falling to the water below. I see that she knows this, and together we are locked in a moment of shared memory.

"I'll try not to," I say.

52
The Day Of

Jessica Watts felt young and alive and vital, the banner in her grip, her voice croaky from shouting. She was energised by the swell of people around her, all teachers, all wanting the same thing. She hadn't felt this wonderful since sixth form, when they staged a sit-in in the refectory to protest the school's rugby club having a wet T-shirt competition at their end of term barbeque. That was the summer she fell pregnant, when her life course changed. But now she was back where she belonged.

The sound of singing, many people chanting as one voice, was good to hear. It made her proud to be a teacher, proud also that she had decided to mobilise the apathetic staff at Bramsholme Primary, a school where no-one fought for anything much, because defeat was almost inevitable. But not today.

Ending her relationship with Roger had been the right thing to do, he had become too controlling, creepy even. The problem was she had outgrown Dave, but Roger wasn't the answer, this was. A purpose.

The train back to Hull leaves King's Cross in one hour, but she doesn't want to go just yet. Doesn't want this day to end. She's felt young, a better person, being here. She doesn't think about Noah, not today. She's given him ten years of her life and wants just one day for herself.

Just recently things had got bogged down at home, she made mistakes including getting involved with Roger. Too involved, she'd even started cooking in his home, cleaning up a bit. Acting more like a wife than a mistress. She'd tried to pull away, but he'd persisted and she'd been weak. Also, she'd felt sorry for his girl.

When she'd first met Roger he had been her mentor and she was on her final teaching placement. It was he who had told her to apply to the school when she was qualified, he had sat on the interview panel. It wasn't long before he was making it clear to her that she should be grateful to him. Looking back now, she could see that Roger had abused his power and she felt that ending her relationship with him was a good move. Now she would re-focus. Concentrate on her career, plan how to move on from Dave without using another man as a crutch.

She was head of year now, a swift promotion because she was good at her job. She didn't need Roger, she realised now that she never had.

When she returned home she would give everything she had to the life she had chosen, for her and for Noah. It would be a better life for both of them.

In another city, Roger Palmer watched the end of his fishing rod, circumnavigating the drop of his line into ever decreasing circles of river water, hypnotising him so his thoughts ran on, unchecked, the fishing rod frozen in his hands, his eyes glazed.

His anger with Jess had become a dull ache, and now he was regretting not going to London. Not because he wanted to strike, he was too old for that sort of thing, damn it, and every fool knows teachers are underpaid, shouting outside parliament won't change that. No, he was wondering if he'd done the right thing because his failure to turn up for the coach that morning was a clear message to Jess that he was accepting their relationship was over, and he just wasn't ready to do that. He appreciated that it would be hard for her to tell her husband, but she didn't love him, she loved Roger. And it was natural she was worried about Noah, but he could have reassured her, he would love Noah like his own son. Cheryl liked the boy, they were both only children and would enjoy having a sibling. Sometimes women needed to be told what to do, they were like children in that respect.

What a mistake he'd made, not getting on that coach. Maybe he could have saved their relationship, if only he was there, sitting next to her on the long journey. He could have persuaded her.

This was just a hiccup, but he would fix it. She was thinking about Noah, about the damage it does to a child if parents separate, but what about the damage when parents aren't in love?

Jess deserved a chance to be happy, they all did. They were just two good people in a less-than-perfect situation, but they could be happy if she would only stop fighting it.

Roger Palmer decided he would fix it, do whatever was needed. Yes, people would get hurt. Jessica's husband, for one. And her son was sure to be upset for a while. But Roger was a strong believer in the end justifying the means.

His rod quivered and the float disappeared beneath the water. Something had been caught, his hook had lodged into the lip of some innocent creature. Satisfied, he gently began to lift his quivering prey from the river.

FACEBOOK: FIND HUMBER BOY B

Noah's mum: Our son may be dead but he is the glue that binds us. When I look in my husband's eyes I see Noah, when Dave speaks I hear the voice my son may have had, had he been allowed to age.

Silent Friend: That's very poetic, Jessica, but it's still bullshit. Death rips relationships apart. I know, first-hand, the truth of that.

Noah's mum: I have no idea who you are, but you know nothing about me. You have no right to even be posting offensive messages on this site. This page is a memorial wall, and the dead should be respected.

Silent Friend: You're right, I can't know what you feel. But, believe me, Humber Boy B destroyed my life too, and I'm going to make him pay. Soon.

55
Cate

"It's no longer a matter of if but when," Cate said as she entered the conference room, the words that had been rebounding in her head the whole drive to the police station now bursting from her. "We have to take Silent Friend's threats seriously, or we're failing in our duty to protect Ben."

All the others were already seated, Steve Flynn at the head of his table looking weary and ready for a holiday, Penny eager as ever with a pen in her hand. Ged was slumped in his seat, his chin rested on his palm, elbow on the desk. He looked like he didn't want to be there. Cate didn't meet Olivier's gaze directly – take him at his own game – but she could feel him watching her and at a glance saw he was poised and groomed as always.

"Silent Friend has given an explicit threat," she continued, "and whilst we don't know who Silent Friend is there are plenty of contenders: Noah's mum. Ben's brother, who arrived on his doorstep two days ago… "

"You're kidding." Penny dropped her pencil. "We told him, over and over, that family couldn't know where he is. The little idiot contacted them?"

"He sent a card, just after his release, to his mum."

Penny cursed.

"I know, he was a fool." Cate simply felt sad about the fact, but didn't have the heart to be angry with Ben. He was just a messed up kid who was trying, in a last ditch attempt, to reach for his mum. Stupid, maybe, but very human. "But I went and spoke to the brother, and he agreed to leave. He's back in Hull now."

"But he still knows exactly where Ben is," said Olivier. "The cat, as you British like to say, is out from the bag."

"Forget cats, this is a total dog's dinner," grumbled Ged into his sleeve. "If his cover's been blown and the press get hold of the fact that we placed him in one of Ipswich's most swanky new builds, the housing department is going to look like idiots."

"And you're worried about that?" Cate hissed. "When Ben's life is at risk."

"Whoa." Olivier was actually holding a hand up to Cate. "That's inflammatory. All we have is a handful of threatening comments on Facebook, nothing has actually happened."

"So are you suggesting we just wait?" asked Cate, still not seated, instead leaning forward on the desk so she and Olivier were directly eye to eye. "All the signs are telling us we need to act. Ben needs to be ghosted out of Ipswich, somewhere safe. A new area where he can start again."

"We can't afford it." Steve paused after stating the simple fact, waited whilst everyone turned to face him. He shrugged, "It's taken a wad of the budget to deal with everything so far, to move him again would mean we'd wasted everything."

"We can't afford not to," said Cate. But as she looked around the table she saw that no-one else was thinking this way, and Steve was the chair of this Risk Management meeting. She was just one voice, and no-one else seemed to be understanding.

They were still determined to follow the 'wait and see' policy and she was Cassandra, calling out what she knew to be the truth, no-one willing to listen. Not until it was too late.

Steve called the meeting to a close and Cate was in no mood to hang around, unable in her frustration to engage in small talk. Briskly, she walked from the police station to her car, glad to be in its confined space, in control. Driving soothed her, as did the fact that she was going back to her own building which felt like a place of refuge. Within the probation office she was no longer a lone voice; other people saw the world as she did.

Cate went first to the tea-room and was pleased to find Dot in there, as well as Sue and Janet, both probation officers whom she had known for years. All listened, all agreed that the Risk Management strategy was foolish and negligent. Then they returned to their own heavy caseload and Cate sat, staring at the notice board and wondering what the heck she should do now. Her colleagues' sympathy, though a powerful balm, didn't change the fact that moving Ben was not within her control, and when he arrived for his appointment she would have to tell him so. She was still in the tea-room, holding a cup of cold tea, when Dot came back in.

"Still here? I'm sorry Cate, I know this isn't what you want to hear just now, but Ben's in the waiting room."

Cate glanced at the clock and saw it was exactly one o'clock. Ben was always punctual, a legacy of being raised in an institution maybe. Still, she didn't move and Dot sat next to her, placing a comforting hand on Cate's leg.

"Maybe the police are right. Maybe no-one's coming for him and it's all just hot air."

"I doubt that." Cate put her mug down, the tea was untouched. "But at least I can prepare him for the worst."

Dot gave her a sympathetic smile and the two women returned to their jobs.

Ben looked different today. He sat straighter in the chair and his hair looked like he'd had it trimmed. He was also wearing a trendy-looking pair of canvas shoes, the same brand Amelia wanted, though she coveted the ice cream design and Ben's were simply red. Cate noticed but didn't dwell on these minor changes. "Ben, I'm afraid I have bad news. There have been some threatening messages on Facebook, and the arrival of

Adam has really compromised things."

"But he's gone," Ben protested, albeit weakly. Cate also noticed the colour rise on his neck, and wondered if he was hiding something.

"I hope so, Ben. But Adam's knowledge of where you live is still a weakness in your release plan. Without knowing who Silent Friend is we can't judge how real the threats are, so I think we have to take them seriously. I'll be honest with you, there was a Risk Management meeting at the police station this morning and I asked them to move you."

Ben looked stricken. "Leave Ipswich? But where would I go?"

Cate waved her hand. "It's not an issue, the rest of the team didn't see it as necessary so you're staying put. Which means we have to keep you safe another way."

"What way?" Ben sounded afraid. "Do you mean back to prison?"

"No, there aren't grounds for that. But we do need to work out who Silent Friend is. Before he, or she, finds you. I want to try and help you, Ben. We need to unmask Silent Friend. But to do that you have to trust me."

Trust. She could see from his reaction that Ben trusted no-one.

"So, let's make a start. What about Adam? He knows where you are, so he's the first suspect. Would he have any reason to want to harm you?"

"Adam… we were close once. Before Noah died. But he lied in court, he made out he was totally innocent. But… "

"But what?"

"Well, Adam was just saving himself. Maybe I should have done the same."

"How could you have?"

"I could have told them about Cheryl."

Cate recalled that this was the name of the girl who had also been in the vicinity of the bridge that day, Roger Palmer's daughter. She was framing a question in her head when Ben spoke again.

"I don't think I know about people."

"Join the club." Ben looked surprised and Cate carried on, "The more I do this job, the more unshockable I become. There's nothing you could tell me, Ben, that would even make me blink. Whatever happened on the bridge that day, I need to know. Because Silent Friend knows you, so it follows that you must know Silent Friend. Let's work out who it is, and then maybe the police will act. It could be your only option."

56
Ben

I'm not sure what to do with a girl.

Only from films, or talking with other inmates. People go on dates, they go to museums and see bands together. They go on walks, or for meals, and hold hands and kiss. Stuart never did that for Mum, and neither did my dad as far as I know, so I'm not sure what a good place for a date would be. I know couples go to the cinema but the last time I did that it ended in Noah's death, there was even a study that said us watching a horror film had something to do with what came later, so I can't face the prospect of sitting in a dark room with a huge booming screen. I don't think I'll ever go to the cinema again.

I can't afford to take Cheryl for a meal. So I improvise and take her to the best place I know. The aquarium.

Cheryl stares at the carp, her face a perfect mirror of their dumb faces and black-hole mouths. "Sorry, Ben, I'm not really getting the attraction."

I'm getting it wrong, she isn't enjoying the date. I need to make her understand, but first I check no-one else is close by. "Maybe because they're prisoners like I was. And underwater, like Noah."

I've often thought about this, why I feel so relaxed around these fish, and it's the only conclusion I've come to.

Cheryl is still facing the tank so I can't see her expression.

"I saw enough of these when I was dragged out fishing with my dad. I think they're ugly."

"They are," I agree. "Really ugly."

"Like you." She turns, pushes herself against me playfully, surprising me so it takes me a moment to understand the game and push her back, against the tank.

She grabs my shoulders, pulling me to her, we stand nose to nose and I can feel her strength, this dancer who has always been athletic when I've spent eight years wasting my muscles in a prison cell. I struggle then, uncertain and uncomfortable, but not so hard that I work myself free. I like the feel of her hand on my shoulder, her body close to mine, her face so near I can see the dimple on her chin. Her mouth, opens, her tongue hot and quick in my mouth. How do you kiss? What am I supposed to do with my tongue?

But Cheryl knows. She shows me, moves me, though I'm unsure whether to close my eyes or not. My senses, all alive only to her, see and taste and smell only Cheryl. My brother's girlfriend.

"Now then, Ben, don't go scaring the fish."

I jolt away from her at the sound of Leon's voice. There he stands, awkward, smiling too, and jangles his keys.

"Ahem, Ben. I'm going to hit the road, or the missus will be on at me for being late for tea. You okay to lock up?"

He's never let me do this, and I take the keys from him with a mixture of pride and apprehension. It's a huge responsibility, and Leon is trusting me.

Off he goes, whistling to himself, leaving me holding the keys. Cheryl has a wicked gleam in her eyes.

"Old pervert. He shouldn't have been watching."

Cheryl kisses me again, next to the large glass windows, onto a world of water and rocks, all types of fish, swimming amongst floating jetsam, getting along, bumping noses and not minding. Peaceful.

And though she kisses me my eyes are watching the river fish, fish of the Humber, the type that gets hooked on lines or caught in nets, the type that Noah saw as he fell, bubbles from his nose and mouth.

Cheryl lifts my T-shirt from my body and I shiver, warm only where her skin touches mine. She takes the keys from my hand and drops them to the floor, they land with a clatter of metal that reminds me of prison doors closing.

"I've never done it in an aquarium," she says.

"I can't… what about Leon?"

"He's gone," she says, kneeling before me and kissing my chest. My waist. "Don't worry about him. Think about me."

And I know that if Leon knew what we were doing, sliding onto the floor under the watchful eyes of the fish, that he'd never have given me the keys. He showed me he trusted me, a sense of responsibility, and I'm abusing it.

But Cheryl has pulled off her knickers, there's no barrier now, and the possibility of her is close and now and I can't stop. All these years, no-one to touch, and she's below me, her skin is all along mine. Legs are laced together, torsos twinned and her lips again, sucking me in, inside. Watched by the fish, I make love to Cheryl. If that is what this is.

I don't stop until I can no longer move, until my body is shuddering its release and the world, the entire population, could be watching us and still I wouldn't, couldn't stop.

She twists to free herself, but I'm drowning in her. What have I done? She is Adam's girlfriend. More than that, she is the reason Noah died. And now she's my lover, she's taken me over.

I need to be free.

She pulls away from me, wadding her dress swiftly between her legs to stop the flow of me from her, and then pulling it back on, smoothing it down.

"What's wrong, Ben?"

I want to tell her that it's Adam, who we both betrayed, that it's the fish with their beady eyes. That it's Noah, that

I should never be happy after what happened, why should anyone want to kiss me? Why, of all people should she and I be together after what we did?

I leave her there. I run from the aquarium in my new red shoes, the keys forgotten on the ground along with my duty to lock the place, and wish that Silent Friend would find me now, get it over with. I don't deserve it any other way.

57
The Day Of

Cheryl didn't care that the wet sand was sticking to her thigh, that she was sat in a puddle, that it was cold and her towel was soggy around her shoulders.

Fuck the world, fuck everyone. Why did it always go wrong for her?

She pulled the towel tighter around her neck and told herself it was a cloak. A golden one, fit for an Egyptian queen. No, it was an invisibility cloak that would enable her to do anything and get away with it.

A gust of wind made her shiver, then scowl. She couldn't control the goosebumps on her arms and legs, or her chattering teeth. Her stomach hurt badly now, there were dragging pains low in her abdomen and she wanted to cry. She wasn't a queen, or invisible. She was just a teenage girl with no power at all.

Things had been bad since Mum left. Her father was always so busy marking work and looking after her, looking after her too much like she was his project. It had always been just the two of them, suffocating and awkward, so she had been happy when Jessica started coming round. Things had changed for the better. And when her dad said that Jessica was moving in, Cheryl thought this would be the answer to everything that was wrong between her and her dad.

She had experienced a taste of what it would be like to have a normal family. In her imaginings she didn't say 'Jess' but 'Mum'. When would she be allowed to call her that, would it be just after she moved in, or would they wait for a while?

And Jessica would bring Noah so she would be getting a brother too.

Cheryl couldn't remember what it felt like to have a mother, but she liked the idea of it. Someone to talk with, someone who had make-up, someone she could ask about boys and why her stomach hurt so badly and if it could be her first period.

Cheryl wanted Jessica to move in desperately.

But then Dad and Jess had started arguing and she'd wanted to stop them, to tell her dad that he shouldn't shout and get angry because then they'd be alone again.

Last night it had been really bad, and now her dad was so sad. Jessica had said it was over, because she couldn't do that to Noah.

Do what? Would it be so bad for him to live with Cheryl and her dad? Why was Noah so special, that he could ruin everyone's plans?

Why couldn't Jessica see that Cheryl needed her, she really did? More than her dad, even, Cheryl was desperate to have a mum.

And now it was ruined. Noah had wrecked everything.

58
Now

FACEBOOK: FIND HUMBER BOY B

Administrator:
This page has been suspended, pending enquiries regarding illegal or abusive activity.

59
Cate

Cate started the car and began to drive towards town, still unsure if she was actually able to face her sister. She would drive in the right direction, and see how far it got her.

It had been twenty years, she didn't even know who her sister was anymore. All memories of Liz felt ancient, all tied up with how Liz had been as a child, obedient, quiet.

Though they were only a year apart in age, Cate had always thought of herself as much more independent, she was the one who got a Saturday job at fifteen while Liz stayed at home in her room. Cate was motivated by freedom, but Liz had seemed content to remain a child.

In her teens, Cate had taken on the role of the sensible one, making breakfast for her and Liz, laying a plate and cup for Mum who might not get up until midday.

With Dad working away, it had often just been the three of them in the house, but when Dad was around, everything was different. Mum would be up early, make-up already on, cheerily chatting as she cooked bacon and eggs. When he left again, as he always did, her mask of cheerful domesticity would slip and she would once more disappear into her bedroom. Cate preferred it when Dad was around, though she found it hard to hold his attention for long, she just seemed to be in the way. She told herself that this was just how it was when you were the oldest. She just had to try harder to be good.

Cate had always watched out for Liz, played nurse to her patient, rescued her from the bad guys, and later at school had comforted Liz when she was bullied. Liz was always being bullied; there was always someone who wanted to crush a bit more of her fragility, or who envied her prettiness. Yet even while Cate comforted Liz, part of her was jealous, knowing that what made her a victim also brought rewards.

Later, it was Liz who was first asked out on a date, the first of many. To Cate's disbelief she never seemed interested. Cate would answer the telephone to hear a nervous teenage male on the line, "Is Liz there?"

"Liz, it's for you. Some boy."

She would appear from her bedroom, whispering, "Tell him I'm out. Please, Cate."

And at first she would. But then she got fed up with being her sister's social secretary and would answer, "Yep, she's here – Liz, its some boy for you," forcing her sister to take the receiver.

Liz would hold the mouthpiece like it was hot, "Hello? No, I can't… No, sorry." Always, the hesitant refusals. Cate thought she just wasn't interested, but then there was Rob, whom she knew Liz liked. He was in Cate's year at school, and good-looking with dark lanky hair and hazel eyes. He would dawdle after school, walking beside them but ignoring Cate, and she saw how her sister would play with her hair when she looked at him, how she started to put lip gloss on in the toilets after lessons. These walks after school were torture for Cate, who either trailed behind like a spare part or sped up, leaving Liz and Rob meandering behind. Sometimes she would be home a whole twenty minutes before Liz appeared, looking a little flustered and flushed. But then the phone calls started and, to Cate's surprise, Liz came to her, "If Rob ever calls, I want you to tell him I'm busy."

"Busy where?"

"Anywhere! In the bath, doing homework. I don't care – but I don't want to speak to him."

"Lover's tiff is it?"

Liz's reply was a look of such anger and resentment that Cate was shocked, "Sorry I asked."

But the next day, as usual, Rob was with them on the journey from school. For several months the pattern continued, with Liz refusing to speak to him on the telephone or go on a date until finally Rob got bored and moved his attentions to Melissa in the year below Liz. From her bedroom across the hall, Cate heard Liz crying for several nights afterwards. She just didn't understand it.

When she reached sixteen, Cate no longer wanted to be hampered with her younger sister. Liz never seemed to have her own friends, only wanting Cate for company. "These are my friends, not yours," Cate would tell her. "Get your own mates." Cate did such a successful job of distancing herself that she was not shocked when Liz failed to return home on her seventeenth birthday. Her presents remained unopened, a cake untouched as evening turned to night. Finally, late, there was a phone call, which Dad answered. She only heard his side of the conversation but it was enough to tell her that Liz wasn't coming back. That she would not tell him where she was.

To think that they had grown so far apart that she had no idea that Liz was thinking to leave saddened Cate. Over the following days she had gone into her sister's room and seen the evidence of long-term planning. A row of hangers in the wardrobe. Empty drawers. Receipts for a young person's rail card, bought two months ago. A bankbook revealing a withdrawal of £900 a week ago. All that time, Liz had been squirrelling away money.

Cate never saw her sister again.

Now, out of the blue, Liz wanted to meet. And Cate knew that, however angry she was for the years of anxiety when there was no news, she was desperate to find out why she left.

She parked at the back, the area for residents in the Great

White Horse.

In just a few minutes she would know.

Just as she walked into the pub, her mobile rang, a call from Penny. Cate lifted it to her ear, thoughts immediately tumbling to Ben and what might have happened.

"Penny?"

"Bad news, Cate. I need you to come to the police station."

The receptionist at the Great White Horse waited politely for Cate's attention. Her sister was somewhere upstairs, and she was just moments from seeing her again, after twenty years. "Now?"

"Right now, I'm afraid. It's Ben. Something's happened."

60
Ben

I'm running from the aquarium, not sure where to, when I'm grabbed from behind. The punch, when it impacts, is both unexpected and clean, a direct hit to the kidneys that makes me shudder and turn, only to feel the weight of a fist pummel deep into my gut.

My attacker is male and large, at least larger than me, as I try to push him away only to encounter solid thick girth and no movement back, an awkward dance of wills that I have no way to choreograph. Then comes a crack, like wood splitting, like a branch snapping and then I am like the carp, floating, unthinking, unfeeling in the black, immense, cold sea and it is bliss.

Hazy words reach me from a distance.

"Oh shit, we need to call an ambulance."

A girl's voice. Cheryl? I open my eyes, blink, close them again as a sharp pain like a needle runs through my senses. It's not Cheryl but a stranger, a woman I don't know who is with a man with a white beard. I think of Father Christmas, then my head throbs and I think only of pain. They are both bending over me.

"Give me the phone, I'll call 999."

I struggle to sit, lay back again, try to speak though my mouth is swollen and full of a sweet, thick taste that I realise is blood.

"No, please. I'm okay."

"Like hell you are." The man's phone lights up as he touches the screen. "Your nose looks broken. Ambulance please," he says into the phone, then after explaining that my condition is not life-threatening there is a pause, "Seriously? That long?"

"What did they say?" The woman asks the man as he hangs up the phone, less anxious now she has established I'm not going to die. I can see her checking her watch, the moon catches the sparkles along the gold band.

Father Christmas runs a hand through his beard and his fingers come away shiny with wax. "No ambulances are available, they're out on heart attacks or whatever. They suggest we drive him to A&E."

They both look down at me, and I see that she is wearing a velvet dress and high heels. He is in a suit with a bow tie. I'm ruining their plans.

"I'm okay, honestly. I just need to get home."

"Where's that, kid?" The man asks.

Cheryl will be back at the flat, there's only one other place I can think of. I reach behind, wincing as pain stabs my ribs, and pull Leon's hand-drawn map out of the back pocket of my jeans.

"Please. Just take me here. It's my dad's house, and he can drive me to the hospital."

They look at each other, back at me on the ground, and the woman says, "If we take him to hospital, there's no way we'll make the party."

Decided, the man lifts me, the woman touching my arm though not doing any good that I can tell, and soon we are at their car, where I'm eased into the low front seat. It's a sports car, so the woman has to wait, but the drive to Leon's house only takes a few minutes and soon the man is being relieved of his duty as I hobble up the pathway to Leon's door. The kind stranger heads back to collect his wife and then on to their party.

The door opens and Issi stands there, a hand quickly over her mouth as she stares at my bloody face. "Oh, Lord," she says, and though I have no idea what I look like, Issi's reaction tells me it's bad. Leon comes to the door and says, "Let the boy in, woman," and then Issi snaps to energetic alert, bustling me into their front room and fussing over me as I explain I was jumped on by a stranger. And that's when I realise my mistake. I didn't lock the aquarium, I left the keys on the ground, I left Cheryl there too. And now this.

My nose is throbbing, my whole face feels as big as a bowling ball. I daren't move my head, my nose hurts so much.

"Oh, Ben, this is awful. Why would someone want to hurt you?" Issi says, then Leon adds, "Did they take anything?" I shake my head. "Not even your wallet?" as though they were one voice.

"Who cares that they didn't take his wallet, look at the poor boy! His nose is broken. I'm calling an ambulance, and the police," said Issi, determined with her lips pursed in disgust at my attacker. "He's not going to get away with this."

"No." I give Leon a pleading look, "Please, don't."

Leon looks surprised, maybe suspicious, and I'm afraid he'll ask me if I locked the aquarium. "So, this just happened after you left work? Did your girlfriend see what happened?"

I shake my head vigorously, then stop because the pain has returned. "She wasn't there. We'd just said goodbye, outside the aquarium. I was walking back to my flat."

He seems to be thinking about this and I wonder too. Was it just coincidence that I was attacked just after I'd left her?

"Issi's right, whoever did this shouldn't get away with it." Then he touches my arm, speaks more intimately, "Unless there's something you're not telling us, son?"

My face, already swollen and tender, now burns. Shame, but not from tonight, old shame. They must smell it on me, they must see through my disguise. If the police arrive, how long will it be before they discover that I'm Humber Boy B and then I'll lose even this. Especially this. I should tell Leon

I didn't lock the aquarium, but I can't. I feel I've already disappointed him enough.

Leon sits heavily in his armchair, "Did you provoke him in some way, son?"

Issi shrieks, "There's no excuse for violence, Leon. Are you saying Ben deserved to get beaten up? Look at his poor face." Leon reaches to pat her hand, but she's too busy moving around me, he can't calm her.

"I know, love. But young people have short fuses. I'm just trying to find out why our Ben here doesn't want the police involved. Is it because you've been in trouble yourself, lad? What with the Community Punishment and everything?"

It feels like thin ice, so close to the truth, but the only way to go.

"Yes," I say, the word cracking in my mouth. "The police might think I started it. I don't want to get in trouble."

I can see this argument is working for Leon, who's a man of the world and reads the *The Sun* everyday. He knows how things work with the police and kids like me. But Issi is still a bustle of energy, dabbing me with wet cotton wool and chewing her cheek as she removes each piece, covered in my blood. I know I'll have to go one step further if I'm to stop her calling the police once she's finished cleaning me up.

I lean forward, though it makes my chest hurt, so Leon can see I'm telling the truth.

"I think I did provoke him, Leon. I didn't handle it well, so I deserved this. But calling the police will only make it worse."

It's my only lifeline. Even if I disappoint Issi, that isn't as terrifying as coming face to face with a police officer.

"How did you provoke him?" Issi has collected up the cotton wool and thrown it into the bin. She's holding the phone in her shaking hand as if weighing up the argument I'm giving.

"I… er… I knocked into him. Accidently, but I think I hurt him."

Issi looks at me like I'm crazy. "Not as much as he

hurt you!" She seems half-crazy herself, angry at what she perceives has been done to me. I've lost my chance. She presses the green button and for the second time this evening, someone calls 999 on my behalf.

"I need an ambulance. And the police, please. I want to report an assault."

61
The Day Of

Adam had always fancied Cheryl, albeit from a distance, but then so did all the boys in his year at school. She was pretty, slim, blonde, she moved like a dancer. Even if he wouldn't know what to do with a girl like that he'd give his right arm to have a try.

He was sure she didn't even know he existed, but here she was, not just looking at him, but talking to him. Not just talking, but touching too. Was she drunk? She was acting a little off, but then he didn't really know her. She was being loud, a little crazy, dressed only in a swimsuit, bringing the fish to them, and encouraging Noah to try to sacrifice it to the Devil.

She was bored, that was it. Her dad was fishing and she just needed something to do.

But why press against him, why put her hand over his jeans, just where his penis was, growing with the pressure. "Do you fancy me?" she asked, feeling him with her fingers.

And then, "How much?"

Being on the Humber Bridge, cars roaring past on the raised road, the river down below, it made Adam feel… it simply made him feel. The wind and the sky and the space. And somewhere, out there beyond the river where the sea begins, heading to colder waters, was his dad. Off again on a trawler, to the adventure that he enjoyed, that he must love, because he kept pissing off and leaving Adam and Ben with their mother even though Stuart knew she barely held it together.

And Stuart had promised him, today was their day. They were supposed to be in Scarborough, a special trip. His dad was a liar. All adults were.

But here Adam was, on the bridge, and from here the sea seemed a long way away. And Cheryl wanted him so he was going to grab that chance with both hands even if it felt weird.

The whole day had been bloody weird, the film, the Ouija board, Noah acting all dopey, Cheryl and the fish.

Adam was just going to ride it and see where it took him because, fuck knows, it had to be better than going back home.

Cheryl didn't stop him when his hand stumbled across her breast, nor when it went lower. She kissed him, wide-mouthed, and as he felt her stomach she moaned. He stopped, thinking he'd hurt her, but she urged him on, touching him too. No-one had touched him before, he had never felt a girl's thigh, the way the skin inside the leg was so smooth, the way it roughened towards the top, the hair.

He pressed his fingers through the thin fabric of her swimsuit, just as she grasped his penis. He stopped wondering how this could be, and just did what felt right, his hand and her hand moving fast, faster. Inside she was moist, fleshy. He thought she liked it, he'd seen this in films, it should feel good for her too.

But when he pulled away, he saw that he had hurt her.

His fingers were covered in blood.

62
Now

Murdered Noah's mum speaks out for the first time in our double-page exclusive:

"All I want to know is why... "

Jessica Watts clutches a photo of her little boy and fights back tears. Just three weeks ago she heard the devastating news that her son's killer is free and living somewhere in the country under a new identity that cost British taxpayers millions of pounds.

"I've been living a nightmare for eight years," said Jessica, whose ten-year-old son, Noah, was thrown from the Humber Bridge to his death. A group of children were on the bridge, and two brothers received convictions. Humber Boy B, who was just ten when he went on his murderous rampage, served an eight-year sentence for Noah's murder.

"Eight years is nothing," said husband Dave, sitting close to his wife. "But what we really want isn't a longer sentence. We need answers. We just want to know why our son had to die."

Full article on page 8.

Join The Sun's *campaign to find Humber Boy B, to help his parents ask the one question that has not been answered. Sign our online petition NOW!*

63
Cate

This time when she arrived at the police station Cate was ushered, not upstairs to the large conference room, but down the corridors near the cells, to one of the windowless interview rooms on the ground floor.

"So what's happened?" Cate tried not to think about Liz, waiting for her at the hotel. She had told the receptionist to pass on the message that she'd be back as soon as she could but she didn't know if it was true or even possible. "Where's Ben?"

Penny waited until the door was fully shut before she began to explain.

"Hospital. There was a 999 call for police and ambulance to attend a house, turns out it was his boss from the aquarium. Ben has been attacked, apparently set upon by a stranger. The constable took a brief statement while they waited for the ambulance but it was only when he put it into the system and filed his report that Ben's name triggered an alert through to Steve, so that was the first I knew of it. I called you straight away."

She was gabbling, and Cate realised Penny felt guilty. Just two days ago, along with everyone else in the room, she had dismissed Cate's concerns and said they had to wait for things to escalate. Well, now they had and Ben was in hospital.

"How bad is he?" Cate asked, hardly daring to hear the answer.

"It could have been a lot worse. Here," Penny breathed out, blowing her beaded fringe from her face, then handed Ben's statement to Cate. "He says it was a random attack. No idea who his attacker was, can't give much of a description. Some bloke just came from nowhere and left him in a bloody pool on the floor with a broken nose."

"What about accents?" Cate asked, looking at Ben's signature at the bottom of a typed page. "Did the attacker speak?"

Penny shook her head, "Hoping for a northern accent, Cate? It's not just folks in Hull who are hunting down our Humber Boy, you know. *The Sun* ran a piece on him this morning. Front page, with pictures of Noah's weeping parents. You see it?"

"I try to avoid red tops."

"Good for you. Sadly, that's where most of the fuel is coming from. That and the Internet. The online campaign has gone viral and it's trending on Twitter. I'm afraid we can't contain it."

"Shit."

"Isn't it, though?"

"The world is watching and Silent Friend has already found him."

Penny held up both hands, "We don't know that. It could be a random attack."

"You're still running with that one?" Cate pointed to a place on the statement. "Even though his wallet wasn't taken?"

Penny looked away, then her radio crackled to life and she listened intently to the incoming message. "Sounds like Ben is out of hospital. Olivier's escorting him, but he asked if you could wait here until he gets back, so he can update you."

"Olivier can't be taking Ben back to the flat?" Cate handed the statement back to Penny with a derisive thrust. She didn't believe any of it. "I feel like I'm going crazy here. The boy needs to be in protective custody. Why don't you want to see what's happening here?"

"Let wait for Olivier. See what he has to say."

Twenty minutes later, still in the windowless room at the police station, Olivier handed Cate a muddy-looking cup of coffee, gave Penny a nod and sat down near the statement. "I'll be honest, Cate, it comes down to money. Ben's witness protection scheme is *trés cher*. Move him again, with a new identity, it becomes *trop cher*. It is more economical for us to accept his version of events. This was a random attack."

"A stranger breaks his nose and it's random? Despite the online campaign, the article in *The Sun*? What if he gets attacked again?"

To Cate's surprise, Olivier looked unmoved. "This may be collateral damage. After what he did we couldn't expect a picnic. But that doesn't mean he is in real danger."

Cate looked from Olivier back to Penny, wondering if it was she who was mad or them. Ben had killed a boy, but he'd only been a boy himself. He'd served his sentence. Wasn't it their job to give him a second chance at life? To keep him safe? She felt she would be wasting her breath to say any of this.

"He's not at the flat. He's with a couple, the man who runs the aquarium and his wife."

"Leon," Cate informed him. "And is that fair, to put them at risk? They have no idea who he is, or what taking him in might mean."

"I don't think they are in danger. And having him stay with them gives us some breathing space."

Cate looked at his smug face and for a second she hated him, they seemed to come from different worlds. How was it that, just last night, it was thoughts of Olivier that filled her mind as she drifted off to sleep?

64
Ben

I'm in Michael's bed, looking at his posters. I'm realising that he wasn't as young as he is in the picture Leon has in the memorial garden when he died. In that picture, Michael is just a boy of about eight, but on the wall is a Nirvana poster, and another one of a topless woman on the back of the door. Also, on the desk is a razor and shaving cream, and other signs that he was a more a man than a boy when he died.

Issi insisted on me coming back to their home once the hospital discharged me. She'd have preferred for me to stay in overnight, under observation, but I wasn't having that and thankfully neither were the harassed staff at Ipswich A&E.

I'm worried about what happened after I left Cheryl at the aquarium. Did she lock up? Did she go back to my flat? She has no idea where I am, and right now that feels like the best thing because I don't know why she's here in Suffolk. I don't know why she had sex with me. I don't even know what she was thinking when she bought me the red trainers. All I know is that since she and Adam arrived, I've had my life hijacked, my nose broken. I'm too tired to really care about anything but sleep. I don't know who hurt me, if Cheryl's involved or not, and I'm aching too much to think about it. At the hospital I got some codeine and an ice pack, and Leon gave me a whisky to bring up to the bedroom with me. Now I just want to sleep.

The nurse at A&E cleaned me up as best she could, but

when I touch my nose it comes away with dark crusted blood. She said it should set okay because it's a clean break, but it felt as though every bone in my face was shattered until the codeine kicked in. When we got back, Issi took my clothes to wash, since they were brown with mud from the pavement and red with the wound from my face. I'm wearing one of Michael's T-shirts and I can tell from this that he was bigger than me, his chest was wider and he must have been taller too because it comes down to my thigh. It's black, with a single cover on the front, Oasis: *Wonderwall*. I try to think back to when Oasis were still popular, but can't. Michael must have died a long time ago.

There's a knock at the door and it opens a crack. It's Leon.

"Just wanted to check if you need anything?"

"No, thanks. I'm fine."

He stands there a moment and then seems to notice the room so he steps inside, finally walking to gingerly take the edge of the bed. "I haven't been in here in years," he says, looking at the topless woman behind the door. "I'd forgotten about her."

I bring the duvet to my chin, then think about the blood still crusted around my nose, and pull it away from my face. I don't want to mark Michael's things.

"He was older," I say softly, "than in the football photo."

"Hmm. It's just that the football day was a good one. His team won the cup and he'd scored the final goal. A day to remember, you know? This," he gestures at the Nirvana poster, the naked woman, "this was a harder time for us, but he was still our boy. I still can't believe that he's not coming back."

"How did it happen?" I ask. I don't need to say any more, we both know what I'm referring to, though I don't know if he'll answer.

Leon clears his throat, a rattle there of history and pain. "Car accident. He'd just passed his test. God knows, I can't even drive myself, I wasn't going to pay for him to have lessons.

231

He was a student at the college, learning to be a plumber, so he'd have a decent trade, but while he was training there was no spare cash. Not with what driving lessons cost, and then you have to pay for the test. So he went and got a weekend job at Tesco, stacking shelves when the store was shut, saved his money up each week. He was seventeen when he started, and he failed his written test twice, but he was determined. He'd had his licence just one week when the accident… "

Leon stops. No more words, instead he sniffs, noisily, supressing emotion and focusing back on the Nirvana poster.

"Issi's been better since you came into our lives." He taps my leg and stands up, walking heavily to the door.

"Goodnight, son," he says. And I don't know whether he's talking to me or to the boy who died.

"Now, this will make you feel better."

I've never had breakfast in bed. The tray is difficult to balance on my thighs and on the plate is a mound of scrambled egg and three rashers of crispy bacon, which I eat with a smile because Issi is watching me. It's good food, maybe the best I've ever had, and every mouthful seems to make her happier. I feel safe in Michael's room, looked after by his mother.

"Eat that, then go back to sleep. That's the best medicine, then you'll soon be right as rain."

"Thanks, Issi, but once I've eaten this I'll go back to my flat and get changed. Then I'm going to work."

"Leon doesn't expect you to work at the aquarium today. Do you, love?" she calls over her shoulder to Leon who is shuffling around the bathroom getting ready for the day ahead.

"Of course not. Tell the boy to rest."

"See?" she says, triumphantly.

I can tell she really wants me to stay, that she's worried about me. Leon, too, wants me to let them look after me, but how can I do that? I can't let them get too close, not now when everything is so uncertain, not when my past is breathing down my neck, breaking my bones. What if it put them at risk too? I make the excuse that I need to go home and pick up the aquarium keys, I need to check that Cheryl locked up, and that everything is as it should be before Leon gets there.

To get back to my flat I have to walk past the place where I was attacked just twelve hours ago. I slow down, as if Silent Friend may still be there. He knows where I live, he must, but I can't run for the rest of my life.

The key in the flat door provokes a noise, a scream, and when I open it Cheryl is stood the other side holding a butter knife, her face white as a sheet with hair that looks like it needs a wash and her dress, the one from yesterday, has creases around the arms as if she slept in it.

"Fuck! I thought you weren't coming back."

Cheryl's eyes look puffy and I wonder if she's been crying, if she cares about me that much.

"Your face! Your nose is three times the size it should be.

"It's broken. I was jumped on, after I left the aquarium. Which reminds me, did you lock up after I went?"

"Of course I did, you bastard. Why did you run off like that? I've been worried sick."

She reaches for me, and then we're holding each other, my cheek in her blonde hair, my mouth on her honey shoulder, and she's saying, "I've never been so scared in my life. Why didn't you come back? Why didn't you let me know?"

She is so upset that it stuns me. She's only been here a few days, why does she care so much? Maybe this is normal, maybe it's me that's off. Maybe this is love.

"I'm okay, Cheryl. I just want to take a shower, then lie down for a while. Get something cold on my nose." It's throbbing again, and Issi's ice pack had been wonderful. I don't have an ice pack, but there is a bag of peas in the freezer.

She gets it for me and I lie down on the sofa, staring at the ceiling. Leon said I wasn't to go to work today, and now

I know the aquarium is locked up I feel calmer. Cheryl has gathered herself too, and she's a good nurse. She gently places the Spar peas over my nose and makes me a cup of tea. She goes to shower and comes out wearing a clean T-shirt.

"That's better," she says, rubbing her hair with my towel. Her T-shirt advertises Pineapple Dance Studios, it falls off the shoulder, is bright pink with sporty stripes down the waist and it's all she wears. I find myself staring at her legs, the peas falling to the side, thinking how toned, how creamy they look. She stops rubbing her hair and stares at me and I realise I'm caught.

"Have you heard from Adam?" I ask and she picks up her mobile, shows me the screen. It says she has eighteen missed calls.

I don't understand why she's not speaking to him, I thought they were in love. I don't understand why she's here with me and not back in Hull with him. And I certainly don't understand why she pulled me onto the floor of the aquarium, why she pressed her body to mine.

She kisses me on the lips. My lips don't move, still awkward even though we are lovers now. She moves her tongue to my lower lip, presses my mouth open and then we are kissing. My nose hurts and my head aches and we're kissing and it's the most wonderful pain in the world.

65
The Day Of

Stuart walked along the dock, wishing the Hull trawlers were still there like before the Cod Wars, back when his dad skippered the *Northern Pirate*. Now the only trawler in the marina was a museum, and to work, Stuart had to sign on with the crews coming out of Peterhead or Grimsby, or sometimes the Icelandic boats. Jobs were hard to come by but there was nothing else he was good at so he knew better than to complain too loudly. Not that they'd understand him in Scotland, with his accent, not in the high winds any road.

As he walked to the marina, where he was catching a boat to Grimsby to meet the trawler, he kept his boots in his eyeline, the gravel crunching in his ears, and didn't think about his boy. He reasoned to himself, though he knew he wasn't being truthful about his motivation.

He just couldn't stay. He was a seaman and the land made him giddy. Home just meant Yvette, with her depression and all the mess, the clutter. The drinking and the temper. On the trawler all he had was a bunk, a small cupboard and that was it. He wouldn't change clothes or shower for three weeks, it was a simple life and it suited him.

Still, he wasn't being completely honest. Not fully.

It was *that child*. That boy who looked like butter wouldn't melt with his white-blond hair and big blue eyes and yet Stuart wanted to smack the living daylights out of him because Ben looked just like his father.

It wasn't the kid's fault, it was Yvette's and it was Stuart's for not being around. But still, he felt the rage inside and the need to get away from it.

Yvette's depression, that too was because of *that child.*

And he didn't know, the boy, that all of this revolved around him. They would have been better off if he'd never been born.

When Stuart was out there, in the North Atlantic, he felt a calm he never did back on the Gypsyville estate. Even though it was the water that delivered the family their problem.

Eleven years ago, Stuart had been mate on the *Atlantic Corsair*. They'd just got the nets in when a storm took hold, and it was all the crew could do to keep upright. The captain noticed that across the water was another boat, a crabber from Iceland. A trawlerman was chaining the pots, right down by the railing, despite freezing water and twenty foot waves.

The captain was a good skipper and he'd seen enough tragedy to be worried. He positioned *Corsair* so they could see the man, even as he and Stuart swore at how fucking stupid the kid was. The boat was rolling, the lad was touching the sea. Then he was gone.

The emergency siren was accompanied by the captain's voice on the tannoy: "Man overboard! Man overboard!"

Stuart and two other men got in their orange gear and into the life raft while the shouting carried on, the emergency bell ringing. The skipper tried to get as close as he could to the drowning man, close enough to throw a life ring, but he slipped below the waves and the ring was tossed aside by the sea.

The life raft was thrown around like a toy and Stuart's hands felt icy. They were risking their own necks for the idiot boy. It felt like a hopeless act.

Then Stuart saw an arm, grabbed it, and pulled the young man to safety.

"You saved my life," the lad said, coughing up sea water, looking pale and weak. His white hair was stiff with ice.

Stuart did save the man's life, and so he felt responsible. They were on their way back to Hull and the Icelandic crabber had three more weeks at sea, so the young man came home with him. He stayed on the sofa, rested. Yvette looked after him. His name was Hugo.

When Ben was born, Stuart embraced his baby son. Even when his hair grew, silvery white, he didn't suspect anything.

But then, that Christmas a few months later, Hugo came to visit with presents for them all, supposedly as a thank you. "I will never forget your kindness," he said to Stuart and Yvette. And then he held Ben, kissed his tiny cheek, and Stuart saw that he had been betrayed.

Yvette denied it, of course she did. For months she said that Stuart was paranoid, an idiot. She said it made her depressed, his jealousy, his anger. That she had done nothing wrong. Then, during a drunken row, she admitted the truth and the hurt crashed in on him like any wave he'd ever witnessed. Sometimes he could forget and could love her again, but other times he had to get away.

The sea made him forget.

The sea didn't lie.

66
Now

FACEBOOK: FIND HUMBER BOY B

Noah's mum: I've had a lot of messages and tweets since *The Sun* article and I want to say thank you, to everyone who is supporting me and for all those kind words. But I need to say this publicly: I do not and never will condone violence. I am a Christian and I believe that only God can punish, and I trust Him to see that Humber Boy B is rightly judged.

I'm posting this because the police came to see me today. Someone has assaulted Humber Boy B. This has nothing to do with me, or my wishes. I simply wanted some answers, not violence.

Silent Friend: Sometimes violence is the only way. A boy like him will never understand anything else, and if he'd had a few slaps when he was younger he might never have killed your son.

67
Cate

Arriving back at the Great White Horse, almost two hours later than arranged, Cate saw that the place hadn't changed much. It was she who had changed. The last time she'd stepped through the doors she'd been wearing Doc Martens with red and black striped tights. She was a sixth form student with back-combed hair who worked the bar two nights a week for some extra cash, and to get out of the house for a while.

Twenty years later, Cate wore a cream linen blouse with black jeans, she'd painted her nails a matt taupe and her hair was straightened and glossy. As if for a date. This meeting with Liz and the attack on Ben had made her nervy, and she'd overcompensated with eyeliner. That at least was the same as when she was eighteen and had just perfected the cat flick. At the bar, where she had previously only ordered snakebite and black, she asked for Grey Goose with Fever Tree tonic and drank it quickly, the ice rattling in the glass as she offered it back to the bartender and asked for a second. This, she didn't touch. She would take this with her up to Liz's room. She hoped that the receptionist had passed on her earlier message.

Cate was just fifty paces away from hearing why her sister had left. Liz had been seventeen when she walked out, leaving Cate the unenviable task of keeping things normal at home, as normal as possible. Prior to Liz leaving their mother drank secretly, but afterwards she did it openly. Her usually controlled anger was given full vent. She seemed to blame Cate – as if she could have stopped Liz from leaving. Her mother's depression was something they had all learned to weather, and although she had previously had very little time for either daughter, once Liz left the family unit seemed to implode and the depression never lifted. Arguments raged between her parents. Within six weeks Dad too had gone, also suddenly, also without a forwarding address.

Cate was in her final year of sixth form and, although she tried to concentrate, her grades suffered. The time she spent alone with her mother was the most difficult. She tried to keep the house clean and make her mother eat the food she cooked, but it was all to no avail. Unable to throw good food away she would eat both their meals. She took the job at the Great White Horse, serving fellow students their snakebites, taking on as many extra shifts as she was able to. Walking slowly back home, she grew to be afraid of what she would find. If her mother was asleep in a drunken haze on the sofa it was bad enough. She would have to haul her into bed and make sure she was comfortable, lying awake through the early hours worried that her mother would choke on her own vomit. But if her mother was drunk and awake that was worse. Then she would have to suffer recriminations, the transfer of blame from Liz to herself. Her mother said things that no daughter should ever hear about herself or, worse, about her father. Next morning her mother would remember nothing, or pretended to, and Cate colluded with the act.

Liz had destroyed the family unit, and never looked back. But now she was here, in Room 3 of the Great White Horse.

The thick carpet sucked at Cate's pumps so she felt she should stand still, even the flooring was telling her she shouldn't walk another step. The light cast creepy shapes up the embossed wallpaper. Cate sipped her drink, the ice cubes knocked her nose. *Fuck's sake, it's your sister. Knock on the bloody door.*

"Hello?" It was Liz's voice, no mistake. She sounded just the same.

"It's me."

The door opened to show Liz. Just Liz, so much Liz, and the same dark hair and blue eyes, but older, slimmer. Cate couldn't help it, she grabbed her sister, hugging her so hard the vodka glass was pressed between their shoulders.

When Liz pulled away, looking emotional, she took the glass from Cate and downed it in one. "Share and share alike," she said, handing the glass back with only ice remaining.

"I'll go back down, get us more."

"That's okay, there's a mini-bar." Liz opened the small black fridge and took out two little bottles of vodka, two of gin, and the Schweppes tonics. She placed the clinking booty on the table and went to get a second glass from the bathroom. Cate was already re-filling hers as she wandered around the hotel bedroom. The room was large, overlooking Ipswich's high street, the jewellery shop opposite was a local trademark and the place where Tim had bought her engagement ring all those years before.

Cate looked around. Whatever Liz did for a living she could afford a superior room. The bed was a four-poster, with dark chunky wood and rich red and russet bedding. There was a pink sofa and two armchairs. Despite all of these comforts, the room was stuffy and Cate couldn't bring herself to say it was nice. She preferred the modern austerity of Olivier's room at Novotel.

"So," Cate sat on the sofa, next to her sister. They both examined the other, fascinated by what time had changed and what remained the same.

"You're not ginger anymore," Liz said, as if this was the most important thing to say after such a long separation. "More auburn now."

"Hmmm," Cate acknowledged. "Red hair gets darker with age."

"Does that mean your temper has mellowed too?"

241

"Not according to recent evidence."

Liz laughed and it broke the tension, but also made Cate feel sad for all of the anger and resentment she felt towards her, all the years she had not known where she was or why she went. All the laughter they might have shared.

"Why are you back in Ipswich, Liz?"

"I'll get to that." Liz had clearly thought about how to handle the meeting, she was very much in control. "First, I want to know about you. Mum told me you have a daughter."

"Amelia. She's ten, eleven next month," Cate replied, deadpan. Liz hadn't just walked away from being a sister and daughter, she had rejected her role as auntie too. "She's with her dad this evening."

"Your husband?"

Cate winced, and thought of that engagement ring gathering dust in a velvet box at the bottom of her sock drawer.

"Mum didn't tell you I'm divorced?"

"I'm sorry, she probably did. There's just been so much on my mind, so many new facts to take on board that I forgot. God, I can't imagine you as a mother."

"Not just. I work as well."

"Artist?"

Liz's departure had changed Cate's plans. When September came, Cate's longed-for escape to art school did not happen. Her mother could not bear the thought of being alone and Cate feared for her safety if she left. With Liz and Dad both gone, what choice did she have? She rejected the place at Glasgow that she had so coveted, and applied through clearing to the local college in Colchester. The courses on offer were limited, not offering the fine art degree she would have chosen, but the one that appealed most was social work. She started the course in September, returned each night to her mother, and worked weekends at the Great White Horse.

"Not even close. I'm a probation officer."

"Oh. I wouldn't have guessed that one," Liz said, looking

surprised.

"It felt like a good fit at the time but it's lost its shine since. What about you?"

"I'm a nurse. I specialise in cancer."

"Oh. Well that's great. Children?"

"Nope."

They both sat in silence, the mini bottles now all empty, the sun outside casting an orange glow in the red room.

"Have we finished with the small talk, Liz? Are you going to tell me the reason you left?"

Liz looked at Cate like she'd slapped her, her face folded with pain and disbelief. "Please don't pretend you don't know. I couldn't bear that."

Cate was mystified. "But I don't know. Why did you walk out of our lives and never look back? What did I do?"

"What did *you* do?" Liz repeated, clearly shocked that Cate showed no understanding. "You *knew*, Cate. You, Mum, Dad. You all knew, you all colluded. No-one tried to help me and in the end I had no choice. I had to leave, for my own sanity. My own survival."

Cate slammed her drink on the table and placed her palms on her knees. "Okay, enough. What the hell are you talking about, Liz?"

The sisters stared at each other, the gap of understanding a wide abyss between them.

"Okay, Cate, if you want to play this game I'll go along with it. If it makes it easier for you."

Liz walked to her suitcase on the luggage rack under the window. She clicked it open and lifted out a wooden jewellery box, ethnic in style, carved with exotic flowers and long-beaked birds. It had brass corners and a small key to keep the contents locked safe.

"I remember that," Cate said, as Liz turned the key. "You used to keep it in your wardrobe, and you'd go mental if you thought I'd so much as touched it."

Cate's curiosity was piqued when Liz opened the box and

placed it on her lap. Inside was a pile of envelopes, and Cate saw her father's unmistakable handwriting, bold lettering in heavy black ink.

"You kept in contact with Dad?" Cate asked. She had not heard from him often over the years, cards at Christmas was about the sum of it, and she felt a stab of old jealousy that Liz was still his favourite.

"These are old letters. From back then."

When Cate's father left home, just after Liz's disappearance, she'd assumed he would return, that it was a bad patch between her parents. It never occurred to her that he too was gone for good. She could see how impossible her mother was to live with, had some sympathy with him, but surely he would not abandon them? She knew that she was not his favourite daughter – it was obvious that he loved Liz more, and always had done – but he wouldn't stay away forever.

As the weeks dragged on she approached the first milestone without him, her eighteenth birthday. Even her mother had made an effort by staying sober at least most of the day and she returned from a morning outing, unusual for her, producing a gaudy pink birthday cake with a fondant unicorn on top. The cake was intended for a child and Cate wondered if this was how her mother saw her, or merely how she wished she were still. Or maybe it had been the only cake left on the shelf.

After watching Cate feign pleasure and force some of the cloying sugar into her mouth, her mother, satisfied that she was performing her maternal duties, handed her the cards that had arrived by the morning's post. Cate opened them without joy. They were from various aunts and uncles who she only saw at weddings or funerals. Wishes and greetings from across the galaxy, it seemed to her then. But her mother had a secret.

When the cards had been displayed on the mantelpiece she produced something else that had arrived in the post, looking nervous and unhappy as she handed it over. Cate's heart burned with righteous certainty when she saw the envelope, the line of postage stamps revealing that it had been posted abroad. She had hoped it would be from her dad. In fact, it was from Liz.

"I wrote to you, from Greece. A birthday card," she now said. "I begged you to get in touch."

"I was angry." But how had she forgotten? Liz had made contact and Cate had not replied. She had not even read the entire card, but thrown it in the bin along with the remains of the unicorn sponge cake.

The two sisters considered each other, and Cate saw in Liz the girl she was at seventeen, the sister she had loved so much. Inside something stirred, feelings long since denied. She had grieved for Liz, lost her twenty years ago, and this was a resurrection of sorts. Why then were they not hugging, full of joy? Liz shut the lid of the jewellery box, closing in the pile of letters as if they were soiled and she did not wish to see them.

"Cate I want you to read these, not now, but when you get home. The police have taken all the copies they need."

"Police?"

Liz nodded. "There's no going back for me. I want to know if I can count on your support."

The bulk of the jewellery box was unpleasantly balanced on her legs and she thought again of her father's handwriting. She tried to hand the box back to Liz.

"I don't think I want to know."

But Liz refused to relieve her of the box's weight.

"Because you already do. And you always have. So please, can we stop pretending? You have a chance, Cate, to make it up to me. Finally, you can be on my side."

At home, Cate got herself another drink before she lifted the lid, carefully removing the envelopes with the tips of her fingers. Some had ripped corners, some were neatly taped down, and she felt some regret at having to tear through them.

The first letter was dated twenty-five years ago, when Liz would have been just twelve.

Darling daughter,
You looked so pretty yesterday in your summer dress. Just like a princess from a fairy tale. If only it were that simple, that you could be rescued from a tower and live happily ever after! But, as in all stories, there is a witch in the kingdom. We must not tell her anything, my darling. I fear it would kill her. And you know how weak your mother is. Keep this safe.
    Dad.

Cate read on, each letter helping her to finally understand why Liz had never had dates, why she never wanted any boy to call her at home. What Cate had jealously interpreted as a father's love for his favoured child was actually an ugly, terrifying thing. And when Liz fled, their father had decided to leave too, no longer interested in the family left behind.

Liz had said that Cate had always known. She believed that Cate had failed her, had wilfully ignored what was going on. And maybe she was right. So now Liz was involving the police, and she wanted Cate to help her. To be on her side, as she put it. Cate put the box aside and buried her face in her hands, not sure if she had the strength. Not sure she could.

68
The Day Of

The four children climbed the steps up to the narrow walkway and then began to make their way along the bridge. Above them, on the road, cars thundered past, ignoring the fifty mile an hour limit. The few drivers who did notice simply saw a group of kids messing around. Nothing to worry about, nothing they would even remember if it wasn't for what came later.

On the path the children ran their hands along the steel tubes, the vibrating metal that supported the bridge. The only colours were the green painted steel and the orange warning signs. Looking over the river they could see East Hull in the distance, the flat roof of Hull Royal where all four had been born, the glass turret of The Deep aquarium where Ben had celebrated his tenth birthday. Their lives were set out before them.

Out in the water, red buoys moved to the swell of the tide, their bells calling out, though there were no boats on the river, just the children to listen to their warning.

Noah knelt on the gravel to re-tie his shoe lace, then placed his forehead on the dead fish and began to mutter a prayer, but backwards. Cheryl snorted.

"You can't just conjure the Devil like that!"

Noah looked up, black eyes glinting defiantly. "How do you know? It worked for us once. It's going to happen

247

again. I'm going to ask him to remove the curse. The fish is a sacrifice, in my place."

"Bollocks. The Devil's not going to come to this bridge just for a dead fucking fish, is he? He's got more important things to do."

Noah ignored her, stood against the railing and held the fish, more dead than alive, over the water.

He wasn't afraid anymore. It was as if watching the film had made him brave, or at least made him feel there was a force out there bigger and stronger than him. It reassured him, the feeling that someone else was in charge even if that person was the Devil. Noah wanted proof, that there was something out there.

He thought of his mum, down in London, fighting for teacher's rights or whatever, but he wanted to do something even more immense. Like save a life. Even if it was just a fish.

"Throw it then, lad," Adam said, pushing his shoulder.

Noah lifted the fish high to the heavens. One glazed beady eye seemed to consider him, he felt its grey heaviness pulse in his hands.

"A sacrifice to the dark lord!" he shouted.

Cheryl doubled over in hysterics. "Who the fuck are you, Harry Potter?"

Noah hurled the fish over the side, but it landed with a splat on the other side of the barrier, on the concrete lip that jutted over the River Humber.

"Good one," groaned Adam.

"It's dead anyway," said Ben.

But Noah put both hands on the barrier and pressed his body up, his right leg quivering as he raised it to try and swing over.

"Stop it, Noah!" cried Ben, grabbing the fabric of his T-shirt.

"Jesus, boy, what the fuck are you doing?" Adam had caught Noah by the belt of his jeans and along with Ben they yanked him back to the safe side of the barrier.

Noah seemed to give in, started to cry hopelessly, afraid of what would happen now his sacrifice had been rejected. He cried for the dying fish. Because he wasn't a hero. Because his mum was marching in London and not with him. Just because.

"Shut the fuck up," said Adam, calmly stepping closer to Noah. "If anyone should be howling off today, it's me."

"Or me," said Cheryl, who was leaning against the concrete platform that led to the SOS telephone. She'd watched the whole fish incident without a word, but now she pushed herself up and moved toward Noah. She grabbed his chin in her right hand, squeezed it so his lips puckered.

"You think you rule the world, don't you? Think you can control everything, because Mummy loves you. Little brat."

None of the boys saw the slap coming, but it hit Noah hard on the left cheek. He reeled, arms circling, falling back against the barrier.

Adam gaped at Cheryl, shocked and awe-struck, confused by the girl's sudden brutality.

"What you chowing at him for? He didn't do owt to you."

Cheryl held her hand, like it was she who was the victim. Her eyes suddenly filled with tears.

"He did. He ruined everything." She glanced at Noah, and saw his lip was bleeding where her nail had caught it, then looked at the floor. "Just by existing."

Noah held his palm to his bloody lip, still crying. Staring at Cheryl as if the Devil had indeed appeared.

Adam gingerly went to comfort Cheryl, delighted when she didn't stop his hand touching her wrist. He asked softly, "What's wrong, lass? Why are you so mad at him?"

She allowed herself to be comforted, walked into his hug then turned to Noah.

"My dad's fucking his mother," Cheryl spat. "She's supposed to love him. She said so!"

Noah looked up, his face contorting as upset shaded with

indignation. "You're a liar! My mum is a Christian and my dad knows everything and he'll be after you if you say things like that. So you better watch it."

"It's you who'd better watch it," she said, then her voice became muffled against Adam's chest and whatever she said next was lost. She whimpered, still in pain, and bleeding too now.

The dead fish lay forgotten on the concrete shelf.

Down below, the warning bell rang once again.

69
Now

FACEBOOK: FIND HUMBER BOY B:
FOR ANSWERS, NOT VENGEANCE

Noah's mum: I saw her today, HBB's mother. She was in the high street, doing her shopping I suppose though she looked totally lost, staring into the window of Boots with her carrier bags dangling from the ends of her fingers. At first I thought she hadn't seen me but then I realised she was doing her best to look the other way. I crossed the road to Boots, stood directly behind her to see if she had the nerve to speak to me. Our eyes met in the glass of the shop window but she didn't turn around.

She was supposed to be looking after Noah that day, I'd trusted her. I found out at the trial that she'd spent the day in bed, spent the money I'd given her for Noah's lunch on a bottle of vodka. Depressed, they said, plagued by migraines. And she looked depressed today too. But her son's alive, isn't he? What's she got to mope about? Her son is free.

Silent Friend: She should hang her head in shame for birthing such evil.

Noah's mum: She should. But it wasn't just one thing that led to my son's death. There are lots of people who let Noah down that day. I am trying to come to terms with that. But what I'm struggling with most is HBB being free.

Silent Friend: Jessica, I am sorry. I am one of those people.

Which is why I won't let you down again. I see you are asking for answers, not vengeance. But what if vengeance is the answer?

70
Ben

I wake to a vision so golden I think I must be dreaming. The sun is spying on us between the gaps in the curtains, casting a sheen over Cheryl's pale skin and yellow hair. Our shared sweat from last night has dried like glitter on her breasts and stomach.

I don't move, daren't move, because this moment is so special. A girl, a beautiful one, in my bed. Maybe my face is swollen and my nose is broken but something good has happened too.

Adam pops into my head, uninvited. My brother, who loves Cheryl. The thought nudges at me – *you bastard, she wrote to you in secure, she visited you. You got out years ago.*

Can it be that in the end I've come out on top? Because she chose me, she could have left with him, but something made her stay. My nose throbs and I wonder if it could have been Adam, if he was the person who attacked me. Whoever it was wore a balaclava. I remember that. Why wear one, unless it was a face I would recognise? Or if not Adam, then someone acting on his say-so. Someone he told where to find me, maybe someone he met that day in the library. Or, could it have been Stuart? He never liked me, and he blamed me for what happened on the bridge. Yes, he would certainly break my nose with no regrets.

Cheryl stirs, opens her eyes, shades her face with her arm and sees me watching her. "That's creepy. Stop it."

"Sorry." I adjust my position, roll onto my back, but she places her hand onto my bony chest and tugs me back onto my side so she can see me.

"Stop being sorry," she says. "You've spent eight years being locked up. That's enough sorry for a whole lifetime."

"Not everyone thinks so," I say, bitterly, and she looks at my puffy face, my swollen nose. On the pillow are flakes of dried blood.

"Then think of me as your guardian angel," she says, touching my tender face. "My job is to protect you."

And as she says this, her lower lip quivers, her eyes narrow and an unexpected tear falls from one eye, down her pretty face to her chin.

"What's wrong?" I ask, though really I'm wondering if this is because she loves me. People cry for someone they love, I saw that with Noah's mum at the trial, I see it with Issi when she talks about Michael. Does Cheryl love me?

"Nothing," she says, sniffing so the tears stop. "Honestly, I'm sure it will all be okay. Now."

And she must mean Adam, getting away from him and choosing to be with me. If she means anything else, I don't want to know.

71
Cate

"There's something the Risk Management meeting refused to accept, Paul. That whoever Silent Friend is, it isn't just a stranger who's horrified by what Ben did. It's someone who knows him, who knew him back when he was ten."

Drained from another sleepless night, Cate realised that she had been fooling herself for years. Deep down she had always known why Liz left. And this has led her to the conclusion that, in Ben's case too, the answer is in the past. That it always is.

Paul mulled this over, whilst adjusting his cufflink, shaped like a black and white humbug. "I agree, that's likely. But how are you going to uncover who that person is? You're not a detective."

"I don't need to be. If I can just unpick enough of Ben's story to find this person, before it's too late, that's the only way to save Ben. He's a sitting duck and no-one but me is acknowledging that fact."

She may have ignored the truth of her own childhood, but that didn't mean she couldn't have clarity about Ben's. She was one step removed, a professional. It was harder to see clearly when the subject was your own family.

"It all depends on Ben, though, doesn't it?" said Paul. "If he's willing to open up to you."

"It all depends on me," corrected Cate. "If I can make him feel safe enough to want to."

Ben took his seat and watched as, sat at her desk, Cate took three marker pens, blue, red and green, and wrote the three boys' names on the large sheet of paper in front of her.

NOAH
ADAM
BEN

She had hesitated over 'Ben', knowing it wasn't his name then, having seen his given name repeated in the witness statements many times, but if she started to use this name in her head, or on paper, what would stop her slipping up when she was with him or in a meeting. So, Ben it was. She added ages:

NOAH, 10
ADAM, 14
BEN, 10

The relationship between the three boys had led to what took place that day, if she could only pull it apart a little it may reveal itself. She drew circles around each name, overlapping them when they shared something: *friendship. Siblings. Same school.*

Noah was Ben's friend, not Adam's.

Adam and Ben were half-brothers, same mother, different fathers.

According to the witness statements, Adam should have been in Scarborough with his dad, but he'd gone back to sea on a last-minute call.

"Why wasn't Stuart going to take you to Scarborough?" she asked.

"He hated me," said Ben.

"Why's that?"

Push, one more step. Ask the question he doesn't want to answer but hold his gaze so he knows it's safe.

"Because I wasn't his kid. I'm half-Icelandic."

"How's that, then?"

Ben leaned back in the chair, closed his eyes. "Stuart saved my dad's life, out in the sea. And he came to say thanks. Got to know my mum. Then when I was born, with this blond hair, Stuart realised that she'd played away."

"And does this man know he's your father?" Cate asked gently.

Ben opened his eyes and gazed at the ceiling, as if in prayer. "Yeah, he knows. But he lived in another country, and Stuart didn't exactly make it easy for him to keep in touch. But even if I didn't have his DNA, I'm Stuart's son really. He raised me. And he hated me."

Cate thinks about this, how the family dynamics would be forever altered by Stuart's discovery that Ben was not his. Being a child was hard at the best of times, but feeling loved was something that could override almost anything else. Ben hadn't received love from Stuart, and only a half-hearted attempt at it from his mother if the witness statements were accurate. The most important relationship was with Adam.

"So what was it like, back then? Was Adam a good older brother?"

"Suppose. He looked out for me."

"Maybe. But he tormented you too, I bet. Older siblings can be a nightmare."

Cate thought again of Liz, the unwelcome nagging thought of how she'd failed her younger sister.

"He'd push us around a bit," Ben looked away, not willing to say more. From loyalty or because he was repressing the truth, Cate didn't know.

"Sometimes even total strangers can be kinder than siblings," Cate added.

"Strangers weren't kinder to Noah," Ben stated.

"True."

Many people had seen the unlikely trio that morning and said nothing, failed to intervene, despite them stealing from

257

a shop, sneaking into a cinema and watching a certificate 18 horror film. No-one intervened on the bridge, even with Noah's increasingly bizarre behaviour, carrying a half-dead fish. Cars had thundered past, noticing, not noticing. Not stopping, or making a call. A cyclist had to swerve to avoid Noah, by then crying on the pavement, but she was too intent on training to stop. Joggers saw Noah's bleeding lip but didn't want to get involved. Just one person could have changed what happened, but no-one was kind or concerned or compelled, not enough anyway. Everyone told themselves it was just kids messing about. People will always tell themselves the narrative they most want to hear, but as a probation officer, Cate was trained to fight that urge and dig to the darker corners of why Noah had died.

Cate tapped her pen onto the desk. "What I don't get, Ben, is how the jury found Adam not guilty. Four years older than you, and I've seen him. I mean, he's tall. Plus he had a bit of a reputation, didn't he? Stealing milk, truanting from school, shoplifting. He must have been the one to lift Noah over the side of the bridge. Wasn't he?"

"No," said Ben. "No-one lifted Noah over. He climbed."

72
The Day Of

Adam couldn't stop the thought that kept bouncing back at him, every ten minutes or so, about where he should be. In this parallel universe, where his day had turned out as it should have, he had spent the day at the beach and then he was in Peaseholm park. In his mind it wasn't raining in Scarborough, the sky there was blue without a cloud in sight, and of course his dad was in a great mood. All day he had been with Ben and Noah only in body, most of his thoughts were an hour away, up the coast, having the day he'd longed for. Even in the cinema he wasn't really concentrating on the possessed woman watch her husband sleep as objects moved around her, instead he was in the park with his dad, cheering as the battleship guns smoked. The peach alcohol had helped, and so had the hunger and the rain. He felt strange, like he was in a dream.

And the dream, the unreality, continued when Cheryl took his hand. How did that even happen, how was it she even knew who he was? She was so pretty, so confident, that even thoughts of Scarborough seemed like nothing compared to the reality of her.

After she showed them the ugly fish she'd kissed him. He could tell it wasn't her first kiss, she knew just what to do, and in that swimsuit it was easy for him to feel her bottom, her boobs. She let him touch her, so deeply that she bled. He felt bad about that. Things had started to go wrong then, she'd got sad. Adam tried to fool around, then he got serious. "What's up?"

"Just today."

He put his hand on hers. "Have I hurt you?"

"It's not you, it's my dad. I can't stand being alone in the house with him, it's awful."

She looked like she might cry and that reminded Adam of his mum. He hated when women cried, it was pathetic, besides, Cheryl had no clue just what a bastard a father could be. Stuart would win the prize, always pissing off, never saying when he'd be back or even if. And how was their mam meant to feed them then? She couldn't work, not after being signed off with the depression and those bastard migraines. There was only one way she could earn some brass, and that was something she'd promised the social workers to stop. The last time she'd brought a punter home, Adam had lain with a pillow over his head to hide the noise, then followed the man out. He'd waited until the bloke was almost in his car and then set about him, made sure he wouldn't ever come back. But there were always others who would.

"So why is your dad so awful? Because he's fishing and doesn't care where you are?"

"That. Also because he doesn't even think it matters what I feel. He doesn't get that what goes on with him is about my life too. You know?"

Adam thought this sounded pathetic, but it wasn't what Cheryl was saying, it was the way she was having to sniff back the tears, the way she looked so broken, that made him think there was something else. She reminded him of his mum even more then, and he didn't know why.

"I thought everything was going to change. I could have had a new life. I thought Jessica was going to be my new mum. But she's chosen him instead." Cheryl cast Noah a narrow look, picked up a piece of gravel and tossed it at the boy's head. Noah, feeling it land, flinched but didn't look up. Since she'd slapped him he was frightened of her.

"Him?" Adam was struggling to keep up with the cryptic nature of the conversation, but he was getting the gist, after all, he had problems at home too. He wanted to show Cheryl that he got her. She may be cleverer than him, out of his league, but they were on the same wavelength when it came to crap parents.

"My dad was supposed to take me to Scarborough. But when I woke he'd gone. He and Mum are always rowing, but still he should have taken me. It's like he doesn't even see me."

"That's it!" said Cheryl, suddenly animated. "They don't even see us, me and you, we're the same like that. It's like we don't exist, not unless they want something from us. Then they see whatever they want, just a fucking toy. It's like we're not even human."

Four children, leaning over the bridge. A teenage boy and girl, then two ten-year-old boys, in a line according to size, staring down at the river below.

It was as if nothing existed beyond that bridge, that for them the world had stopped, right there hanging over the River Humber on a steel platform many feet in the air.

Inside each head, thoughts were humming.

Inside each heart, pain and hurt. The pain of being human, but felt more keenly for the company of other children who had the same sickness. No-one to snap them out of it when the snap comes.

73
Now

Noah's dad: This is a message from both Jessica and myself. We have been advised by the police that all posts on this page are being monitored.

Since the article in *The Sun* we've been overwhelmed by all the messages of support. But we have been concerned about some of the messages we have received, from an anonymous source, and we want to make clear that we started this site to get answers. Not to be vigilantes, or to instigate any violence.

Silent Friend: You always were pathetic, Dave.

74
Cate

Olivier stroked Cate's leg with the tips of his fingers, from the sole of her foot to her knee, his eyes never leaving hers. "Sleep now," he said.

Breathing in the bedroom, a light breeze rustling the blinds. Growing darkness as night deepened.

Eyes wide open in the dark, Cate spoke. Because he couldn't see her face, and she didn't want his pity.

"My sister's back. Liz left just a week before I turned eighteen, I haven't seen her since then."

Silence and breathing. "Are you happy to see her?"

A sigh. Cate released herself from under his hand, rolled onto her back. "I should be, but it's complicated. She's back because there's going to be a court hearing. My father... "

She stopped, thinking she'd said enough. Olivier was a police officer, this was an old story. His hand found her body again, running over her shoulders, supporting her.

"And she wants me to be a witness."

"Well," he said, speaking softly, "you have spoken in court many times, I imagine."

"But not about something so personal." She waited, but he did not speak. Olivier was letting her find her own way through the dilemma. "The other thing is, I really can't remember. She says I knew, but if I did I really suppressed it. How can that be possible?"

"It's very possible," said Olivier softly. "We humans are

good at telling ourselves only what we wish to hear. How many of the criminals we work with have families, parents and spouses, who will not believe the evidence before their very eyes? We are all capable of such self-deceit, I think. And you were young, Cate, so you can be forgiven for protecting yourself in this way."

She moved closer to this man, who seemed to understand her, needing to be held once again. Wrapped inside his warmth, she could forget everything else except what the body desired.

After a leisurely Sunday brunch of scrambled egg and bagels, Olivier left, back to his hotel room where he told her he had work to do. After he'd gone, Cate retained that feeling of being wanted, of a fresh start. Though the sky was a dull grey and the weather was chilly, Cate felt nothing of the sort. She was ready for something to change, and she started by pulling the bag from the closet that contained the autumn and winter clothes that she'd stored back in the spring, digging out a light jumper in the prettiest yellow, the shade that had started to appear at the top of the ash tree in her garden as the leaves turned before falling to the ground in a firestorm of rust and red. September was almost over, summer was certainly behind them, but this new season brought a mellowing she loved. Things were changing, with the return of Liz, her relationship with Olivier. New buds of human connections, a distant promise of fresh life where she had thought the root was dead.

This time when she passed through the bar area of the Great White Horse, people were scattered around tables wearing long-sleeved shirts or cardigans, drinking hot drinks. She continued up, knocked on the door of Room 3 and heard Liz moving around before the door opened.

Though it was now afternoon, Liz stood in bare feet, draped in a heavy peach robe that fell to the floor extravagantly, and rubbed her eyes sleepily. Her dark hair was tangled around her face and she looked every bit the kid sister Cate had loved so very much.

"Cate," Liz said, surprised and then pleased.

"Hi." She paused, thinking that Liz had been in bed all day. "Are you okay? I thought we could grab a coffee, but if you're sick or something…?"

"I'm fine, I was just having a nap. Come in and give me a minute to get dressed." Liz padded to the bathroom door, her robe dragging behind her, and then Cate heard the shower running. The room was a hot mess of tossed bedding, clothes and empty spirit bottles. There was a smell, too, antiseptic and sharp.

Liz was soon back in the room, wrapped only in a towel, rooting through her suitcase for clean clothes.

"When does the chambermaid arrive?" Cate asked, looking at the unmade bed and gathering the empty mini-bar bottles into the nearby bin.

"I sent her away, she woke me up. It shouldn't be allowed, knocking at nine-thirty on a Sunday morning. I told her, as long as you re-stock the mini-bar, I don't care about the rest." Liz glanced up as she pulled on her knickers. "This isn't exactly a holiday, you know."

"No," Cate acknowledged.

Liz finished dressing, yawned and reached for her bag. "Coffee calls. And I'm starving."

In a window seat of the Starbucks next door, the sisters sat opposite each other, each cradling a large white mug. Cate's contained cappuccino, Liz had espresso. Double. And a panini with cheese and bacon.

"So," said Liz, clearing her throat. "I take it you read the letters?"

Cate passed over the carrier bag she'd been clutching. "Yes." Inside was the jewellery box and its contents, which she was happy to hand back to Liz. Even having them in her home had felt like a burden, the thought that Amelia may discover them terrified her. But it made her realise, too, that she was lucky their father had left when he did. At least he'd never met Amelia, she didn't have to think about the implications of that. She searched for words to explain all these emotions, how the letters had made her feel, but Liz's face revealed enough pain for them both.

"I'm just so sorry, Liz."

"Me too."

They both sipped their drinks. Outside the world walked past, some still refusing to wear jackets but regretting it as the air whipped around them. Others in trench coats, they'd seen the weather report that morning.

"So," Cate said. "What happens now?"

Liz leaned forward, her face rested on her palms as if she was too tired to sit without support. "He's already been interviewed, and denied everything of course. But the Crown Prosecution have agreed to proceed, they're happy with my evidence."

"So, there is definitely going to be a trial?"

"That's why I'm here, Cate. To ask you to speak in the witness box, to say what you know. What you saw."

"I didn't see anything."

Liz's mouth loosened, her eyes hardened. "You're either lying or delusional. Either way, I wish you wouldn't."

Cate closed her mouth, closed her eyes, "I'm not lying, Liz. I think I knew something, but I locked it away. I want to help, but… "

"Do you?" Liz leaned over the table, knocking her empty cup into a spin on the table so Cate had to reach forward to steady it. Liz grasped Cate's hands, so they both had the cup in their shared grasp. "I need you, Cate. I need you to remember."

"What about Mum?"

Liz shook her head, released Cate and sat back as if to assess her anew. "She wants to help, but my legal team don't think she's a good witness, not with her history of drinking.

She says she'll keep sober for the trial but I can't count on that. If she arrives tipsy they'll easily be able to discredit her, and that will damage my case. It's only you. Or else I have to do this alone."

Cate felt it, the weight of what Liz was asking, but also the hopelessness of it.

"I can't remember, Liz."

"Then try," Liz spat. "It's the least you can do. At least promise me you'll try."

75
Ben

"Issi was hoping to see you, son. She's a bit upset that you haven't been round to see her."

Leon folded his paper and placed it on the desk, picking up his tea and taking a sip, "She asks me every day about your nose, and I'm not so good at that kind of thing. You know, I say you're fine and she tells me you can't be. Asks me to tell her more, you know, how the police investigation is going and all that."

Ben shifted the mop beneath his feet, grateful that Leon wasn't asking him a direct question.

"Thing is, son, if you don't go see her I'm afraid she'll turn up here at the aquarium. And if she sees that all I do each day is read the paper and drink tea I'll be for the high jump, or even worse she might decide that she wants to join me from time to time. And this is our space, isn't it lad?"

I feel ashamed of myself. Issi looked after me that night, I should have gone to see her, but I've been too busy. Too taken up, eaten up, absorbed with Cheryl. I don't know what she sees in me, I don't know why she's even here, but I don't care. All I care about is how soft she feels, how she moves, her mouth on my skin.

"Ben? Are you listening, son?"

"Sorry. Yes, I'll go see her as soon as I finish here today, I promise."

Issi's face lights up when she opens the door and that makes me feel like a right idiot, that I didn't give her another thought after she'd dabbed up my blood and placed ice over my wound, given me Michael's bed, generally looked after me better than my own mother ever had.

"Come in, come in." She's breathless as she stands aside, welcoming me back into their cosy home. Once I'm sat in Leon's armchair she lightly touches my face, twisting my head gently towards the light so she can see it.

"Oh, that's better! Almost back to your handsome self."

"I don't know about that." I duck my head and she ruffles my hair affectionately. Suddenly, I feel suffocated, like I can't breathe and I'm glad when she moves away and the moment of tension passes. "I'll get us a drink."

Once we're sipping tea she comes out with it, the question I've been dreading. "So what did the police say?"

"They say that unless someone comes forward, they've got nothing. They don't know who it was."

"Well, that's not good enough! Did they check the CCTV in the area?"

Issi must be into crime dramas, but I know about CCTV from the Humber Bridge, those grainy pictures of us all crossing. The pictures that were published in the press, of Adam kissing Cheryl just before Noah landed in the water.

"They must have. He was wearing a balaclava anyway, so… "

I run out of ways to say that he's not getting caught. Issi looks more upset than I feel and I wonder if she's thinking about Michael.

"Did anyone get arrested?" I ask. "For Michael's car accident."

Her mouth goes small as a pebble and her eyes fix me with a hurt accusation. "Leon told you he died in a car accident?"

"Yes."

"Okay," she says in an outward gust of breath, but her face

269

shows it is anything but. This is pain, this is what mothers feel when they lose a son, and it's hard to see it up close.

"I'm sorry, I shouldn't have said anything."

"We're all sorry. But it can't change anything."

"No."

Michael is there with us, suddenly, a teenager in a Nirvana T-shirt, twirling a key ring in his fingers, his new car waiting outside. I can hardly bear to remain seated, it's so awful. Then Issi starts to cry, and I don't know whether to walk out or go to her. So I just sit still, waiting for her to stop shaking, for the tears to stop falling. I feel like I caused it, which is wrong, I'm thinking of another mother, another boy who died. And then I'm crying too, and Issi thinks it's because of her and she opens her arms to me, I go to where she's sat on the sofa, kneeling at her feet and we're both crying, rocking, a grieving mother, a boy killer. And I thank God that she doesn't know and promise I'll do anything, anything at all, for her to never find out.

76
The Day Of

"My dad legged it, off to sea like he always does," Adam said, as if he'd finally accepted the fact. "The twat didn't even wake me to say he was off."

"At least you have a mum," challenged Cheryl. "Mine left us with my dad. Just the two of us in the house, he treats me like his property."

Noah, who had been listening, sat cross-legged on the floor of the footpath that ran the spine of the Humber Bridge, messing with the laces in his red trainers. "It's my mum who ignores me. She's in London, she left me to do whatever I wanted. She doesn't even care."

"She organised for my mam to look after you," corrected Ben.

"Exactly," Noah sniffed. "No offence, Ben, but if she really cared about me would she leave me with your mum? Everyone knows she's mental."

Adam looks up blankly, as if wondering about reacting, then decides he can't be bothered.

All four of them are silent at this, lost in the mutual agreement that they're all invisible, neglected. United by the crapness of their parents.

"There's nothing we can do," said Ben. "It's just the way it is."

But Cheryl had a different view, she had an idea. Suddenly, she jumped up and grabbed Adam, pulling him to

271

the railing. "Come on," she said. "All of you. Follow me. Let's make them notice." Cheryl called, positioning herself directly below the CCTV camera and pulling Adam to her for a full-mouthed kiss, tongues and teeth and eyes wide open. They all gaped: Ben, Noah, the camera with its one all-seeing eye, as Cheryl appeared to devour Adam, her hands on his face so he couldn't pull away, a kissing technique she must have learned from a film and practiced on a mirror. When she finally released him, Adam reeled drunkenly, staggering back into the railing where he turned to face the water and gave a jubilant whoop.

Cheryl bent over the railing, laughing hysterically, then grasped the metal barrier with both hands and jumped up in one swift athletic movement, twisting as she sat upon it, her bare feet entangled with the metal struts. The towel fell to the ground and she sat in just her swimsuit, hands either side of her body as she leaned backwards, over the water, still laughing madly.

"Would they notice this?" she cried, adrenalin making her brave and stupid.

"Stop!" the word was a struggle for Noah to say, his chest felt tight as he watched Cheryl leaning back. "That's dangerous." his eyes were wide as saucers.

Cheryl looked over at Noah, enjoying his fear and the feeling of power it gave her. A wicked expression darkened her face like she might try and do something even more crazy, spooking Noah so much that he had to get away from it. He tried to run, wanting to be safe at home, but tripped over his shoelace and landed flat on the floor. Tears came as quickly as the blood and he curled into a ball, his lip already split and now he had a bloody knee.

Two joggers ran past.

The joggers, a man and woman on a lunchtime run, saw the boy's tears, the blood, the crazy-looking girl in her swimsuit sat precariously on the railing. Neither stopped. Neither

272

spoke to the children, or to each other. Not until later that night when, back in their own homes, they each watched the nine o'clock news.

A text message: **Oh shit. Did you see the CCTV image? That was them.**

Then: **Say nothing. Best not to get involved.**

77
Now

FIND HUMBER BOY B:
FOR ANSWERS, NOT VENGEANCE

Silent Friend: You need to change your header to Humber Boy B: Found.

A person is not defined by what they did in the past, but what they do now. I cannot change what happened to Noah, but I have an opportunity to achieve justice for his family.

Noah's mum: Who ARE you? How can you claim to know what we want?

Silent Friend: Because I know you, Jessica. And I will never let you down again.

78
Cate

Penny finished reading out the latest message and the room fell silent. Ged was the first to speak.

"This Silent Friend sounds like a right nut job."

"Hmmm," agreed Steve, tapping his fingers on the edge of his chipped Suffolk constabulary mug. "That's what concerns me. And we still don't know who he is, but he obviously has some link with Jessica from the way he's speaking to her, even if it's only in his head. And he claims to have found Ben."

"I think," said Cate, adjusting her voice so it was both louder and more certain. "In all likelihood, Silent Friend is someone from Ben's past. These messages sound like someone with a personal reason for involvement. I've been working with Ben to try and find out who it could be."

Olivier leaned forward, lifting his pen. "Good detective work, Cate. We may poach you from the probation service. And do you have a name?"

"The problem is," Cate admitted, looking at her own notes. "There are several. This crime left many ripples, and so many people were affected. If we are assuming that Ben's attacker was Silent Friend… "

"Which at this stage is still an assumption," Olivier stated.

"Yes, but if we don't, then the possibilities are so random that I don't know how we'd fathom the depths. We need to start with something."

Olivier lifted his chin and then nodded. "Agreed. So, who is on the list?"

"Well, Roger Palmer for one. After the murder, which he witnessed, he never returned to work and had to be signed off with stress. He'd tried and failed to save Noah, maybe he thinks that now Ben is out it is his chance to get justice."

Steve looked at his notes. "Yes, that sounds possible. We could send someone to speak with him. Who else?"

"Ben's step-dad, Stuart. And we shouldn't rule out his natural father, Hugo. An Icelandic trawlerman, who might not like his son's behaviour."

"Seriously?" Ged said. "You think the kid's own family could be behind this?"

Cate sighed inwardly at the assumption that a parent wouldn't do such a thing, even though most evidence suggested that your own parents were far more likely to hurt you than a stranger.

"After the murder, Stuart sold his story to the papers, said his step-son was evil and he wished he'd never been born. That sounds like one angry man to me."

"Okay," Steve made a note on his yellow notepad. "We'll check him out too."

"Anyone else?"

"Well, the most obvious people are Noah's parents, or someone else in the Watts family. After all, they have more reason than anyone. And these public statements on Facebook about not condoning violence could just be game-playing."

"Hull police have already interviewed Jessica and Dave about the Facebook page, but we could check further," said Olivier, nodding his assent to Steve. "Even if it's not them directly they may have some idea of who it is, maybe somebody from their church group, someone from the fundraising committee for the skate park."

"Agreed," said Steve. "Good work, Cate. Feels like we're getting somewhere."

Cate then braced herself, what she had to say next was the

most pressing issue, and she was expecting resistance from all quarters.

"Ben is still a sitting duck. His block of flats is just yards from where he was attacked." She paused, looked from Olivier to Ged. "I'd like him moved to a place of safety until we've established who Silent Friend is."

Ged slapped the desk with his palm, "It can't be done. We're putting too much into this as it is."

"Plus," Olivier added, "Ipswich isn't huge. If Silent Friend is watching Ben, he knows he goes to the aquarium, to your office. We can't move him, Cate, to do so would only prolong things. We have to be proactive. If we hide him in plain sight we can catch our man when he makes a move."

"That's crap," said Cate, registering Olivier's affronted reaction but continuing to look around the table. "Ben needs to be transferred, not just from the flat but from Ipswich. We have a massive problem here and we can't just carry on as if it we don't, a ticking bomb is about to go off under us, and if Ben ends up floating in the Orwell it will be us who are accountable."

"Calm down," said Olivier, reaching a hand across the table to touch hers before realising what he'd done and pulling back.

But Cate was livid. "Calm down? Don't patronise me, Olivier. Just do what I ask."

"No, Cate. This has to be a police decision, and you have to respect that."

Ben wasn't getting moved, she may as well be speaking to a brick wall.

79
Ben

Back in my flat, I'm standing at the window, looking down.

I catch my reflection in the glass and tentatively tap the tender skin around my nose to see if it hurts when I press. The corner of my eye catches on something, someone moving quickly around a van that's parked on the marina. I watch until he moves again, this time ducking behind the restaurant sign for the barge that's moored to my right. Though I can't see his face, his body movement strikes me as familiar. I think I know him.

"Cheryl?" I call, quietly, as though the person down on the marina can hear me, or in case he's watching me right now.

"Hmm? I'm just in the bathroom."

"Come here. Please."

She must hear the urgency in my voice because I hear her pad up behind me, pausing at my shoulder. "What is it, Ben?"

"Someone is over there. Watching us."

"Oh, shit," she walks to the window and I tell her where to look, but he's gone. "I can't see anyone."

"He was quick, but I saw enough. I recognised him. I think it's Adam."

"It can't be. I spoke to Adam an hour ago and he was in the city sports bar watching Hull Rovers on the big screen they have there."

"Or said he was."

She concedes the point, but my thoughts circle around what she just said.

"Why were you speaking to Adam?"

Cheryl sighs, her head on one side like I'm being difficult, and steps towards me on her delicate bare feet, stopping when her nose is almost touching mine. I can smell the peach scent of her shampoo, feel the warmth coming from her body.

"He hasn't stopped texting or calling, I was trying to get him to stop. He wants me to go home. Back to Hull."

She says this like it's nothing, like we're not lovers and she isn't talking about breaking my heart. Like she hasn't already broken Adam's.

"That's it, then. Adam's here to take you back."

But the idea of losing her pains me, deep under my ribs, and the question I should ask hurts my throat, each word catching like a knife.

"Will you go back with him?"

Cheryl turns her back, returning to the bathroom. "We don't know what Adam's here for. I'm not your brother's keeper. And he's not mine."

Which leaves me feeling that she's not answering the question, the real one.

"Why are you here, Cheryl?" I ask, to the closed bathroom door.

"Cheryl?" I hear the toilet flushing, water running in the sink. No answer comes.

Before going to my afternoon shift at the aquarium I visit Issi and we sit in Michael's memorial garden. There's a drizzle in the air but this corner patch is protected, as if the last of the summer has been trapped just in this spot. We sit together on the concrete bench, and though we aren't touching I can feel Issi's warmth and smell cooking fats and butter. There's a cake in the oven, I can smell its delicious vanilla scent, and Issi's floral apron is dusted with flour. I'd give anything to keep this moment, like in a snow globe I once had in prison.

It was a gift from the French teacher at Glen Parva, but got smashed by another inmate before New Year. In the few days I had it, I enjoyed the way everything in the globe – a scene from Paris with a tiny Eiffel Tower – was perfectly frozen. I'd have liked to freeze my life that way, before I stepped onto the Humber Bridge.

The glass has to shatter at some point, though.

"I'm in trouble, Issi."

Her breathing comes in deep raspy gasps. She should exercise more, eat less, but her heart is better than any I've ever known.

"Is it to do with this?" She touches my face gently so I can feel the warmth of her hand but it doesn't hurt.

"Someone is after me, Issi. But I'm not sure who."

Issi focuses on the concrete footballer, but I can sense the thinking that's going on inside. "Why, Ben? Why would anyone be after you?" Then she shifts her position, so she's facing me fully. "What have you done, son? You can tell me."

I'm as close to telling the truth as I've ever been. Issi is so soft and loving and I do want to tell her, desperately. And all because she called me 'son', and I want to hear it again. I want to say that I was just a kid, that I didn't know what I was doing, but inside, all of those years of hiding and lies are so strong, so fixed, that it's like an inner scream: *Shut up! Don't tell her! You'll lose everything.* But the glass is close to breaking.

Her eyes flick from mine, to my bruised face, back to my eyes. Finally she taps my hand with hers, then holds it fast.

"I want to tell you something, Ben. It's hard for me, but I want you to know the truth. Leon told you that Michael died in a car accident when he was just eighteen, didn't he?"

I nod. I hold her hand, afraid of what's coming.

"What he didn't tell you was that Michael caused that accident. He'd been drinking. And it wasn't just him in the car, there was… " she pauses, tries to suppress a sob that comes anyway. "His girlfriend, Lorraine. And another friend, just seventeen. Paul's in a wheelchair now. He won't speak to me, though I've tried many times. Michael was to blame, but he's not here, so I take the blame instead."

I process what she's telling me, try and adjust my thought of Michael, the sainted son who died too soon. He was to blame, a drink driver.

"What happened to the girlfriend?"

Issi shakes her head, the tears are coming now and she's crying too hard to answer me. She just reaches for the footballer, touches his foot, and then I know.

Michael killed himself and his girlfriend, left another boy disabled. He's not an angel. He's like me.

Issi is still crying, so I want to comfort her, reach her somehow, and before I can stop myself I say, "I killed someone too, Issi. I was just a boy, and so was he. I'm Humber Boy B."

80
Cate

When Ben didn't turn up at the probation office, Cate waited just twenty minutes before getting in her car and driving to the waterfront. The steering wheel slipped in her hands and she found herself breathing through her mouth, short, full breaths. With each minute the distance shortened and the likelihood that Silent Friend had found Ben seemed to increase. She parked the car quickly and badly outside Wolsey block, one wheel ramped on the kerb, and the door slammed with such speed that Cate actually stumbled.

Pull yourself together. If it's happened, you can't change that. Get a grip.

Slowing her pace, Cate looked up at the top flat, but the window was high above and she could see very little at this angle. Was Ben in there or was he lying in an alleyway somewhere or, even worse, in the back of some car? Cate had no trouble believing what Silent Friend was capable of, she had seen enough of what humans could do, especially when angry. And Cate may not know who Silent Friend was, but she knew whoever they were they had anger running in their veins.

The lift swooped down in seconds and opened the jaws of its glass box. Cate stepped inside, felt the ground thin beneath her as the glass platform elevated her to Ben's level.

"Ben?" she knocked, listened. Knocked again.

There was a sound, definite movement from within the flat. "Ben. Open the door now."

She could hear muffled voices. There were two people in the flat, there could be a struggle taking place, and the door remained closed.

She slid her mobile from her bag and scrolled for Olivier's number, gasping when he picked up on the first ring, "It's me. I'm outside Ben's flat but he's not opening. I'm frightened something's happening in there."

Olivier ended the call abruptly, promised to send backup.

The hallway was like a greenhouse and Cate felt sweat gathering under her shirt as she waited. She could hear odd sounds coming from the flat.

When the lift door opened behind her she expected a police officer in uniform to step out, but it was Olivier. He gave her a swift kiss on the lips, then banged hard on Ben's door.

"Police. Open this door now, or we will force an entry."

Slowly, the door opened and Ben peered out. He was red in the face, wearing boxer shorts and a T-shirt, bed-headed and in need of a shave.

"Ben," Cate said, exasperated, "you missed your parole appointment and then you didn't answer when I knocked! Don't you realise that's two breaches of your licence?"

"I'm sorry. I… " He scratched his chin, looked at his feet.

"I heard voices," she continued, "someone is in there with you."

"No, I… I was talking to myself."

Olivier looked the boy up and down and Cate realised this was only the second time he had seen Ben in the flesh, and the last time was at the hospital when he would have been covered in blood.

"So everything is okay, then?" Cate asked sceptically.

Worried Olivier would be pissed off, Cate started to apologise for wasting his time but he held up a hand. "It's good to be cautious. In fact, I suggest we take a look around your flat, Ben. Just to be sure that you are truly fine."

Ben looked stricken and Cate had the idea that he was in fact hiding something. He looked afraid. Olivier seemed to realise this too, and he walked past Ben, edging into the flat with the skill of a professional snoop.

Cate could see sweat appearing on Ben's forehead and then he said, "I'm sorry, Cate," just as she heard Olivier say from within the flat, "I think you should put some clothes on, *Mademoiselle*, and come into the lounge."

Ben and Cheryl are sat on the sofa, Cate is perched awkwardly on the only chair in the room and Olivier is stood by the window, gazing out.

"I'm confused," said Cate, looking at Cheryl for an explanation. "You came to visit with Adam and he's gone back to Hull, but you're still here."

Cheryl, who had pulled on a dress but was still showing plenty of flesh, stuck her chin out defiantly. "Last I looked, it was a free country."

"Not for him," said Cate, pointing at Ben. "You missed a parole appointment, Ben. And having a relationship with someone who was a witness at your trial may not be strictly prohibited but it's certainly not smart. This is supposed to be a fresh start, and Cheryl is a direct link to your past."

Cate sighed, contemplated whether or not what she was about to say was wise, but decided that Ben needed to know the danger he was in. "There was an article about you, in *The Sun*. Feeling is running higher than ever, so you need to keep the lowest possible profile."

The message has got across, Cate can see the fear in Ben's eyes.

Olivier kept his back to them, hands in pockets, and seemed to be simply watching the marina. "Cate, I think we should go now," he said, turning and checking his watch. "But no more missing appointments, young man. Next time your probation officer knocks, open the door. *D'accord?*"

"Yes, sir."

"Someone is watching the flat," said Olivier once they were in the lift. "I could see a man, down on the marina. It may or may not be connected to this girl. Either way, Ben is under surveillance."

"Shit. Now Ged has to move him."

"That wouldn't help us catch Silent Friend. Nothing has changed, Cate, we all accepted it was likely that Ben's identity had been compromised. But something needs to happen for us to take action, and Ged will say the same. You know this."

"Something *has* happened. His nose was broken."

"Yes," Olivier said, "but we need something that is more clearly personal to Ben, to his past. We still don't know that this person is Silent Friend, realistically anyone who read *The Sun* may be our stalker, so we need to wait for him to make a definite move."

Cate felt herself tensing, anger grabbing hold. "You want Ben to be bait."

Olivier shrugged. "If we move Ben, we know nothing. If we wait, we can get an arrest. It's better that way."

"Not for Ben," Cate said, but Olivier didn't answer as he led her from the lift and outside into fresh air. "Now, we are not working. For twenty minutes we talk about other things, okay?"

Not calmed, but still finding that she wanted to be with Olivier, Cate allowed herself to be led to the café further along the marina.

Olivier took Cate's hand in his; he leaned forward as if to kiss her fingers but then pulled back. When he looked at her she feared what he was about to say.

"I want to tell you that I am leaving Suffolk."

"Oh," Cate realised her face had dropped, that she felt a wave of sadness at the coming loss, even though she had known from the outset that it would happen. "When?"

"I should have already left but I negotiated extra time to oversee this case, but once we have arrested Ben's attacker I will be flying home. For good."

Cate's insides felt suddenly empty at the prospect of Olivier leaving. She had just started to allow herself to feel something for this rather arrogant man who was turning her world around, and he was leaving.

Olivier rubbed her fingers between his own, gave her some warmth, which she felt rise up her arm towards her heart. Her eyes warmed with tears and she realised she was close to crying.

"You could come to Luxembourg?"

"It's not somewhere I'd thought to visit," she said, hesitantly, still trying to master her emotions. "But I could fly over one weekend when Amelia's with Tim."

"No," Olivier lifted her chin gently and she felt each of his words like a kiss. "I mean for you and Amelia to come back with me. I think we could make it work."

She couldn't comprehend what he was asking. Neither of them had even said, 'I love you', and they had only spent four weekends together, though admittedly neither had slept very much. It was a whirlwind romance, but it was too early to tell if they had the necessary ingredients to become an actual couple. It was a crazy idea, she doubted he was serious.

"How could I come with you? I mean, Amelia… "

"Would thrive. She would be bilingual in no time. Travel broadens the mind at any age."

She felt dizzy, unsettled that Olivier was actually toying with her in this way. "I can't leave Suffolk. My career is here."

"So take a break," said Olivier, as if it was nothing. "Negotiate a period of absence so you have nothing to lose. Take a chance. If it doesn't work, you can always come back."

"He actually said that?" Paul was, for once, lost for words.

"I know! As if my career didn't mean anything."

"My God, Cate, not THAT. Our careers don't mean anything, you know that. I mean he actually asked you to move to Luxembourg to be with him. That's HUGE!"

"Yeah. I know." Cate gulped back some water from the bottle sat on her desk then began to log into the Offender Assessment programme, so she could change Ben's risk profile to 'high'. She also was going to record what Olivier had said about Ben's flat being under surveillance, the extreme danger she felt he was in, even if it changed nothing.

"Forget OASys, what did you say to Olivier?" Paul looked dismayed, like she'd switched off the TV just when the storyline was getting juicy.

"Actually, I didn't say anything." She worked on the keyboard, typing fast. "The idea's crazy."

"Perfect!" He tugged at a lock of her hair to get her attention, "You do crazy very well, my dear."

"You don't think I should actually be considering it?" She turned towards her friend, confused that he seemed to be taking Olivier's offer as a genuine possibility when it would mean turning her and Amelia's life upside down. And she could just imagine what Tim would say to the idea of her taking his daughter to live in Luxembourg.

"I certainly do, Cate. As the man himself said, travel broadens the thighs. Must be all the croissants."

"Mind. Travel broadens the mind."

"That too."

At home, Cate was helping Amelia with her spellings. Helping was perhaps the wrong word, as Amelia was struggling and Cate was at the end of her tether, so Amelia was now bent over an A4 pad, her hand moving like a slug, because she was being forced to write BECAUSE fifty times.

"Amelia, what on earth are they teaching you at that school?" And then, quick as a dog on a bone the thought that always followed: *I'm not spending enough time with her. I don't read with her enough.*

And a new thought, one she would never have dreamed of before today: *I could take a career break, concentrate on being just a mum. Concentrate on being in love.*

The doorbell rang and Amelia ran for it as if it had saved her from a terrible fate. She open the door and yelled, "Grandma!" with extra pleasure because she sensed a reprieve from spelling. Cate realised that it was now her turn to suffer.

Entering the kitchen in a breeze of purple satin and musky perfume, her mother purred, "Catherine," then seemed to bend and kiss her but all Cate felt was a vague waft of heavily perfumed air across the top of her ear. Was her mother attempting to camouflage the smell of booze?

"Hi, Mum."

"So," she sat at the dining table and pushed Amelia's school notebook aside to make space for her elbows, as if settling in for a cosy chat. In fact, Cate realised, her mother looked thrilled and her purple blouse looked new. She was carefully made up and her hair looked freshly coloured. "I hear you've seen Liz."

"I've been to the hotel, yes. And we had coffee in town last Sunday."

Her mother's face was flushed, and on this occasion it looked like pleasure and not alcohol. "Good." She turned to Amelia who had found her iPad down the side of the sofa and was scrolling through it, one earphone in her ear, the other dangling. "And did you see your Aunt Elizabeth?" she asked Amelia.

"No, but Mum says I can soon."

"Of course you can!" She turned back to Cate. "It's been so wonderful, we just had lunch at the new place near the church in town, do you know it? Run by the mentally disabled, so you have to be prepared to wait, but very cheap." Cate winced. "And then we did some shopping. All these years, this is what I missed."

A pause, a moment for them both to acknowledge that Cate had been around. Cate was not the gap in her mother's life though, that space was reserved for Liz alone.

"Amelia, why don't you go play in your room?"

"Hey?" Amelia lifted her head, mouthing the words of whatever song she was listening to, then said, "I'm nearly eleven, Mum. I don't *play*."

"Go listen to your music in your room, then."

"'Kay, Mum. See you later." Amelia disappeared fast, delighted with this unexpected turn after her terrible performance with BECAUSE.

Mother and daughter waited until they heard the sigh of a closing bedroom door, Amelia's voice signing along softly to music only she could hear.

"You seem very happy, Mum. You look good too."

Her mother's mouth remained tightly pursed but her eyes lit with pride. Carefully she said, "I'm back at AA and haven't had a drink in six days. I want to be sober for the court hearing."

"You're going?"

"Going? My darling, I'm a key witness."

This was a change from what Liz had told her. "But did you know?" Cate's heart felt leaden. "And you did nothing?"

The question hung between them, so Cate wished she could snatch it from the air and stuff in back into her mouth like a gag. She wasn't sure she was ready for her mother's answer.

Her mother looked pained, then defiant. "I tried to block it out with drink, but now that Liz has given me a second chance I'm going to be there for her. Her team say I have to be sober for it to stand in court, and I've promised I'll do it."

Cate found that she couldn't speak, words simply failed her. Her mother had known, then. The final chance for their relationship was that she too had been ignorant to the abuse, but that possibility was gone. This was really happening, her father in court, her sister and mother in the witness box. Unless he pleaded guilty there was going to be a trial.

"What do you think Dad will say?"

Her mother's face resumed a familiar look of contempt. "He'll deny everything. Like he always did."

So. A trial. Hours and days of painful testimonials, memories resurrected from childhood, paraded before a jury for their scrutiny and judgement. One word against the other about events from decades ago, and a jury who would have to decide whom they believed.

"I can't speak in court, Mum. I didn't know... I wouldn't be any use." All she has is vague memories, the feeling that Liz was better loved. None of this amounted to anything in a trial. And it could be misconstrued, distorted by the defence.

"Of course you'll be of use. Finally, your career giving some tangible benefit to the family. You're the only one of us who has ever been in a court room."

"But this would be different. Personal. I think it's best if I'm not there."

It crushed her, the feeling that she was turning her back on Liz just when she had a chance to build a relationship with her. She longed, just once, to be making decisions that were easy. And her mum was judging her, she felt it.

"Cate, you will be there because your sister needs you. And so do I. Please don't let us down."

81
Ben

Cheryl is checking her phone, tapping a text message to someone, but when she sees I'm awake she closes the screen and places it on the bedside table.

"Was that Adam?"

She hesitates then says, "Yeah. 'Fraid so."

"He's here, isn't he? I know it was him I saw."

"Don't be stupid, I told you he's in Hull. You're just imagining things." Then, as if to close the matter, she says, "He has got a job to do, you know."

I don't know, not really. She could be lying, he could be outside the flat right now, waiting for a moment to pounce on me. But if it was him who attacked me, why wear a balaclava? Why not let me see his face, after all, I'd asked for it. His girlfriend is lying naked in my bed, making me feel things I never thought possible, that I didn't think I deserved to feel.

Despite the fact that my face is bruised, even though I know someone is out there looking for me, Cheryl being here is something good. When I start to doubt this I think of her kissing me, and tell myself I'm just being paranoid.

Cate is meeting me at the aquarium today. It's a review meeting, or so she says, to see how the placement is going, and our official story is that I'm on a Community Punishment order for driving offences. She didn't go into more detail than that, and Leon won't ask. He made it clear at the start that he doesn't want to know what I did. But now I've told Issi and I can't be sure that she hasn't told him.

The kettle is boiling and Leon is already on page four of *The Sun*, so I walk past him into our staff room and start to make us tea. When I put his mug in front of him he shakes his head.

"That's terrible."

I look into the mug, but the tea looks the right colour to me. "Do you want me to make another?"

But then I realise his eyes are on the double-paged article lying next to him. "What makes a kid do something like that?"

I don't move, don't need to. That article is about me, it's the one that Cate warned me about. When I try to sip my tea my hand shakes, and some spills onto the print, darkening the words. There's a picture of Noah's mum, she used to be so pretty but now she looks older and haggard. She's clutching a framed photo of Noah. Worse, there's another photo of Noah and me, in his garden, holding his scooter between us. I can see, and it must be obvious to Leon, that the kid on the right is me. The same white-blond hair, the same blue eyes. The same small, runty frame.

I squeeze my eyes shut, step backwards. Did Issi tell him? If Leon knows I'll have to go and never come back. I simply can't think or talk about it. Not here, this aquarium. My safe place.

Just then the door slides open, and there stands my probation officer, smart in her navy suit, obviously not here to see the fish.

"Morning. I'm Cate," she offers Leon her hand, which he takes and pumps vigorously.

"Morning, love. Leon. The boy's just made tea, and I have to say he's pretty good at it. You want one?"

She looks at me then, smiles. "Hi, Ben. Milk no sugar, thanks."

I return to the staff room and I hear Leon say to Cate,

"You see this? Terrible thing. But then, you must know all about it?"

Oh shit.

I pour the water into a clean mug even though it's not re-boiled yet, and leave the teabag in rather than waiting because I want to get back to Leon and Cate quickly. When I do she looks shocked, unsure what to say, so I push the tea at her and say, "Yeah, it's awful." She understands. Leon meant she knows all about crime generally, not this one specifically, though she does because I'm standing here.

We exchange a look.

"What I don't get is why?" Leon is still reading the article. "Explain to me why a ten-year-old boy would do something like this?"

Cate sips her tea, which I know must taste awful, tepid and weak, but to her credit she doesn't show this. "I think that a child only does something that terrible if their experiences of life have been terrible. If they've been badly treated or neglected."

"Abuse, is it? Seems to be everywhere these days."

"No!" I say, before I can stop myself. Both of them are staring at me. "That's no excuse," I add.

"Not an excuse, but a reason," Cate says softly. Cate continues to speak, gently peeling back the layers of my protection and leaving my shitty childhood exposed. "His dad wasn't around, his step-dad didn't love him. His mum had mental health problems that she medicated with alcohol so she wasn't as attentive as she should have been. It all adds up, Ben. That's the thing."

And I splutter, emotion in my chest rises and bursts from my mouth. And then I'm crying and she's holding me steady.

"It's okay, Ben," she says into my ear so Leon won't hear. "It's over now."

But when we pull apart, Leon is looking from the newspaper article back to me and I see that he knows already.

82
Cate

Cate saw the pained realisation in Leon's eyes, the horror as he looked back at the newspaper, then the gaze of sheer disappointment as he turned to Ben.

"How could it happen, Ben? You seem like a good kid. Why would someone like you do an evil thing like that?" He lifted the page of the newspaper with his index finger as if it was foul.

Cate could have intervened, but Leon had asked the question she too most wanted answered. And though she wouldn't have planned for this to happen, she wanted to see the outcome.

The aquarium door slides open and a mother comes in, clutching the hand of a toddler in dungarees who is sucking an orange lolly, the same colour as his hair. The mother who gazes wide eyed at the nearby tanks, her voice singing, "Won't this be fun, Rolf?" and then comes to an abrupt halt at the desk, seeing Cate, Ben and Leon.

"Are you open?" she asks uncertainly.

Leon looks at the boy with his lolly, who still hasn't given the fish a second glance, and says, "I'm sorry, love, but we're closed just now. Staff meeting. But we'll be open after lunch and I'll give you free entry. How's that?"

The woman's frown softens and she reaches for her sticky child. "Let's go play in the park, Rolf. We'll come back later."

The boy takes her hand, clearly unconcerned that his trip

to the aquarium is off the table.

Leon follows them out, waves goodbye and then locks the door.

"Okay. Now we can talk." He sounds exhausted, but Cate can also see that he really cares about Ben as he leans across the desk and holds Ben's wrist. This makes Cate nervous as she watches Ben struggle to explain the unexplainable. It means that Leon has more emotion invested, could be more easily disappointed. And Ben needs all the support he can get.

"I was only ten. Noah was my friend, it wasn't like I set out to do anything… It was a weird day. Everyone was acting off, first Stuart left even though he had promised to take Adam to Scarborough, then Mum said she had a headache and was staying in bed even though she'd told Jess that she'd look after Noah for the day. It was like every adult we saw hated us or didn't trust us or didn't even see us."

The water filters gurgle in the tank nearest them, the lack of natural light suddenly feels oppressive and it seems to Cate that Ben has grown younger. She can see him, at ten. Confused and unwanted with too much time to kill.

Leon looks like he might weep. He is still holding Ben's wrist, as if this gesture could undo the damage done.

"Please tell me you didn't do it, Ben," he pleads. "Tell me it's not like they describe in the newspaper."

Ben doesn't speak. But his mouth quivers, his face seems to melt with pain.

"I think I just wanted to see what would happen." Ben looks down, shuffles his feet.

"But how was he even there?" Leon asked, frowning. "On the wrong side of the barrier."

"He climbed over. He wanted to be noticed. We all did."

"*I just wanted to see what would happen.* That's all he had to say for himself?"

Paul leaned back, his arms behind his head. A look on his

face that was both weary and cynical. But Cate didn't feel either, she thought Ben had answered Leon as well as he was able.

"The thing is, Paul, it was so obviously the truth. You know, I could just tell that he was as confused as we were, but that it was an honest answer. It was an impulsive move, without any pre-meditation."

Paul sighed theatrically. "So, that's it? A random act where a child ends up dead. That's bullshit, Cate. It's just not good enough."

Anger came quickly to Cate, surprising her with its force. "Not good enough for whom? For Ben's family? Because they're in the mix too. His step-dad? Who never loved him, his mum who neglected him. And what about Noah's mum, leaving him in the care of the neighbourhood alcoholic… "

"Careful Cate. Victim, remember?"

"Yes, and my heart aches to think of what she's going through. Any parent knows that we all have days where we aren't our best selves. Jessica Watts was a good mum, but she was busy. She made a bad judgement call, asking Yvette to babysit. Noah wanted to be noticed, Ben said, that's why he climbed onto the bridge. He'd probably seen people do likewise and get on the news, the poor kid just wanted attention. There were four kids on the bridge, and all of them took their own history to that moment. It was simply a terrible tragedy."

She stopped, exhausted by it.

Paul put it far more starkly. "No, Cate. A murder."

"Yes, it was. But not in the way you would imagine."

"I think you like him too much."

"I think someone should, if he's going to stand a chance out here."

83
The Day Of

Cheryl ran. As soon as Noah began to climb over the barrier, she turned and ran because she feared what was coming next, even though she willed it too.

It was as if the pain of the fall, the frustration of the day, had all exploded and Noah decided to end it the swiftest way he could, and even if he changed his mind she knew that other forces had been conjured.

The bridge is long, and as long as she is on it, she will feel more to blame for what takes place. So she runs harder, bare feet on concrete, her gymnastic body moving to its limits, the swimsuit riding up, the towel long forgotten.

It takes forever to leave the bridge, the rain is now strong and steady and relentless as she scrambles down the riverbank. But still, she can see the bridge, and this makes her panic.

She runs to where her father is stood by the water's edge, his mobile in his hand. He sees her and looks relieved but also furious.

"I've been worried sick. Why didn't you take your phone?"

They can both hear it, ringing in her bag just a few yards away.

"Where did you go, Cheryl? You should at least have put some clothes on!"

She was in trouble, she'd been gone too long. She wanted to go home, to leave this place behind.

"I asked you a question, Cheryl. Now answer me. What's going on?"

She pointed, up to the middle of the bridge.

"The boys, Dad. Up there. I think one of them is going to jump."

Roger began to collapse his fishing rod, zip up his coat against the rain and pack up his things. "Don't be silly, Cheryl. Now let's clear up and get out of this rain. We can talk about this at home, I haven't finished with you yet."

"Maybe I'm not happy with you."

Roger looked up to see his daughter, standing in the rain in just a swimsuit, staring at him with a look that was on the precipice between temper and tears. He was genuinely surprised to see her this way and took a step forward, but she held up her hand, palm towards him.

"No, Dad. Nothing you say can make this better."

"What?" he asked, perplexed. "What is it you think I've done?"

"We had a chance Dad, to be with Jess. But it's going to be okay. I've thought of a way… she could love you again, Dad. She could love both of us. And then you can stop hating me. I think she'll come back to us now."

She was shaking now, crying too, and Roger didn't know what to say or how to comfort her.

"Cheryl, what are you talking about?"

She didn't answer, but instead jumped into the cold water, no longer thinking about the boys on the bridge but thinking only of the family she might have had. She slapped her bare feet into the gravel, not caring that it stung, and tried to wash away the blood from her thighs.

They both looked up when they heard the scream.

84
Now

FACEBOOK: FIND HUMBER BOY B

Silent Friend: No-one has posted on this page for a while, so I'm thinking I'm the only one who really cares. Or maybe you others just want to leave the dirty work to me? I have him now. See the photo if you don't believe me. Looks different than in the other pictures, but then you haven't seen him since he was a boy, have you Jess?

I promise you this is our man. Now what do you suggest I do with him?

85
Cate

"I don't like doing this," Ged said, as they stepped out of the lift. "It's not good practice to enter a tenant's property without permission."

"We both know this isn't a usual case, though," Cate said irritably before adjusting her tone. "And I'm grateful."

It was Leon who'd called the probation office, just after nine-thirty that morning, to say Ben hadn't arrived at work. He'd shut up the aquarium and walked to Ben's flat, thinking he was ill and might need help, but no-one answered the door when he rang.

If Ben had absconded, it would be an immediate recall to prison for breach of parole licence. The only other option was far worse. Silent Friend had found him.

Ged knocked on the door, "Come on, Ben! Open up."

Silence. Cate waited, understanding that Ged needed to go through this process, though inside she was screaming at him to use the bloody key.

The key in the lock, he stopped, and said, "What if he's killed himself? If he's just hanging there. I don't want an image like that in my head."

Cate nudged him out of the way and turned the key herself. The door swung open and she stepped inside.

The flat was sparsely furnished but what there was had been knocked askew, the sofa was at the wrong angle, as if it had been pushed aside during a scuffle. Ben's few possessions were randomly scattered on the floor. "This isn't Ben," said Cate. "Look." She walked to the kitchen, where order remained, and showed Ged the line of tins, cereal boxes, bread. Obsessively straight. In the bathroom was a similar line of shower gel, shaving foam, shampoo.

But the lounge was wrong.

Ged followed behind her as she went from room to room, cautiously, as if they still might find something unpleasant.

"You think someone came in here and got him?"

"I think we shouldn't touch anything, just in case." She dug in her pocket for her mobile and began to dial. "I'll let the police know."

When she heard Olivier's voice on the other end of the line she spoke quickly.

"I'm in Ben's flat. It looks like a struggle may have taken place, but he's gone."

"Okay. I'll be there as quick as I can. In the meantime, Cate, you should wait outside."

"So, any sign of the girl?"

Olivier's first words as he stepped out of the lift, as if continuing a conversation that prior to that point had taken place in his head.

"No sign of either Cheryl or Ben. Nothing in the flat."

Olivier offered Ged a hand to shake, and gave Cate a kiss on each cheek, throwing her thought pattern askew. Olivier however, was thinking very clearly.

"We have to consider the likelihood that they have simply left. Decided to make a break for it, somewhere no-one knows either of them."

"I thought that too, until I saw the flat."

She would have preferred this option, but she couldn't believe it. Not when Ben's few belongings were still in the flat. Under his bed was the duffel bag he'd carried when he left prison, and inside she'd found letters from his mum and

301

his dad. If Ben had left of his own volition he wouldn't have left those behind.

"I think Silent Friend has him."

"But you don't know that, Cate."

Cate felt that Olivier was once again correcting her, making her feel irrational compared to his cool logic.

"Ben absconding is more likely than him being abducted, statistically."

Cate snorted. "There are reliable statistics for a case like this?"

"Okay, Cate. Let's analyse this. Is there evidence of foul play?"

Cate couldn't say a definitive yes, she simply had a gut feeling. "Well there wasn't a note, if that's what you mean."

Olivier smiled, "I always enjoy your British humour. So sharp."

But inside Cate wasn't smiling. She was once again feeling the frustration that her perspective was not being taken seriously. Ben was in real danger, and they needed to act swiftly. He could be anywhere.

86
Ben

I'm back in the prison laundry, trying to scrub white shirts. But they are heavy to lift, sodden with water, and when I do lift them from the water they bleed red dye onto my hands, no matter how hard I rinse. I scrub with white soap that turns red in my hands. Then I see it's my hands that are bleeding, that it's my hands that are turning the shirts red. I am the problem.

A pressure wakes me, a hand over my face, so even when I open my eyes the world stays dark. The hand is large, covers my forehead too with a pressure, so I'm a prisoner again.

Then a voice, female and soft. "Don't hurt him."

Cheryl. That's when I know I'm not in prison, it's much worse than that. I'm free and someone is about to hurt me and no-one is coming to help.

The hand over my mouth smells of nicotine and something salty too, maybe sweat. The palm moves so it covers my eyelids.

Next, something is being pulled roughly over my head. It feels like a hat but it covers my whole face, right to my neck where the wool is itchy on my skin. A balaclava, but with the mouth and eye holes at the back. That's when I know for sure that this is Silent Friend. The same man who hurt me, left me bleeding on the ground when the couple came by. Now returned to finish the job he started.

I can hear movement in the bedroom, light footed and quick, and I know that it's Cheryl but I don't know why she is letting this person blind me with the balaclava.

I feel his hands on my shoulders, lifting me from the bed.

"Let him put some clothes on at least." Cheryl sounds panicked, like she's not sure if she has any authority in this situation. She's scared too, but something in her voice makes me think she knew this was going to happen.

"He needs his shoes," she says, with a certainty that tells me she knows what is going to happen to me.

And that's when I realise, this is where my story ends. It was all leading up to this moment. How could I think Cheryl had chosen to be with me, and not realise that it was part of something, a plan to get me? I strain my ears to Silent Friend's breathing, knowing that I have heard it before. Cate said I must know who he is, if only I can remember. Someone from my past, now in my present.

"Okay, Ben," says Cheryl. "Just do what he says."

"Adam?" I ask, my voice coming out muffled from the fabric. "Is it you?"

But there is only silence is the room as I am manhandled towards the lift. I try to refuse, back away, but I have no choice. The world drops beneath me as I am taken downstairs, finally travelling in the lift for the first time. And also the last.

87
The Day Of

Cheryl did not think again of what she had done. How she had held the tip of Adam's penis in her palm, her fingers were working the shaft, when she leaned into him and said, "But if I do this, you have to do what I say."

But Adam was thinking of it, could not do anything else but remember the feel of her hand. It was a moment he had previously only fantasised about, bent over one of his dad's mags or after catching a scene on the TV that had aroused him. But now, a real live girl had held him in her hands and he would do anything, anything at all, for her to finish what she started. To be with her again. He wanted it so much that his mouth was salivating at the thought, his fingertips felt electrified as they remembered the feel of her waist, so small and slippery, the swimsuit allowing him to canvas her hips and bottom easily.

She had wriggled her fingers, moving her hand too roughly so he gasped with a pained pleasure. He had no longer been able to hear his brother speaking and joking with Noah, he could no longer hear the cars thundering over the bridge. He could hear nothing but the pulse in his ear, see nothing but the skin of her perfect smooth shoulder, and taste nothing but its salt, his own appetite creating a drool on her skin. The world shrank to only them, the moment pixelated to not even her hand but his urge, the rising need, the power he could no longer stop, the pulse and push of his desire that she was coaxing, controlling.

"Promise me," she had said, when it was already too late.

Adam would do anything she asked, if only he could have that feeling again. Because somewhere in his torn heart she had made him feel loved. It was water to him, it was bread. Love was the very air that was missing from his lungs.

The Devil had moved the glass on the Ouija board. He believed it now, because only the Devil would make the price so high for just a little love.

88
Now

FACEBOOK: FIND HUMBER BOY B

Silent Friend: An eye for an eye, and a tooth for a tooth. Isn't that what the bible says, Jessica? So how to deliver justice to a murderer who threw a boy from a bridge.

Where to take him? What to ask?

Noah's mum: If you're telling the truth, then the person asking him questions should be me. You're not God. You're not even the victim.

Silent Friend: Oh, but I am.

89
Cate

Cate sat at her desk, berating herself for being so useless. There was simply nothing she could think of that she could do, nothing that would help find Ben, now missing for six hours. She hadn't heard from Olivier so she had no idea what the police may have discovered, if anything. Amelia would be out of class by now, being greeted at the school gate by Sally and Chloe. Friday night with her other family, playing with toys she was strictly speaking too old for but still loved, no doubt her and Chloe would spend the evening moving miniature animals dressed like humans around their perfect houses.

If only real life could be that easy, if she could peer into the doll's house of Ben's life and find out who he was with.

Cate tried to work, she had a pre-sentence report to write on a drunk driver and a risk assessment to complete on a burglar due out of prison next week, but her eyes couldn't focus, her brain was too preoccupied with thoughts of Ben. And she was hungry, it was long past lunch and she'd not eaten since breakfast.

Grabbing her jacket, Cate at least felt energised by being on the move. She told Dot she was going to the Buttermarket to get a late lunch, but to call her if there was any news on Ben. Dot waved her off with a warning to take an umbrella, it looked like it would rain, but Cate didn't stop.

Buttermarket Shopping Mall was heaving, and unaccustomed as she was to the Friday afternoon crush of shoppers, she felt disorientated as she pushed and 'excuse me'd' away from groups of school kids high on the promise of the weekend and mothers with prams clutching bags of food. Signs everywhere announced sales and bargains. Cate began to feel headachy. She needed a drink and some food, and braved the café in search of both.

It was only when she had paid for her meal that Cate saw there were no seats, before her was a group of toddlers waving sippy cups and squeaky toys at each other's heads whilst their mothers chatted earnestly, dabbing their breasts with sheets of muslin and drinking double espressos. She had obviously gatecrashed a mother and child meeting. Just then the table nearest to her was vacated. It was the only empty table in the place and other people were already approaching it with their plastic trays piled with food. She grabbed the nearest chair, avoiding eye contact with the sulky teenage couple who nearly beat her to it, and tore open the plastic shell of her sandwich, wedging the limp offering from the box, shrivelled prawns falling from dry bread. It looked awful, she couldn't eat it.

Cate winced as she sipped her stewed coffee and pushed that away too. To the relief of the couple, still standing with their tray, she left the table, negotiating a path through the hordes of shoppers and out of the precinct. Outside it was pouring, she should have heeded Dot's warning. Thin shards of rain stung her eyes. She pulled up her collar, put her head low in her jacket and ran down the pavement, failing to look properly as she stepped off the kerb and into the path of a speeding Mazda. Just as the car was about to slam into her body a hand came from nowhere, grabbed her shoulder, and pulled her to safety.

The car driver furiously sounded his horn, and people nearby stared at her. Suddenly sensible about what could have happened, and leaning into her rescuer's embrace, Cate swore at herself.

"You must be more careful, it would not do for there to be no Cate in the world."

The man who had just pulled her to safety was Olivier.

"What? What are you doing here?"

"Dot told me where to find you." He kissed her cheek, but she didn't respond as he said her name again.

"Sorry! It's just, I'm sorry, I'm a bit distracted. I was just going back to the office."

"I think you need to gather yourself a bit after stepping in front of that car. In Luxembourg we believe a glass of red wine can cure most things. And I too missed my lunch. Come on." He took her hand, pulling her through the rain to the nearest place, an Italian restaurant. Being inside was a relief, as she stood, hair dripping water down her face. Olivier helped her peel off her jacket, handing it to a waiter who they followed to a table. He placed one arm on her shoulder to ease her into her seat. She looked up, still shaking, "If you hadn't grabbed me… "

"But I did. I saw you leaving the food court but it took me a few minutes to catch up. Terrible crowds, I hate this about Ipswich."

Cates shook her head slowly. "If anything had happened to me, what about Amelia?"

"Nonsense. Don't torture yourself like that. Some medicinal alcohol will sort you out."

"I don't know." Cate rubbed her eyes, thinking about Ben. Where was he? If only she could find him.

Olivier called to the waiter to bring a bottle of red wine, asking for the grape and year with expertise. "I've been here a few times before," he explained. "Better than eating at the hotel." And, as if on cue, a waiter arrived. Olivier ordered without checking for her preference, an assortment of salad, pasta and breads and then he poured her a glass of gleaming ruby wine.

She caught his expression and wondered how he could

look so relaxed. "I can't stop thinking about Ben. What if he's in danger, Olivier? Shouldn't we – or someone – be looking for him?"

"We – the police, that is – are. They are checking out all of the witnesses from the case, as well as the names you gave. This is not your problem to fix, Cate. Please relax. There is nothing for you to do but enjoy good wine with good company." His fingers found her hand and she returned his smile. "There, so much better." But inside she was still worried sick.

She took another mouthful of the wine to loosen her up. "How do you manage to keep so calm? If anything happened to Ben, we'd all have egg on our face."

"Ha, I do enjoy these expressions. Yes, we would be in the egg, as you say. But I find I can still sleep, as long as I have done my job as well as I am able. Also, it helps that I like swimming, I like music, both very relaxing. And I love Friday evenings on the sofa with a jazz CD playing and a very old bottle of wine." The image was a pleasant one. "But it's no fun alone, so maybe we could do this together, once we have eaten?"

"At the Novotel?"

"It's only a small sofa, but I think we could make it work. Unless you have to be home for Amelia?"

"Nope. She's with her dad all weekend." Cate could feel the warm alcohol flowing through her veins now, the tension draining from her limbs.

The waiter appeared, saw their intimate pose and quickly delivered the order. The food was delicious, colourful orange carrots and yellow courgettes ribboned into the pasta. Olivier divided a portion onto her plate and she tasted it, it was the best food she had had in a long time. Cate was so intent on eating that it made her jump when she felt his hand move away a damp curl of hair that had fallen onto her cheek. Outside other people ran in the rain, heads bowed or hidden under umbrellas, but the restaurant was warm and delicious and, despite herself,

Cate had to acknowledge that so too was Olivier.

She couldn't find Ben, as Paul had already told her, she was no detective. So she would instead take Olivier's prescription for a Friday evening and try to enjoy her new lover before he left her for good.

90
Ben

The car keeps moving and my stomach lurches, bile rises and seeps into the fabric. I'm curled on my side in the boot, my nose pressed to the parcel shelf, pulsing with fresh pain.

I can't move, my stomach lurches again and empties itself, I try to breathe as I retch. It smells meaty and then I need to piss, I need to shit. I can't stop, my body is emptying itself in terror and my bowel is an open passage. The stench of my waste is overwhelming, I wish I could pass out, I wish the car would stop and they would get it over with. I decide I want to die, in just a few hours they have reduced me to this moment. I'm ready now. It's time to let this misery end.

Minutes stretch to hours, the road beneath the car sounds smooth so I know we're on a motorway, driving a long distance and on the metal bonnet above me I can hear heavy rain. Minutes pass and I can't stop shaking. All I see is blackness. I can't breathe through the balaclava, which is wet over my mouth from saliva and vomit. I could die here, I'm going to die here, and still the car keeps moving.

We slow, stop a few times, so I think we must have paused at lights, we must be in a town. I can hear the tyres splashing through water, the car slowing at the impact. I can't tell how many hours have passed but the idea that we have arrived terrifies me.

The car stops and I think it is now, this is it. They will take me out, shoot me, throw me, throttle me. In whatever way they choose. I will not see another day.

The boot opens and it is dark and wet, so I can see just two silhouettes through the fabric of my blindfold.

"Oh fuck," says Cheryl, stepping back and holding her nose. "It stinks in there." I can't make out her expression, but can just about see her blonde hair, damp with rain. I long for her to touch me or give me just one kind word.

Her companion comes forward and I can hear heavy feet. Then a hand on my shoulder, tugging me to look up. I respond, or try to, but I'm wobbly. As I lift my head a gust of wind catches inside the boot, a force that knocks me back down.

Cold air, strong wind, heavy rain. And then I hear water, pushing impatiently against the shoreline.

It is in that moment that I know where we are.

I am home.

91
The Day Of

Yvette had finally got around to pulling on some clothes and was wandered around the house looking for Ben and Adam, remembering that she was also looking after Noah, because her old schoolmate, Jessica, was going to London for the day. Lucky bitch. Adam would be taking care of Noah, he knew she wasn't well and he was a good lad, that one.

Poor kid. Stuart should never have promised him a trip to Scarborough, he never really meant it. When the call came in late last night saying there was a Grimsby boat needing a mate, he didn't even hesitate. She'd told him that he couldn't keep letting the lad down, but Stuart wasn't bothered about that. And then the row, always the same, about how he was the only one keeping the family together, and didn't he have to work just to bring some food into the house.

Bloody martyr. That's what she'd said. "You reckon you're a bloody martyr, or summat? Doing it all for us."

What about all the weeks when they had to just get by on their own? Just the three of them? And she was ill, proper ill. The doctors had signed her off on the sick, but no-one seemed to show any sympathy. The migraines were like nothing on earth. Tablets didn't work, nothing knocked the pain on the head like booze. She felt a twinge of guilt, knowing Jessica's money had bought the vodka when it was supposed to pay for Noah's lunch. Then she looked at the clock on the DVD player display, it was 3.47pm. Way past lunchtime now.

The last dribble of vodka kicked like a mule, warm and strong like all good medicine.

Still, though, where were the boys?

The house felt so empty without them.

92
Now

FACEBOOK: FIND HUMBER BOY B

Noah's mum: The skate park is going ahead. All the finances have been agreed and today I am visiting the site, to see where the building work begins tomorrow. I'm going to take the Hull Rover's scarf from above Noah's bed and tie it to the railings of the bridge and say a prayer for my boy.

Because he's not here, in my home. It's so quiet, with Dave out at work. I'm going to the bridge because that's where Noah is, his spirit. His soul is in the River Humber. And though it hurts and I cry, it's better than the emptiness of the house without him.

93
Cate

Cate woke in the darkened hotel bedroom hearing activity in the corridor; cleaners or other guests already awake. As her eyes adjusted she could see the standard objects around her, the TV, the dressing table. Her work clothes from yesterday mixed with Olivier's on the floor. She shifted gently, not wanting to disturb him, feeling unaccustomed muscle tension in her legs from their lovemaking. It felt good, until she remembered Ben was still missing. But now her brain was alert to a new thought. She had experienced this before, the way a problem can unravel and resolve during sleep, how upon waking things seem clearer.

Cate turned on her side, taking a moment to look at Olivier's toned body, his tussled dark hair, his long eyelashes. She could allow herself a moment of sentimentality, before he was awake, because once he was, everything would change. They had work to do.

She touched his chest, feeling the steady beat of his heart beneath her palm.

"I know where Silent Friend has taken Ben," she said.

She was worried he would dismiss her, that this time would be just like in the meetings when he would say they needed evidence, not gut feeling. But she misjudged him. This time he agreed with her.

"I want to go with you, Olivier. I know this case better

318

than anyone, I've read every witness statement and I know the exact journey the boys took before Noah died. Somewhere on that route, that's where they will be."

Cate sifted through the details of what they knew so far. Silent Friend was someone from Ben's past, someone who knew Jessica Watts. Cate's belief was that this was a person involved with the case, and as they had now kidnapped Ben it was logical that they would take him back to the scene of the crime. Because this person wasn't a simple vigilante, this person had some emotional involvement. They would want answers. Their goal may be to kill Ben, the ultimate justice, but they would make him face what he had done first.

Olivier took a quick shower and, still damp, swiftly began to get dressed simultaneously fielding calls on his mobile. "The Humberside police have been alerted, and they will be speaking to Ben's family too. We can't rule out him having gone home."

"He hasn't gone home," Cate said. "It's Cheryl. She's the anomaly, the person from the past who doesn't fit. Why was she even here, why did she stay when Adam left?"

"You think she's Silent Friend?" Olivier turned away but she saw his suppressed smile in the dressing table mirror and Cate remembered his dismissive approach to female criminals.

"You know what, Olivier, if I was placing money on it I'd say she is."

"But she didn't bust Ben's nose. That was a man."

Cate rose from the bed, clipped on her bra and reached for her shirt. "She's involved. Silent Friend doesn't have to be one person."

"Cheryl and Adam?"

"That's possible," Cate smoothed the creases of last night's clothes, sifting through the witness statements in her head, stopping with the one that had affected her most, Cheryl's dad, who had tried to save Noah.

"It's her father," Cate said, suddenly excited. "Silent

Friend said he'd let Jess down, but he wouldn't do it a second time. He tried but failed to rescue Noah! This is his way of making up for that failure. Cheryl was his scout. You need to alert the Hull police. Ben has been kidnapped by Roger Palmer."

"We can be there in four hours if we don't hit traffic."

"We?"

"You're the best detective I've got Cate."

Cate discovered that she knew it would be this way. Almost as soon as she took the case, she knew she'd end up visiting Hull.

Ben had always seemed like a boy who needed saving and now, whether she was capable or not, she would have the chance.

They stopped for petrol once they hit the A14, bought coffee and a sandwich each, and were just getting back in the car when Olivier's phone rang.

"DCI Massard, speaking... I see, did you check with the neighbours? Okay. Thanks."

He clipped the phone into the hands-free holder and put it on speaker, then re-started the car.

"No sign of Roger Palmer?"

"Neighbours last saw him two weeks ago. His house has free papers and flyers sticking from the letter box."

"It's him."

"Sounds like it. Tell me Cate, have you ever thought about a career in the police force?"

Cate bit into her sandwich, swallowed a swig of bitter coffee and winced. "Absolutely never."

94
Ben

Through the fabric of the balaclava I can see light, the sky, though it is spitting rain. A dark silhouette as the monster leans over me, not a monster, a man. Around me in the car boot is my own puke, my own piss and the stench of my bowels. I want it over. I want him to kill me now, the only thing I fear is prolonged suffering.

He grabs me by the upper arm, yanks me up, but I'm weak and shaky and it's awkward. He lifts the balaclava, so I can finally see and breathe, but this is when I'm most terrified because now I can see his face. And if he is letting me see his face he must plan on killing me, so I try not to look. He doesn't care, he just wants me out of the car, so in a final heft I land in a heap on gravel and dirt. I see shoes: his, sturdy brown shoes, the kind men wear for fishing, and Cheryl's green pumps. I lift myself to a dog position, head down and heave, but my stomach is empty and nothing comes out. Then I look up and face my assailant.

Roger Palmer is looking down at me.

"God, what a mess!" Cheryl is talking about the car boot, or me. Both would be true.

I lift my head and it's there, the shame of my nightmares, my stomach twists despite the hollowness, my head swims and I know why I'm here and what it is Roger Palmer is going to do. But I can't walk, I won't make it. He may as well just do it here, on the river bank. I can't climb to my destiny, it has to come to me.

I'm hauled up by my shoulder and I stumble until a hand steadies me, then I stand, leaning on the car. He has a large black umbrella that he opens against the wind and the rain, the fabric flaps like an enormous wing, hiding us from view.

"Are you sure it's him?"

A woman's voice calls from the driving seat of a parked car. Before anyone answers the car door opens. I turn my head to see who it is but my eyes are watery and unfocused, she is just a shape walking towards me, a blur. Hanging from her hand is a scarf, red and white, Hull City Rovers. I know who she is then, and she says my name, my old name. Just when I thought everything was as bad as it could get, I discover a new level of pain.

She comes closer, standing just beyond the protection of the umbrella, but clearly not caring about the rain dripping in her eyes. Noah's mum, Jessica. It's her. But she looks older, more than the eight years that have passed. Her eyes are world-weary, her mouth is downturned. I did this to her. I made her skin sag and wrinkle, I made her look that sad. Both of her hands work around the Hull Rovers red scarf as if for comfort and I think of Noah, because he was their biggest fan. Whatever she does to me, it will be in his name.

She calls me by my old name again and it is worse than a punch, worse than a knife. She doesn't sound angry. She sounds so very sad, just saying that one word. And it is worse than if she was shouting or punching me, because I know, I can see, that what she wants is the one thing I can't give her. She wants her son back.

Roger Palmer holds the umbrella with one hand, but the other has a firm grasp of my forearm. Noah's mother breathes heavily following behind as we climb the gravel bank towards the bridge. Ahead is Cheryl, leading us, taking the rough path easily, her slim but strong legs carrying her upwards. She doesn't care about the rain, she never did. But what she does care about is still a mystery to me. How is it that I held her just twenty-four hours ago? She kissed me, made love to me.

I see now what a good actress she is, that it meant nothing to her. I'd like to see her face, to know for sure how she feels, but she can't be happy at this moment. She also has secrets.

The bridge is busy, as it always was. Cars speed along the road sending torrents of water splashing down onto the walkway. Roger may now look to them like he's frogmarching me, he's simply at my side, but close enough so if I try anything he'll soon grab me. The car drivers won't care anyway, I know that from personal experience. No-one is coming to save me.

I have no desire to escape. The inevitability of my story ending here is so clear to me. I keep walking, my gaze fixed only on Cheryl, listening to the red lorry, yellow lorry zoom by. My only wish is that Adam was here. I'd have liked to say goodbye to him. It would be better, the three of us should be together when justice is meted out, real justice, not the phoney kind in court. The woman who is judging me today loved Noah, so I won't fight my sentence.

We walk farther along the pathway that goes across the bridge to Lincolnshire, with the road above it and the water down below. It's been eight years since I was last here and everything is the same. Cheryl must feel it too, she grips the railing as she walks, as if for support. Then she says, "This is it."

The exact spot where Noah climbed over the railing. The place from which he dropped to the water below, never to come up again.

Cheryl and me, Roger and Jessica, we huddle under the umbrella. To the passing drivers we may look like a family on an outing. But what a family we are, united by death and vengeance, yet I feel closer to these three now, as close as I felt to Adam the day Noah died. Why does no-one talk about this, the way a death can unite people? Why is it such a dirty secret?

I know, from the court case, that CCTV cameras will have filmed us as we arrived, and in my head I imagine the footage. It will be played on the news, maybe even tonight. *Humber Boy B murdered by his victim's mother.* No-one will blame her.

95
The Day Of

Nikki was getting a stitch when she arrived at the bridge, but her personal trainer had said to work through it, so she cycled hard, blocking out the pain in her side as she tuned in to the beat of 'Eye of the Tiger', promising herself that when she got to the other side she could stop for water. She was training for the London to Paris bike ride, already had her sponsorship page open. Last night her boss had pledged a hundred pounds and she didn't even think he liked her, but people always admired effort. She was raising money for disadvantaged kids, planned on hitting five grand, with the added bonus of getting fit.

She hated it when people got in the way of her bike, and up ahead a group of kids were taking over the pavement. She found the best thing was to put her head down, adopt a racing pose and power through.

Why weren't they in school, anyway?

The music and the speed transported her, fast pumping feet on pedals, slowing only as much as they needed to for the kids.

Whatever they were up to, it was no concern of hers.

She had a sponsored race to train for.

It was only the following day, when she saw the papers, that she realised she was the last person who could have stopped the murder of Noah Watts. She raised even more money for the charity, selling her story of this fateful bike ride to *The Sun*. Life can be funny like that.

96
Now

Silent Friend: Dear Jess, I am so sorry for your loss. I think about that moment each and every day. That moment when you lost your son to the River Humber. You said you wanted to know why it happened and I want to give you that chance. Meet me in twenty minutes.

Noah's mum: I don't even know who you are.

Silent Friend: I was your future, my dad and I both were. We would have all been together now, one happy family, if things had happened as planned. We'll be waiting for you, you know where.

97
Cate

The sign announced they were approaching Hull but she knew it anyway, the seagulls were swooping frantically overhead and she could see the Humber Bridge in the distance, curving upwards as if to the rain-torn heavens, the fall on the far side hidden from view. Olivier let a low whistle escape from his teeth, "So much water," he said. "It's always strange to me, after living in a land-locked country."

"How far is Luxembourg from the sea?"

"Oh, four or five hours to the coast, Belgium or France. But we have rivers and lakes. And there is no wind there, it is better than the sea."

Cate cracked her window and breathed in the salty drizzle, letting raindrops hit her cheeks. No, it could not be better than this. She loved the coast and for a moment forgot why they were here, and simply enjoyed having Olivier next to her, talking to him. In the four hour trip she had enjoyed listening to his stories from home, the pictures he painted of Luxembourg and his apartment there, the visits to his parents in their art nouveau home in Nancy. It sounded quaint, like a fairy tale, so different from the stories of her own childhood, the imploding family drama that was about to take place with Liz and the imminent trial of her father.

"What is it, Cate?"

Without noticing it her thoughts had surfaced, she was sighing, she was gazing out of the window blindly. Olivier placed a hand on her thigh.

"Cate?"

"I was just thinking how much I wish I could escape. I wish I could fly away sometimes."

Olivier squeezed her leg, and said, "But you can, Cate. You are free to do as you wish."

They drove over the bridge, a huge arc of motorway in the sky, but as they began to descend the curve, Cate cried, "That's them, look! Four of them, by the barrier down on the footpath, with the umbrella."

"I can't stop here, not without alerting them."

Olivier drove off the bridge then swung round and down into the viewing area. Part of it was cordoned off with steel barriers and a sign that announced a skate park would soon be built there.

Olivier reached for his radio and began to ring in the sighting.

"Wait," Cate said, and he paused. "If you ask for back-up we'll have a road block situation, you won't give Roger any options if he feels boxed into a corner. Ben is sure to be thrown over the side. Can't I try first, to talk to him? Without the drama?"

Olivier looked up to the bridge.

"A police siren will just escalate things," Cate said, based on instinct and not experience. Nothing in her career or life had prepared her for this. "Please, Olivier. Let me try."

"I can get a trained negotiator here, Cate. That would be better."

"Olivier, please. I know I'm not trained, not in that way, but I know this case. I know Roger Palmer's witness statement as well as if he'd described to me first-hand what he felt that day. And I know Ben. That must give me an advantage?"

Olivier checked his watch. "I'll wait here. If you haven't talked them off the bridge in twenty minutes I'm calling for back up from the local team. Go."

Cate checked her watch. It was a quarter to twelve.
Her twenty minutes started now.

98
Ben

I look to where Cate is half-running along the puddled walkway, towards us. But she is too late, eight years too late.

I want to tell her to turn around because this is where I should be. All roads, all choices, were always going to lead back to the Humber.

99
The Day Of

Noah had acted without thought beyond the desperate need to be seen or to feel, and that was why he was over the other side of the metal barrier, stood on the narrow ledge, with his arms wrapped around the railings, the steel painfully pressed to his spine as if supporting his whole body. He felt the closeness of the drop below, he felt alive. More alive than ever before.

It was enough. He was shaking now, at his own daring. He was ready to climb back to safety.

"That girl Cheryl, " said Adam to Ben. "She's fucking crazy. I mean, I know she must be mental or summat. But she's beautiful, too. And she seems to like me. She must, mustn't she?"

As he spoke he was watching Noah holding on to the railing, and Ben wondered what she had said to make Adam act so weird.

Ben looked from his brother to Noah.

"Come on, Noah. Come back over now. It's not funny anymore."

Ben didn't recognise his friend right now. Noah was facing out, staring at the water, and it made Ben nervous. Near him Adam was hopping from foot to foot like a boxer about to enter the ring. Ben felt uneasy.

"Let's make tracks, lads. Come on. I'm nithered."

Neither Noah nor Adam moved.

"Come on," Ben turned to Adam, but his brother's face was Stuart's, the fixed determination that he so feared his step-father for. "What's up?"

"It's her," said Adam, speaking in a voice that came from low in his gut. "She touched me, she kissed me. But I hurt her, made her bleed. She said… she said… "

Cheryl was gone by now, but she had changed the atmosphere. As if she was still here with Adam. Ben could feel her influence on his brother, the way she had swept him along with her. And then Ben thought that Adam wasn't acting like Stuart in this, but like their mother. His head was a mess because someone kissed him, showed him something approaching affection. Big fucking deal.

He grabbed Adam and tugged him, "Let's go home, our kid. Come on!"

But Adam leaned into Ben and hissed, "Cheryl made me promise. She said I should just do it, he's such a fucking runt anyway."

Runt. The word their mother used for Ben. It was he who was the runt, not Noah.

"Do what?" asked Ben, though he could see the murderous intent in Adam's eyes.

"Do what the Devil said," said Adam, stepping towards the younger boy.

Noah, turning to climb back over the railing, saw Adam moving towards him. The younger boy, wide-eyed, began to scream.

It was as if the horror film was playing before his eyes, only this time the Devil wasn't invisible, throwing objects around in the dark. This time the Devil was wearing a Hull Rovers rugby strip and answering to the name of Adam. In his panic and fear Noah slipped, fell down so he was holding onto the bridge by the railings, one of his legs dangled over the edge and the red trainer fell from his foot. And Adam still kept moving forward.

"No!" yelled Ben, trying to stop his brother, seeing Adam's

life run before him as a wasted thing. "I won't let you!"

I won't let you. The final words as Ben took his brother's place. He didn't feel himself act, just like he hadn't felt himself push the glass that had conjured the Devil. But the worst happened and only when the boy had lost his hold on safety, and was falling back into the sky, did Ben realise what he had done.

100
Now

FACEBOOK: FIND HUMBER BOY B

Noah's mum: When I started this page I thought I wanted to see Humber Boy B but I have no words. Because nothing he can say can bring my son back.

This is my last message. After this, there will be nothing more to say.

A black umbrella, as still and as secure as a roof, is waiting for me. Under it is two bodies with no heads. The heads are hidden inside, untouched by the rain, and belong to my two Silent Friends. Beside them, stood with head bowed out of the protection of the umbrella with rain dripping from his hair to his cheeks, from the end of his nose, is a young man. How can a person look so normal, just a boy I would pass in the street, when he ruined my life?

I must go now. I need to call him by his name, I need to look in his face. And then there will be just one more thing to do.

101
Cate

By the time Cate reaches the group on the bridge, ten of her twenty minutes is already gone. She slows a few paces from the scene, trying to work out what is actually happening. There is a woman, and Cate recognises her, she's seen her Facebook pictures.

When she is close enough Cate feels afraid, wonders why she ever asked Olivier to let her do this alone. This is beyond her control, and Ben's eyes are already dead, his slight body already wedged by the greater force of the man beside him, who is hidden under an umbrella, his beefy hand on Ben's shoulder. He must be Roger Palmer.

"Ben," Cate offers, desperately opening her arms because it is all she can think of to do. "Come to me."

But he isn't going to move.

Ben looks drenched, but not just by rain, by the past and its weight that clings to his clothes, his skin, his hair. Cate goes closer to the woman, sensing her stiffen.

"You must be Noah's mum."

"I'm nobody's mum. Not anymore."

Cate slowly approaches Jessica, who stands as still as a statue, her face a mask of grief. Roger looks at Cate, but then back to Jessica and she sees devotion there, mixed with something ugly. Anger or regret. She can feel his energy, his resolve, even across the distance of yards.

"Roger, I read your statement. I know that Noah's death had a terrible effect on you, that it stopped you working, caused your depression. But whatever you're planning today can only make that worse."

Roger faces Cate, and she sees the sag in his jowls, the tired eyes, the lines. This is a ghost of a man.

"You know nothing about me."

"I know more than you think. I know that killing Ben won't help you. You have your daughter to think of."

"And what about her?" Roger said, pointing at Noah's mum. "You think anything you say can stop her? She has no-one to consider, not now."

The loss of a child, the most terrible thing in the world. And if that child is murdered there can be no peace. Cate believes these things, yet she also believes there is a better way than this. She cautiously approaches the barrier, where the woman is leaning over.

Ben's death feels close, pressing on them all, and Cate knows that only Jessica can save him. Roger will only stop if she says so.

"Jessica, please?"

The woman shakes her head, hunches her shoulders. "Nothing is changing my mind," she says.

Cate feels how the seconds are speeding by, the sand is almost drained from the glass. Roger holds Ben's shoulder with one hand, the barrier of the bridge with the other. Ben is just one swift throw from the fall. The barrier comes to Ben's chest but that is nothing, no barrier, to the deep drop in to the swirling river below.

Jessica faces Ben, clears her throat, tries to speak to him, but her voice is a thin reed that the wind cruelly whips from her throat leaving her speechless. Cate knows, because she is a mother too, the question she asked: Why?

Olivier had promised to give Cate twenty minutes but he should be here, his strength could match Roger's and save Ben. Instead, she is all that stands in the way of Ben's death.

In a movement that makes them all jump, Roger lets go of the black umbrella. It flies like a huge black bird into the sky and then drops to its warped destiny, a clatter of metal bones and vinyl wings as it catches on the rails.

Cate watches Roger, now abandoned to the elements, a naked revenge etched on his deeply depressed face.

But what of the girl, what of Cheryl? Who stands shivering just behind her father. Was Roger going to murder the boy, with his daughter as a witness?

"I'm sorry," Cate says to Jessica, pleading with her. "I'm sorry that Ben killed your son. But he was a child himself."

Ben, finally prodded to life, says, "I didn't. He climbed over the barrier himself. It's the truth."

Jess shot towards him, propelled by anger, and grabbed Ben by the neck.

"You lying shit. You fucking little… "

"No!" Ben places his hands over hers so it looks like they are both throttling the life from him. "I'm not lying. He slipped. I'm not lying."

"The truth, Ben," Cate says. "You need to tell Jessica the truth."

And that's when his whole body slumps and he begins to shake. "I'm sorry. I'm so sorry. But I couldn't let Adam… I wanted to help Adam. Because… "

He stopped speaking. Words would never explain properly.

102
Ben

Finally Jessica releases me, collapsing into sobs, and I grab onto the steel railing for support. Roger holds her and I catch my breath, looking out over the Humber where seagulls scream and dive. The wind blows my hair over my eyes, but still I can see too much of the water. Too much of the past is flashing before me.

A hand rests on mine and I think it's Cheryl.

"Just breathe," she says.

It's not Cheryl. It's Noah's mum. She too is breathing deeply, trying to control her emotions as she stares out over the cold water.

"I've been here so many times," she tells me, "just to get a breeze of him, just a pulse of my boy. I want him back so much." And her hand tightens, gripping mine as if for support, as if it was Noah's hand.

I want to say I'm sorry again, but there's no use. Sorry isn't enough, it's an insult.

I press my stomach to the barrier, feeling hollow and still sick, though I know nothing can come up. I just want this over with.

"Please. Tell me why you murdered my son."

And I take a breath of cold air, I close my eyes. That question, which I knew she would ask, I cannot answer. Because my answer won't help. Won't bring him back, won't fully explain. When I do speak I'm surprised at what I say, as

338

if somewhere inside of me there was a reason I wasn't even aware of.

"I'm not a bad person. It was just a bad day."

And then she slaps me, not hard because she misses and scratches my chin, but I see in her eyes that she wants to hurt me. I'm aware of Roger and Cheryl, flanking us like bodyguards, behind us but ready to pounce if I try anything. Cate is standing there too.

Noah's mum moves, in a swift motion I wouldn't have thought she was capable of, and wrenches her body up, one leg over, then the second, until she is over the barrier, standing on the wrong side just as Noah did that day. Her back is pressed against the barrier, her arms wrapped around it. She turns her head to look at me.

"Tell me!" she demands. "How did it happen? Noah was here, right where I am. What happened next?"

And her eyes are dark, just like Noah's. It's that moment again, when he stood just there. And I remember, I do, but it's still not good enough.

"It was a fucked up day," I say desperately, "Adam, my brother, he'd made this promise. To her!"

And there, a gasp. Then Cheryl is beside me, screaming, "Don't blame me! Don't you dare! It was just a joke, I didn't mean it! Don't be so fucking stupid."

Noah's mum leans forward and I think she'll fall, but then I see her arms are still wedged around the steel ruts.

Roger moves towards his daughter, he looks wild, crazy. "What are you talking about, Cheryl? What was a joke?"

Cheryl is looking desperately from Noah's mum to me, then back to her father.

"It's your fault!" she screams. "I was just a kid, but you were the adult! Didn't you think it affected me? Both of you. I just wanted a family, I would do anything for that. This last month, sending those messages on Facebook, I've felt like we have been a family. We've been united, haven't we?" And she smiles, sadly, at Noah's mum. "I've made up for my mistake, by bringing Ben here to you. Haven't I?"

Roger and Jessica exchange a look and I recall what Adam told me that day. They were going to move in together, but Jess hadn't wanted to upset Noah. Cheryl was blaming him for it. Just a family situation, just a domestic.

"It was your fault, Cheryl," I say, feeling it for the first time with clarity. "You were the one who really murdered Noah."

"Don't," Cheryl shakes her head, struggles to get the words free. "Don't say it was me that caused it. I asked Adam, not you, and I never meant it. I never asked you to do anything."

"But I loved my brother. I couldn't let him wreck his life." My hand went involuntarily to my mouth, as if to stop the words that were now tumbling out. Finally, the truth. "I couldn't do that to him, but I could do it to myself. Because I'm no good, and I never have been. It never mattered what happened to me."

On the bridge there was a moment of stillness. They all felt it, that Ben was saying something true and ugly and sad. And so very wrong. Because it had mattered, what Ben did, a great deal. Everyone stood on the bridge had felt the impact.

Tears are streaked down Jess' cheeks, either from the wind or emotion, I don't know.

"Do it to me," she orders, her eyes fixed on mine. "I want to join my son, and I want you to do to me what you did to him. Push me!"

She wants to die. She wants me to be responsible.

"Stop!"

Quick feet move toward us. Cate reaches for Jessica.

Here to rescue me, just like she said she would. But it is not me who needs to be saved.

"Please, Jess," Cate begs. "Climb back over the rail."

Noah's mum looks hypnotised by the water below. Her arms are shaking. She turns, looks like she is wondering what to do. But then she lifts her head, listening. Police sirens are approaching.

"You're not going to help me, are you?" She turns her face to Roger. "None of you will put me out of my misery."

And then I see what I must do.

I step towards Jessica and push her hard, much harder than I pushed her son, sending her to rest with Noah. I do as she asks. It is what she wants.

103
Now

A figure falls from the Humber Bridge. Not a boy, but a woman.

The survivors on the bridge each cling to the railing, looking down, calling to the wind. But there is nothing to be done.

Humber Boy B watches, as his future once again becomes certain.

104
Cate

Ben sits beside Cate in the back of the police car. The silence ticks by.

"You'll be taken to the police station, then remanded," Cate tells him.

He doesn't answer.

"There's nothing anyone can do now. It's finished."

And she may be talking of Noah, or of Jessica. Both of whom are lost forever.

"She wanted me to do it, she'd planned it all along," Ben said, shaking his head in shock. "I thought they were going to kill me, but instead, I helped her die. And that was worse."

Olivier helped Cate from the car and put a blanket around her shoulders but she still felt cold, her teeth were chattering. Cate's helplessness at not being able to stop Ben pushing her, the shock of seeing Jessica's body fall to the cold river below, finally released from her grief.

Oliver looked out to the river, where the Humber Rescue team were pulling Jessica's body from the water.

"She made her own choice today, Cate. She wanted her son's killer back in prison and she's achieved that. He'll never be free now."

Cate sighed, leaned back.

Olivier held her close. "There are no good answers to any of this. I'm sorry, I wish there were, but that's the sum of it. People, we want things to be neat. We want right and wrong, good guy and bad. Cowboy and Indian. But life is just a mess."

She knew he was right and moved further into his embrace so he could soothe her with words.

"Cate? You can't change what just happened on that bridge, but don't let it take your life too. Take the chance you have."

He left her then, returning to his work as a detective. He would take statements from Roger and Cheryl, who had both already been taken to Hull police station where they would be charged with kidnapping and false imprisonment. She herself would be required to give evidence, but there was no doubt that Ben would be returned to prison for life.

The only question was about her own future, hers and Amelia's. But Olivier had reminded her that she, like everyone else today, had a choice. And she was going to choose a different path. A better future.

Arriving back in Ipswich many hours later, Olivier didn't come into the house with Cate. She simply wanted to strip off her clothes, take a shower and go to bed. Before she left the car she reached her hand out and he grasped it, kissed her fingers.

"This wasn't your fault, Cate. Remember that."

She watched his car pull away and turned to the house, where Amelia was waiting with her grandmother. Cate needed to see her daughter, needed to hold her. Watching Jessica fall from the bridge, it had made her feel the fragility of life, the need to clasp love tight as it was so vulnerable.

"Hey, Mum."

And because Amelia had not been on an exhausting trip to Hull, had not seen a grieving woman fall to her death, she tried to walk past, but Cate grabbed her daughter, smothered her with a hug, kissed her cheek.

"Okay, Mum, you were only gone a day."

But in that day everything had changed.

105
The Day Of

"I can't do it," Adam said. He stopped walking forward.

Ben had never seen his brother this way. So upset, shaking and his voice wobbling.

"Fuck, I can't do it."

It disturbed Ben, to see Adam like this. He'd always been the strong one, making sure Ben got food, getting him out of bed each day, taking him to school. Adam had been mother and father and best friend. And now he was dissolving. Right in front of him.

"Adam, it doesn't matter."

But Adam howled. "Fuck him, leaving like that. Fuck her, for letting him."

Ben knew this wasn't about Cheryl, not only anyway. It was today, this fucked up day that had been wrecked from the start. They should have all stayed in bed, done the same as their Mum, refused to get up and see the light.

Adam was on his knees, crying, shaking. Ben couldn't comfort him, he didn't have the words. And he would do anything, anything at all, to help his brother.

And there was Noah, the wrong side of the barrier, still screaming. He'd slipped down, standing on the ledge though one foot was missing a shoe, hanging on desperately to the railings, sobbing in fear and frustration at the whole mess of it.

It was too easy.

In that moment, that split-second, it was simply too easy to step forward and give him one single shove.

Ben watched Noah plummet and felt what he had done, the tingling power that grew, swelled along his arms and to his chest which was flooded with relief at his own strength. The adrenalin rush hit him hard. His whole body shook, violent shivers so he had to grab the railing as he gasped in air. He wanted to run, to jump in the air. He wanted to ride the euphoria for as long as it lasted, he had never felt it before.

The CCTV camera caught the brothers running from the scene. And they caught Ben grabbing his brother, in what looked like an ecstatic embrace.

106
NOW

FACEBOOK: FIND HUMBER BOY B

Noah's mum: I am getting ready to meet an old friend and I hope he will keep his promise. If he does, then I will finally get the chance to see my son's killer, and to ask him the one question that has been burning inside me since he got released from prison.

The question may not be the one you expect. No answer will ever be enough to that particular question, and I'm not foolish enough to believe that anything that boy says will explain or excuse what he did to Noah.

My question to him is about his guilt, and if he feels any. If he is willing to show me that he does, and face the consequences.

This is what I want, and if you are reading this and it has already happened then I want you to know that I'm sorry for any pain it causes. And I don't expect you to understand.

All I can ask is that you forgive me. I couldn't live any more if he was free.

It's as simple as that.

107
Cate

Cate picked up her bag and placed inside all the things that were hers, nothing that belonged to the probation service. She'd joined because she wanted answers, that certainty. It was over now. She was going to try a different approach: love.

Because she was human and fallible and Olivier said he loved her and Amelia.

She was going to try Luxembourg.

Cate felt it then, deep in the pit of her stomach, the unpalatable truth festering there: none of the people involved in Noah's death were psychopaths. None were evil. Yet an alchemy of each personality, of each decision, had led to the greatest evil of all.

And Jessica's death, so keenly felt by Cate, had been a direct result. A woman whose life felt empty, and who chose to give it up if it meant her son's killer was back behind bars.

Ben didn't have to push Jessica over the side, even though she asked him to. He didn't have to push Noah. The choices he made were ugly ones, the reasons banal. But in the end Cate felt it was guilt that had motivated him to do as Jessica demanded, and maybe fear of what the outside world held. Either way, he would never be free again.

She was heading towards the exit when a voice stopped her.

"Someone said it once, don't know who, but to have a good system of judgement you must have good men. But not too good."

Cate paused in the corridor, her box heavy in her arms, the photo of Amelia on top.

"I'm leaving, Paul. You're too late."

Paul came closer, smiling. "Not so good, Cate, that they have forgotten what it is to be imperfect."

Cate stared at her friend. "I fucked up, Paul. Another person died and Ben is back in prison."

"But you are a good person. And that's why you must stay."

"I don't feel good. I feel rotten. And this box is heavy."

She had contacted Liz's legal team and said that, no, she would not be standing as a witness against her father, no matter what he had done. Because it seemed to her now that she was someone not to be trusted, her testimony was worthless. Working with Ben's case had done this to her. Cate felt trapped by her mistakes, by her failure to protect Ben from being abducted and taken to Hull where a new chain of events, of which she was part, had ended in another body in the Humber.

"I need perspective, Paul."

"Can you at least put the box down?"

"If I put it down I may never pick it up again, and right now I just need to keep walking. I need distance from this so I can assess just how badly I messed up. Right now I need to be far away from damaged people. I'm too damaged myself."

Paul touched her arm and gently took the box from her.

"Then I'll help you to your car. But let me tell you this, you're good, you know what it is to be human. But if you need some time off, then take it. Just promise you'll come back."

Cate followed Paul from the probation office, but made no promises to return.

Acknowledgments

I have been mulling over the themes in this novel since January 2000, when I first started to work in a special prison unit in Suffolk, set up to deal with boys who had committed crimes similar to the one described in *Humber Boy B*. Like Cate Austin, I was driven by a need to find out why these children had committed such grave acts and although Ben is fictional, as is his crime, I have taken inspiration from the young men I met. I would also like to acknowledge the people I never had the opportunity to meet: the victims. I always kept them in my heart and mind, both as a probation officer and in writing this book.

I am grateful to the ongoing and unstinting support of my writing group: Liz Ferretti, Jane Bailey, Morag Lewis and Sophie Green.

My thanks to Tom Chalmers, Lauren Parsons and Lucy Chamberlain. Legend Press are a beacon of hope for authors, an independent publishing house who champion their writers with gladiatorial passion. I am fortunate to have found you.

And I would not have done so, had it not been for the Luke Bitmead Bursary, established by Elaine Hanson in memory of her son, Luke. His memory lives on through the bursary, and many authors have benefitted hugely from the award. Speaking personally, I could never overstate how winning the bursary changed my life, and gave me a chance to follow my dream of becoming a published writer.

Finally, many thanks to my family. My children, Amber and Eden, joined me on the research trip back Hull, my hometown. Although they loved The Deep they may have felt a bit nervous when I asked them to lean over the edge of the railing on The Humber Bridge and describe how it felt. As way of apology, I'd like to dedicate this book to you.

If you enjoyed *Humber Boy B*, make sure you look out for
the next Cate Austin novel, *Nowhere Girl*.

*From the top of the ferris wheel, Ellie can see everything. Her
life, laid out beneath her. Ellie looks up. She wants freedom.
Down below, her little sister and mother wait, watching as
people bundle off the wheel and disappear into the crowd.
No Ellie. Must be the next box.
But the ferris wheel continues to turn.*

When Ellie goes missing on the first day of Schueberfouer,
the police are dismissive, keen not to attract negative
attention on one of Luxembourg's most important events.

Probation officer, Cate Austin, has moved for a fresh start,
along with her daughter Amelia, to live with her police
detective boyfriend, Olivier Massard. But when she realises
just how casually he is taking the disappearance of Ellie,
Cate decides to investigate matters for herself.

She discovers Luxembourg has a dark heart. With
its geographical position, it is at the centre of a child
trafficking ring. As Cate comes closer to discovering Ellie's
whereabouts she uncovers a hidden world, placing herself
in danger, not just from traffickers, but from a source much
closer to home.

Come and visit us at
www.legendpress.co.uk

Follow us
@legend_press